BEWITCHED

Eliza turned toward him and smiled. "Kissing is not a crime."

"You're right on that score, Miss Lytton, yet I'm concerned—"

"Evidently not concerned enough to stop the assault on my senses," she scoffed gently.

He spread out his hands as if searching for something that would change his past actions. "I don't know what came over me. You bewitched me."

"So the blame is all mine?" She went and stood in front of him and crossed her arms over her chest. Straightening her back, she met his gaze fearlessly.

He thought about her challenge, a smile playing over his lips. "Yes," he said finally. "Your vivacity and the allure of your lips so close to mine made me lose my head."

"Now you're piling injury upon injury."

"If you're not careful, I might kiss you again," he murmured. He stepped closer but she moved away, heading toward the door.

"I never thought of you as a rogue, Captain Hawkins, but I find that impressions can be deceptive."

CAPTAIN HAWKINS' DILEMMA

Maria Greene

ZEBRA BOOKS
KENSINGTON PUBLISHING CORP.
http://www.zebrabooks.com

ZEBRA BOOKS are published by

Kensington Publishing Corp.
850 Third Avenue
New York, NY 10022

First Printing: August 2004
10 9 8 7 6 5 4 3 2 1

Printed in the United States of America

ONE

Captain Leo Hawkins studied the advertisement in *The Times* one more time even though he knew it by heart:

> *Unattached gentleman wanted, preferably young, strong, and quick-witted for traveling assignment and possible further employment of a more delicate nature. Patience and an even-tempered disposition are a must. References required. Generous salary.*

He looked up at the solid oak door of the domestic employment agency and knocked. A discreet sign in the window stated that he'd arrived at the right address, and the door opened immediately. A lanky young gentleman stepped outside, and a stout older woman behind him pinned a beady eye on Leo. She wore a black bombazine gown and a large cap on her gray curls. She looked shrewd enough, but no smile of welcome softened her mouth as she studied him.

"Mrs. Brown, I presume," Leo said and gave a curt bow.

"That's correct." She held the door for him as he stepped through. "Can I assist you, Mr. . . . ?"

"Captain Hawkins, ma'am." He held up the folded news sheet. "I'm here about the advertisement."

"I see." Her voice brooked no nonsense, and he suspected that she would scrutinize every aspect of his life. He didn't relish the idea, but he needed something to occupy his time, and to get him out of the doldrums after he had to sell out. He missed his cronies in Wellington's army; he missed the assignments, the constant activity. His injury had stopped everything, and as he'd spent a year contemplating his life, and finding a way to accept his current circumstances, he'd resented the confinement. He longed to breathe the fresh air of the open country, to move freely as he used to before.

His foot ached with every step across the floor of the foyer, but he tried not to limp. It was a damned nuisance that one of the ammunitions carts had rolled over his foot in the mud on the way to a battlefield. That irony of fate had brought him back to England before Napoleon had been defeated, and he'd had to follow the battles via the news sheets and the correspondence with his cronies. Even as his broken bones healed slowly—never to be quite right again—he had realized his career was over, and he'd never had the chance to be part of the battle of Waterloo, the crowning glory of Wellington's brilliant war strategy.

"We've had quite a few applicants for the position, but no decisions have been made as yet, Captain," Mrs. Brown said and sat down behind a large oak desk in the front parlor, which had been fashioned into an office. Dark, heavy furniture oppressed the room, and the portrait of an old man who might be Mrs. Brown's father or late husband stared down at him with a stern expression.

The weighty velvet curtains muted the noise of the London streets outside, and a murky gloom resided in the room, but Mrs. Brown seemed alert despite her surroundings.

"I'm acting as a liaison for a friend of mine, and I've promised to find the very best man to fill the post," she said.

Leo really didn't care whether he received her offer of employment or not, but the advertisement had intrigued him, and he had to get away from his lodgings, find new ways to support himself. "Would you mind if I ask you a question, Mrs. Brown?"

"Hmm. I normally ask the questions here, but I'm willing to listen." She thrust her round chin forward and gave him her full attention.

"What does this mean . . . a position 'of a more delicate nature'?" he asked and pointed to the advertisement.

She gave him a long, hard stare. "It's not my place to explain, Captain. If you are offered the position, your employer will elucidate on the matter."

"I see," he said, but didn't really see. The sentence had triggered his curiosity so much, he had to pursue the ad. It still did, but he knew Mrs. Brown would not budge.

"Now, if you'd be so kind as to tell me everything about yourself, Captain Hawkins."

He explained about his past successful career in the army and the accident that had put him out of commission, and that he was now looking for a temporary post to get him started on something new. "I find the traveling aspect particularly intriguing, and I am strong and resourceful. I would have no difficulty defending a person seeking a protector. I'm deft with all types of weapons, and strategy is my forte."

She gave him a veiled look. "I don't doubt your strength, Captain. It's obvious to see that you're both disciplined and a gentleman of power, if not as quick on your pins as you once were, but I can't hold that against you. May I inquire about references?"

"Viscount Allerton is my father, and I have connections who move in Wellington's circles, not to mention fellow officers who would vouch for me."

"Hmm, very impressive, but if you don't mind my asking, why would the son of a viscount seek this kind of employment? You could surely find an administrative position with one of your past benefactors?"

"That's possible. For the time being, I'd like to travel—as I explained earlier. I desire to begin my civil life with a lighter assignment—and a change of vistas." He looked around the room. "I take it you're not going to make a decision today."

"That's correct. There are several applicants and we will certainly wait a few days to see if more apply. I realize you have an impeccable background and an impressive military career, but my employer will have to decide whether your . . . well, difficulty"—she glanced pointedly toward the floor—"will be detrimental to the mission."

"Mission?" He grew more intrigued by the minute.

"Thank you, Captain Hawkins." She rose from the desk and showed him out of the room where a maid escorted him to the front door.

Mrs. Brown certainly hadn't asked as many questions as he'd thought she would, but perhaps those would come later. His life had been a straight line since he'd bought a commission in the army, and he had nothing to hide. He glanced up at the gray sky and inhaled the sooty air. He longed to experience the rest of the spring season in the green lap of England, not in this gray and dusty city.

To his delight, a letter arrived two days later at his lodgings ordering him back to Mrs. Brown's agency for further inquiries. Another two days passed and he finally stood eye to eye with his prospective employer. To his surprise, she was a diminutive woman dressed in a sky blue gown and an exotic shawl that depicted all kinds of birds and strange foliage. Her clear blue gaze stared at him in a disconcerting way, and immediately he knew her to be direct in her speech, and a woman who was not afraid to make her own decisions.

Her soft brown hair curled around her temples, and her heart-shaped face transformed from firm to lively as she smiled. Her eyes took on an irresistible gleam, and he found her quite attractive. He also found her womanly curves alluring as the material of her gown clung as she held out her small, slim hand toward him.

He was going to kiss it, but she shook his hand without ado. Her grip was as steady as that of a man, which was unusual, indeed.

"Good morning, Captain Hawkins," she said, and he liked her warm voice.

He bowed, reluctant to relinquish his hold on her hand. "Good morning . . ."

"This is Miss Lytton," Mrs. Brown interrupted. "She's going to ask you a few questions, Captain. Answer them quickly and to the point. We don't want to waste Miss Lytton's time." She led the way to the office and they sat down behind her desk.

Miss Lytton's gaze scrutinized him anew, and he stared just as frankly. She never flinched at his directness, and he grew more intrigued by the minute. He wouldn't mind knowing more about her.

To be honest, he found her irresistible. He had certainly been out of commission far too long. . . .

"Mrs. Brown divulged your background to me, and I see that you're well connected, Captain. The matter is of some delicacy, and I must have your assurance that you won't carry any of this conversation farther than this room."

"Of course not, Miss Lytton."

"I am relieved." Her face relaxed.

"Any and all confidences are safe with me." He wondered why she would consider sharing anything confidential with him after so short an acquaintance.

"I spent fifteen years in Egypt with my father, Sir Walter Lytton, a scholar of the ancient civilization there. I have little memory of my previous life here in England. I lost my mother at an early age, and I'm not versed in the ways of ladies. I worked as my father's assistant in the field, which according to Mrs. Brown"—she shifted her gaze to that formidable lady—"is a very unladylike occupation. Nevertheless, I gained an appreciation for my father's work, and I'm doing everything in my power to preserve what he held so dear. I need a healthy and strong man to aid me on my trip to the Lake Country where I will deliver certain documents to my uncle, who is also a scholar. If the documents were to be lost or stolen, everything that my father worked for would be for naught."

"Fifteen years of research could hardly be for naught," he inserted.

"Certainly you have a point, Captain, but these parchments hold the key to the finds that he unearthed, and once deciphered will throw a light onto the past and bring history forward. I carry on his mission so that his research can be concluded."

"I see. It is a noble cause, Miss Lytton, and your concern is commendable. I take it my position would include guarding these documents on your journey to the Lake Country?"

"You're quick-witted to boot," she said with another smile.

Somehow that smile made his insides melt, and he felt powerless against the novel emotion.

"Guard them with my life, no doubt," he said with a corresponding grin.

She nodded, her smile fading. "With your life. It would break my heart to see my father's efforts vanish into the ancient sands of the Sahara for the lack of validation."

He understood her concern. "Your father worked on a worthy cause, and I'd be honored to aid you—if you'll allow me, Miss Lytton."

She seemed to sink into deep thought, and he wondered what was going through that sharp mind of hers. "My maid Lucy will be in charge of the boxes, but you'll have to make sure they are safe at night."

"That would not be a problem."

She fell silent once more. "I daresay you've had a slew of applicants for the post," he said to break the silence.

"Several, in fact, yet your credentials are quite impressive. I would feel safe in your company," she said, pinning her direct gaze on him once more.

Her approval made his heart swell. Her words lessened his previous agony of broken bones and a broken career. "I prefer to take a rigorous trip across the country rather than to sit at home and stare out the window. I was a very active man in the past, and will continue to be so as I have now recovered from my injury." He glanced at Mrs. Brown who wore an expression bordering on boredom. "There's one question, Miss Lytton."

She looked at him expectantly, those blue eyes spellbinding.

"In the advertisement you hinted at another duty of a . . . well, 'delicate nature,'" he began.

"Oh, yes, well, it will be revealed in due time, Captain Hawkins. No need to know about that now." She spoke briskly as she stood up and held out her hand again. This time, he lifted her fingers to his lips and brushed them lightly. A blush rose in her cheeks, and she pulled away as if burned.

"As I said . . ." she stated, her voice petering off as if she'd already forgotten what to say.

Mrs. Brown handed her a piece of paper, which she extended to him.

He looked at an address on Conduit Street. She lived respectably in Mayfair.

"Captain, this is my address, and I expect you to start your employment on the day we leave. I shall reward your efforts handsomely. With some luck our mission will be concluded in two to three weeks, depending on the roads, and my uncle's disposition. After we have concluded the mission, we shall return to London."

"When did you come back to England, Miss Lytton?" he asked, as he was reluctant to leave. She intrigued him more than he could explain.

"Two months ago. My father died a year ago, and it took time to settle his affairs in Egypt. I admit I suffered a major adjustment as I returned here. I had forgotten how proper and exacting the society is compared to the rather more flamboyant customs of the Egyptians." She took a deep breath. "I felt somewhat like an exotic animal on display at the gatherings that my father's friends invited me to, and I found that I was not well received due to my foreign ways. But it matters not; I'm not bound to what others think of me."

"You're brave, Miss Lytton."

"The weather is another kettle of fish. I'm used to hot, dry air and daily sunlight, and I doubt we've seen the sun here twice since I returned. Lots of fog, though, and drizzle."

"Yes, you're right on that score, but with summer about

to march in, the measure of sunshine should improve," he said.

Mrs. Brown clearly thought their conversation unnecessary as she led the way to the door.

Leo bowed again, excited to have made Miss Lytton's acquaintance. He was eager to start his new position.

Eliza watched him leave, his awkward gait endearing him to her. His straight back and his elegant bearing, not to mention his beautiful brown eyes, had struck a chord within her. She had seen pride in his strong jaw, sensitivity in his long fingers, patience in his deep eyes, strength and maturity in the stillness of his handsome face, and she'd seen the boy he'd once been in the black curls at the nape of his neck.

He'd made a striking picture in his blue coat and pale yellow pantaloons, and she'd also read the pain and the disappointment from his recent difficulties in the slight droop of his beautiful mouth.

"I'm surprised you chose Captain Hawkins," Mrs. Brown said.

Eliza gave her a startled stare. "Why? He's quite qualified for the position."

"Yes, but if he has to move rapidly to protect you . . ."

"I don't anticipate any ambushes or highwaymen attacks."

Mrs. Brown pursed her lips in disapproval. "You can never be sure, Eliza. You're too optimistic at times."

"Be that as it may, I have an intimate knowledge of arms of all kinds. Father taught me to protect myself, but a male escort puts me at great advantage should something occur on the road."

Mrs. Brown huffed and crossed her arms over her

ample middle. "It's not seemly to admit to such unladylike knowledge."

"I never stated I would *use* weapons, but if my life was threatened, I wouldn't hesitate." Eliza pulled on her gloves briskly and the maid put a light cloak over her shoulders.

"Your mother would turn in her grave if she heard you speak thus," Mrs. Brown said with heavy censure.

"You worked in the household when my mother was alive, but I have no strong memories of her, and even though I would not want to shock her, I feel she wouldn't judge me for wanting to protect myself."

"Your mother was a gentle flower."

"I must take after the more robust side of my father's family. I recall my aunts were women of strong convictions, and Aunt Avery helped Father until her death. Never married."

"I'm not surprised," Mrs. Brown said abrasively.

Eliza kissed Mrs. Brown's round cheek. "Thank you for your help, Betty. Wish me luck on my travels."

"You chose the captain for his dashing appearance, Eliza."

Eliza laughed. "I see nothing wrong with that. I like to rest my gaze upon beauty if it's offered."

Eliza could not stop thinking about the intriguing Captain Hawkins after the interview. He would be a fascinating companion, and her sudden interest worried her. She had never been interested in any particular gentleman. Granted, she'd not had much opportunity to meet eligible bachelors in Egypt, yet the ones she'd met had made scant impression on her. Even though the captain had not said much, she'd known immediately that he was the right man to escort her.

Lucy, her capable maid, bustled about the town house on Conduit Street, packing valises and trunks. Every dress was aired, brushed, and folded gently, every hat placed in a hat box, and shoes polished and stowed away. Eliza's bedchamber was strewn with clothes, even though she'd told Lucy to only pack the necessities. "It's not as if we're going abroad; we're only going north for a short period of time."

"Miss, you don't know what social situations might present themselves. You have to be properly attired at all times."

"Pooh, you make me tired with all of your concerns, Lucy."

The tall abigail of middle years and nondescript coloring, but displaying an imperious demeanor, looked disturbed. "I've worked as a lady's maid for many years before I came to you, Miss Lytton, and I assure you that I'm fully knowledgeable of every detail of a lady's attire."

"I'm not," Eliza said with a shrug.

Lucy looked shocked. "'Tis fortunate that I am, then," she said, her nose quivering with shock.

"It doesn't overly concern me. Attire never held much interest to me."

Lucy's blue eyes widened at such a sacrilegious utterance, and her long face fell even farther. "I shall make sure you are a lady to your fingertips at all times."

"Ladylike demeanor does not reside in a dress."

"But it certainly helps," Lucy said, now clearly outraged.

Eliza sighed and went downstairs to oversee that everything she had to deliver to her uncle was packed in sturdy cases. She intended to inspect the packets of research papers her father had written, and found them securely wrapped and packed in a wooden box. On her desk was the letter that her father had saved for her to read after his demise, and it still, after a year, brought tears to her eyes. She scanned the lines, which she already knew by heart.

. . . and it would pain me no end to see you alone and abandoned, dearest daughter. Therefore, I beg you to wed my friend and colleague Melvin Homer. He's rather humorless and dry but a gentleman I trust. I know he's older by a decade, but he would take good care of you, Eliza. He's the man I would choose for you as you share many of the same interests, among them ancient Egypt. He will provide a home for you, and family, too, as his mother and aunts are still alive. I would rest most peacefully if I knew you'd made your vows with him, and he knows I'm counting on him to manage the sizeable fortune that is about to become yours. In fact, to receive your inheritance in full, you will have to marry, my dear, and I've picked Mr. Homer for you. As you read this, you know, alas, that I won't be at the nuptials, but know that I will attend in spirit.

Eliza tossed down the letter and recalled the meeting she'd had with Mr. Homer upon her return to England. She never could abide the man, but out of respect for her father she had decided to give Mr. Homer a chance. He had traveled back to England after Sir Walter died, and she wondered why he hadn't completed his own research in Egypt.

He had courted her with autocratic nonchalance as if already sure of his position as her future husband, and she'd hated every minute of it.

No love letters or bouquets of flowers had arrived on her doorstep to open the path to her heart. He'd said, "You must understand, Eliza, that due to my age"—he'd sounded much older than the ten years that separated them—"I'm not prone to romantic fancies or flowery words. And I see it as a waste of good funds to buy roses that will die within a few days. Ours will be a sedate and proper courtship, and you will be under Mother's vigilant eye at all times. Under no circumstances will I allow you to gallivant about London in wild abandon as you have since you returned from Egypt. Granted, I had to curb my attention until the proper mourning period was over, but I gritted my teeth at your visits to museums and shops with only a maid and a footman as company. I shan't accept any of that when we're joined together in matrimony; in fact, I shall take you back to the country estate immediately where you will stay."

Eliza had stared at his tall, thin form dressed in brown, at his beaky nose and cold blue eyes and oily brown hair, and found that she abhorred him even more after those words. She could understand that her father had enjoyed scholarly exchanges with this man, and had probably not seen his arrogance directed at women as the two of them mostly spent their time together in the field and in the company of other men.

She longed to obey her father, and follow his advice, but marrying Mr. Homer was wholly out of the question.

"I understand your concern about my safety, Mr. Homer, but as you must know, I'm a very capable female. I was my father's assistant for many years, and I'm quite educated and able to deal with varied situations that might appear awkward to a lady less experienced."

"But you are a *woman,* nevertheless, and as such have to yield to a gentleman's greater knowledge and wisdom."

Shaking with anger, she'd taken a deep breath. "Mr. Homer, if you possessed a smidgeon of wisdom, you would not utter these statements. I'm appalled at your arrogance. I have only one thing to tell you now. If you were the last man on the earth, I would not marry you."

His surprise had been palpable, and with an expression of great injury, he'd departed from her house. He had threatened to return when she'd collected her wayward senses, but she'd only slammed the front door shut behind him.

One thought nagged at the back of her mind since she had told Mr. Homer bluntly how she felt. What if her father had written in his will that she had to wed Mr. Homer expressly to gain her inheritance?

Her father's solicitor, Mr. Tyler, had given her a copy of the will, and she reread it as she pulled it out of the desk drawer. To her relief, Mr. Homer's name was never mentioned. A heavy weight had lifted from her shoulders, and she took a deep breath of relief once more.

"Father," she whispered, "I always tried to follow your gentle guidance, but in this matter, I have to follow my own heart. I'm sorry to disappoint you, but Mr. Homer will never walk down the aisle with me."

As she concluded that statement, two strong footmen came in to carry out the boxes that were going to Uncle Claude's estate in Cumbria.

Tomorrow she would be on her way, and if all eligible gentlemen were like Mr. Homer, she'd rather remain a spinster her entire life. She would never submit her own will and freedom to some ignorant man, and she would never accommodate some man who acted solely out of selfishness.

TWO

Leo rode his tawny gelding, Gambler, down Conduit Street and found the chaise and four packed high with boxes. In the bright morning sunlight, the servants were strapping a trunk to the back as he pulled up. He noticed Miss Lytton at the door, her black cloak flying out as a gust of wind passed through. She looked beautiful in the clear morning light, and her smile glittered as she saw him. All around him people bustled and issued orders, but everything seemed to grow still as his gaze locked with hers.

"Good morning, Miss Lytton," he said and slid out of the saddle to stand before her. A groom took charge of his mount.

"You're on time, Captain, which does you credit. We're just about ready to leave." She tightened the button on her kid gloves and examined the contents of her reticule. "Everything is packed, and lodgings and change of horses have been arranged along the way. If the weather holds, we should be making good time." She glanced toward the door, where a lady's maid dressed in gray waited. "Lucy, did you bring the box from my father's room?"

"Aye, miss, nothing has been left behind," the woman said. "Everything is as it should be." She gave Leo a stiff appraisal, and he knew she would guard her charge closely.

Eliza gave him a quick glance. "Did you bring anything besides your mount, Captain Hawkins?"

"Everything I need for the trip is in my saddlebags and a small valise. I'll be riding—"

"I'm bringing a traveling companion, and Jimmy, the coachman, will be of great help. He has an excellent hand with horses."

"Perhaps my services will be superfluous," Leo said with a smile.

"I doubt that," she said briskly. "I would not have hired you if I deemed it unnecessary. I will entrust the general plans for the safety of our journey to you, and I expect only the best on your part."

"You can count on me, Miss Lytton," he said with a bow. He liked the challenge, and he looked forward to the change that travel invariably brought.

A short but sturdy lady of middle years who looked like someone who enjoyed rigorous walks in the country stepped through the door. She wore a dark blue poke bonnet on her gray curly hair, and a muddy brown traveling dress that did not become her. She shaded her hand and looked toward the sky as if assessing the weather.

Leo liked her on sight. Her lively gray eyes fell on him.

"This is Miss Lavinia Lytton, my aunt. She is my companion until we arrive at Cumbria. She looks forward to walking in the mountains, something she does once a year for two weeks."

"It's a pleasure to meet you, Miss Lytton."

"Young man," she said with a quick smile, "call me Lavinia or we will forever be confused with two Miss Lyttons. I don't stand on formalities—never did."

"I'm delighted," he said, and meant it.

The younger Miss Lytton started to move forward. He took her hand as she walked down the steps and led her to the coach. She didn't reject him, but he sensed that she made an inner protest as if unused to the attention. He suspected she had little experience of male attention of any kind. He found her different from the females he knew, and it intrigued him. She seemed determined and full of purpose, the opposite of what was expected of a lady of quality.

A barouche with an older woman and tall, thin man pulled up behind the traveling coach. The man stepped out, and Leo saw Miss Lytton's mouth press into a thin line, and anger flared at the back of her eyes, darkening them. Her chin took on a stubborn tilt, and her back straightened.

"Miss Lytton," the man began. "I see that you're still pursuing your foolish plan to travel north with no one but servants to escort you."

"As you see, Aunt Lavinia is here to lend decorum to the expedition, Mr. Homer. Not that I understand how it affects you in any way."

"As my future wife, I have to make sure—"

"Desist, Mr. Homer. I have no interest in arguing with you further on any of the points we discussed before—as you well know. As far as I'm concerned, I have no interest in furthering our acquaintance. Moreover, I have plenty of protection, as you can see. Good day."

She held her own in verbal sparring. Leo stared at the disconcerted man with curiosity. Miss Lytton's husband-to-be? It didn't appear to be the truth if Miss Lytton's icy expression were an indication. And if he were, he should be protecting her all the way to Cumbria. The man gave Leo a calculating stare, bowed stiffly, and then turned on his heel and marched back to his carriage.

"Dratted man," Miss Lytton said under her breath.

"Has he been bothering you?"

"He's a busybody of the first order who thinks he can dictate my life. He's an old crony of my father, and he brings nothing but annoyance to my house."

Leo sensed difficulties, but the barouche made a smart turn and rolled over the cobblestones in the opposite direction. The older woman turned around and gave Leo a stare full of venom, which he could not understand.

With a deep sigh, Miss Lytton gripped the edge of the door frame and turned her attention to the folded down coach steps. "We might as well carry on."

The servants of the house stood watching as she climbed into the coach. "Godspeed," one of them said, and twirled his cap between his large hands

She smiled. "Thank you, Lawrence."

The maid stepped in behind Miss Lytton and another servant passed a leather valise and a case into her hands as she settled on the seat. The coachman gathered the reins, and a footman closed the door to the handsome chaise painted dark green with shiny brass details on the leather straps, lamps, handles, and steps.

Miss Lytton was far from poor, Leo concluded as he swung himself into the saddle. His foot ached, but joy burst in his chest at the thought of riding through the green countryside and inhaling great gulps of fresh air. He fell in behind the equipage that moved through the narrow streets.

Leo could tell the coachman had great experience as he steered the coach through the crowded thoroughfares and out of London. Their first major stop would be the posting inn at Walford in Buckinghamshire where they would change the horses, but he suspected the ladies would need to pause for refreshments before that. He smiled to himself as he followed the coach.

This would be an easy assignment—much lighter than the dusty fields of Spain that he'd been used to during the war.

The chaise made good progress, and they had left London far behind as Leo's stomach told him it was time for the midday meal. At Harpenden the coach pulled in under a wide gate set in a stone wall, and within, the stable yard bustled with activity. Dogs barked and a farmer's cart trundled by, barely having enough room to leave as the two vehicles met.

Leo scanned the area, but saw no vagabonds or drunkards who might be a potential nuisance at the tables outside the taproom. He took his work seriously, but suspected he wouldn't have much to do besides keeping abreast with the coach. Besides, Miss Lytton didn't seem to be the squeamish type.

Still, he knew that she hadn't told him everything about his assignment, but he would have to be patient. He rode up to the coach window where she was waving at him. "Captain, please inquire about a private parlor."

He did, and found the owner, Mr. Vane, at the inn, very helpful as he offered cold lemonade and ale, and a wide selection of dishes to choose from. The taproom smelled of fried bacon, fresh bread, onions, and tobacco smoke.

Leo helped his employer down and led her into the taproom and to the private parlor beyond that was sparsely furnished with a long table, chairs, and a sideboard. A woven rug of rusty tones softened the hard floor. Miss Lytton settled on one of the chairs and ordered lemonade, a big loaf of bread, and shepherd's pie.

Not one to pretend she had a small appetite, Leo

thought. Most of the ladies he knew only picked at their food and frowned on hearty dishes.

He returned to the taproom and escorted Lavinia to the private parlor. He went back to the coach and found that Lucy would stay with the boxes in the coach. He arranged food for her and returned to Miss Lytton to find out if she had any orders concerning her luggage, but she shook her head. As he moved to join the men in the taproom, Miss Lytton said, her hand indicating a chair, "Please join us, Captain. I suspect we bore you, but I desire your company for dinner. Though I'm acquainted with your past career, I'd like to know you better."

He bowed. "Thank you, I'm flattered." Sitting down, he ordered ale from the young barmaid and decided he would have a portion of the shepherd's pie as well.

"That kind of heavy food will give me a stomachache," Lavinia said. "I prefer a glass of claret and a plate of vegetables, or perhaps a cup of broth and some of that delicious bread I smell." She pinned Leo with her frank gaze. He could see from whom Miss Lytton had inherited her sharp eyes. "Tell us about yourself, Captain."

He laughed. "And worry that I would put you to sleep before you've had your meal? That would be catastrophic."

Lavinia waved dismissively. "I sleep very little, so there's no danger of that."

"What about you, Miss Lytton?"

"I sleep very soundly, thank you, Captain, but I assure you the excitement of the journey still holds me in its grip. I could not sleep even if I wanted to."

Her kind assurance made his heart take wings, and he liked her very well, indeed. He wished at that very moment that he had something to offer besides a captain's pension. Even if he was the youngest son of a viscount, he had very little, and he could never approach anyone as well set as Miss Lytton and not earn the epithet of fortune hunter.

"I have two sisters and an older brother. The family hails from Sussex, and I spent my childhood in the lap of the South Downs. It was an idyllic spot to grow up, and I never saw the flaws of the Allerton ramshackle estate until I was grown. My father still lives there with all the leaks in the roof, and the rotting floors." The description was his way to tell her he had no future prospects.

"I'm sorry to hear that," Miss Lytton said.

"The strange part is that he doesn't care. My sire cares for nothing but the horse races, and we've owned some fine horses over the years. However, Lady Fortune has never turned a benign eye upon my father. He still gambles."

Both ladies nodded thoughtfully.

The barmaid brought in glasses and a pitcher of lemonade, a bottle of claret for Lavinia, and a tankard of ale for Leo. She served the refreshment and left the room. Lavinia drank with obvious pleasure. As she set down the glass, she said, "And what about your two sisters, Captain?"

"Angelica is married to a clergyman in London, and Libby is Lady Wellford. Between them they have six children—all boys." He laughed. "It's sometimes hard to keep them apart when they're all together. They are a fistful of rapscallions. Any prank is game to them."

"Perhaps it runs in the family, on the male side," Miss Lytton said, her mouth curving sweetly at the corners.

He found himself longing to kiss her. "There might be some truth to that, Miss Lytton. I once got a caning for gluing my grandfather's slippers to the floor. He stepped into them and almost broke his arm as he stumbled and fell." Leo laughed ruefully at the memory. "I never imagined the possible danger attached to the prank, but after I couldn't sit for two days, I knew I would never do it again."

Miss Lytton's laugh chimed sweetly. He leaned his elbows on the wooden armrests of his chair and relaxed. "I daresay you've never done something that daring," he said.

"No . . . but I filled my father's slippers with sand once," she replied. "He emptied them and made me sweep his tent every day for a week. It was an endless task."

"Ample punishment, I take it," he said, and laughed.

"As I said—endless. My father was a rather shrewd man with plenty of patience and a firm sense of what was right and wrong."

"I suspect you're rather like him," Leo said.

Miss Lytton hid her smile behind her hand, but her eyes sparkled. "That's a compliment, Captain Hawkins. I admired my father a great deal, and if I inherited a fraction of his talents and traits, I consider myself fortunate."

"If he was as determined as you are, he must've been a strong man."

A veil crossed over her eyes. "Yes . . . to seek for answers in the past, one has to be determined."

"You miss him," he said in a low voice, and she sighed.

Lavinia dabbed at her eyes. "I'll never understand why Walter had to travel to that hot land and dig in the sand," she said. "My brother had rather strange tastes. He insisted that Eliza work with him, and the English governesses he hired for her never lasted very long under that hot sun. But Walter always was . . . well, different."

Miss Lytton pinched her lips tight as she fought her emotion. "I would never wish to change anything that happened in the past." She glanced at the door opening, and as the barmaid appeared, he could hear Miss Lytton breathe deeply. "Ah, food."

The tray was laden with plates of steaming shepherd's pie and vegetables swimming in butter. "There ye are, then," the maid said as she placed the food in front of them. "An' 'ere's the bread."

The dishes smelled delicious, and Leo found that he had developed a great appetite. His current company intrigued him no end. As the maid left, he served more claret to Lavinia and took a deep draught of ale. His stomach growled in a most ungentlemanly fashion. He wished he could spend time with Miss Lytton alone, but he knew Lavinia would not leave her side.

He tasted his food, finding it superb. "I take it you have no siblings, Miss Lytton," he said after the worst of his hunger had been satisfied.

She shook her head. "No. I don't have very many relatives. There's Lavinia, of course, and her sister Delilah, who is married in Devonshire. We don't see her very often and she suffers from gout. Then there's Uncle Claude who's a recluse—a very learned man."

Lavinia snorted, and her cheeks grew rosy from the claret. "As for recluse, that's hardly an exaggeration," she said. "Claude always had his nose in a book, even more so than Walter, but he didn't like to travel."

"Nothing wrong with that, surely, Aunt," Miss Lytton said.

"No, but he has turned into a country yokel. He's no better than the farmhands on his land, outside in all weathers, pacing his fields. That's when he's not studying. Just as your father, he obsessed about the Egyptian culture, and the artifacts he displays at Broadmoor could not be more out of place."

"I see no harm in that," Miss Lytton said in defense of her uncle. "He's a very intelligent man."

"But a yokel all the same." Lavinia gulped down her wine and finished her glistening vegetables. "But he shan't bother me. I'll walk the mountains on my own."

"I never understood the tension between the two of you, Aunt Lavinia." Miss Lytton sent her relative an exasperated glance.

"That's neither here nor there. Claude is a stubborn mule and only accepts his own opinions. Woe is he who displays a different view."

"Like yourself," Miss Lytton said with a laugh.

Lavinia turned up her nose and glanced out the window. Leo listened, amused. "A family of strong people," he commented. "Perhaps it's something to be proud of rather than—"

"Pshaw, don't ingratiate yourself with me, young man!" Despite her strong words, her eyes twinkled, and Leo considered himself lucky to have entered the ladies' lives, even if it was only for a short while.

"You sound just like my father," he said.

"And what about your older brother, Captain? Does he have a brood of boys, too?"

"To his chagrin, Alan has only one daughter. My sisters got all the boys, and all the dogs, enough to support a hunt. Alan is hoping for an heir to carry on the name and the title."

"And what is expected of you, Captain?" Miss Lytton asked as she patted her mouth with a napkin.

"That is a very personal question, Miss Lytton." Embarrassed, he glanced out the window where clouds had gathered on the horizon, promising rain.

"Aren't you expected to marry and carry forward the name? I would expect you to have a lovely fiancée."

"I daresay. I have yet to meet someone who is willing to take a closer look. Besides, in the Peninsula I had few opportunities to meet eligible ladies. I don't see a bright future on that score."

"Surely, it's not that dire," Lavinia said, and drank some more claret. "You're a strapping young man."

"You're making him blush, Aunt. I believe we're too inquisitive; we're embarrassing him."

Leo laughed, startled by her gall.

"You *are* blushing, Captain," Miss Lytton continued.

"I have thick skin, and I'm used to brutal banter from my cronies. If you dig deeper you might find that my background is somewhat dull. I don't have illustrious or flamboyant characters in my ancestry. No one saved a king's head or led a conquering army."

He grew restless and looked outside once more. "It's time to leave, ladies. We might escape the looming rain showers if we set off now."

They gathered their shawls and gloves, reticules and parasols. Leo went into the taproom to settle with the landlord. He glimpsed the maid in the coach, vigilantly guarding the boxes within while balancing a plate on her knees. The coachman, Jimmy, was chatting with her, but she seemed standoffish, a lot more so than her mistress.

Leo escorted the ladies outside, and Jimmy hurried to assist them into the coach. Within minutes the equipage had entered the narrow, hedge-lined road where birds twittered in the greenery and sunlight dappled the road.

The clouds grew slowly thicker and chased away the sun as they proceeded down a slope and entered a valley dotted with elms, linden, and rolling green hills.

Leo's spirits rose with every hour that passed, and life seemed possible again after a year of joyless living. He would soon be soaked, but it didn't matter. In the Peninsula he'd been drenched more times than he could count, and the mud had caked everything, including his books.

The coachman hurried on the horses as if speed would save them from the weather. Within half an hour the sky opened and rain poured. The world turned dark, dripping, and gloomy, but the earth smelled fresh and the air sweet. Leo saw a small hand wave at him in the coach window as he rode beside the vehicle. Miss Lytton looked at him with concern.

"Yes?" he inquired as she pulled down the window.

"You're wet, Captain. We ought to halt the trip before it grows completely dark."

"There are some hours until that happens," he said over the hissing of the rain.

The weather did not improve until they entered Walford, a small hamlet off the main pike. Leo's clothes were damp despite the heavy cloak he'd worn, and he smiled grimly as the rain stopped abruptly as he jumped out of the saddle. His boots sank in the mud in the stable yard, and he studied the muddied sides of the coach that had pulled in before him. This was not an auspicious beginning of their journey, but not unexpected. So far, the spring season had been rainy.

He shook off his rain-soaked hat and went to assist the ladies.

"I'm very disappointed," Lavinia complained as she stared at the thick evening sky. "I had so looked forward to a bucolic, sunny trip up north, but the Hand that rules disappoints me again." She sighed. "But what can you expect."

She looked tired as Leo handed her down.

"At least we made progress, and here's The Wind and Whistle as planned." She pointed at the sign by the front door of the posting inn. "Needs fresh paint, and there's certainly no wind tonight."

The air hung damp and heavy, brooding in the silence of the countryside. The horses clopped through the mud as hostlers led them away. In the light from the lanterns by the coach door, Leo noted that Miss Lytton's mouth drooped and there were dark smudges under her eyes.

Her small hand lay trustingly in his as he helped her down, and that warm feeling curled around his heart once more. It wouldn't do to house any warmer feeling for the lady, as the whole prospect would be doomed from the start. He looked into her eyes, and the awareness of him reflected back, and his breath caught in his throat. There was *something* about her that he couldn't explain.

"Captain, this is not an indication of what is in store for us, I pray?"

He knew she meant the weather, but he could apply her statement to his feelings. "It most certainly is not, Miss Lytton. We'll see the sun upon the morrow."

She smiled and followed her aunt toward the inn. He escorted them inside and made sure they were shown to their rooms with brisk efficiency. The maid straggled behind, carrying a box and a leather case. Her expression was grim, and Leo instinctively didn't like her. He helped her upstairs with her load, and then hoped he had the evening to himself.

He eyed the warmly lit taproom with pleasure. Some food and ale would soon shake off the cold that tried to penetrate all the way to the bone. *Middle of May should be warmer than this,* he mused as he went to make sure his horse was housed and fed. He retrieved his valise from the coach and turned back toward the inviting lights of the inn. Wondering what was going through Miss

Lytton's mind, he stared up at the windows behind which her room was located.

Eliza shook out her damp gown and hung it on a hanger in the armoire as Lucy tut-tutted with disapproval. "'Tis not your place to take care of your dresses, Miss Lytton. That's my duty."

"I forget these details." Eliza sat down on the bed and sighed. "Why do we live with such complications?"

"Manners, Miss Lytton, manners."

Eliza pulled up her legs onto the patchwork coverlet of her bed and plumped the pillows behind her. She brought her writing case to her lap and unscrewed the ink pot and opened her journal. So many impressions crowded in her mind to be recognized, and she was eager to put them down on paper. She described every part of the day, and when she came to describing Captain Hawkins, she hesitated.

> *The captain is all that is polite and considerate. I am slightly taken aback at his handsome appearance, and cannot but be surprised that he's not married. He does not push himself forward in any way, but he's very charming. I find it difficult to admit to myself that I'm not wholly untouched by his gentlemanly ways. He's the epitome of a dashing officer, and if it weren't for his sadly injured foot, he would be perfect. Yet, I'm glad the imperfection has marred him as it makes him more human. He touches me in my core, and it disturbs me no end. I don't know how to explain it.*

She got no farther as her aunt entered the room and sank down on the only chair in the small chamber. As the ink on the page dried, Eliza closed the journal. "How is your bed, Auntie?"

"Rather lumpy, but I have slept on more unforgiving ground in my day. As you walk through the mountains, you have to use a rock for a pillow more often than not. But that's neither here nor there. I'm famished even though we enjoyed a large midday meal."

"We shall dine shortly in the private parlor downstairs."

"You're writing down the day's events, my dear?"

Eliza nodded. "Father taught me that habit. He wrote everything down."

"No details slipped by Walter. Now, tell me the truth; the whole page was about the handsome Captain Hawkins."

Eliza did not want to lie, but she had no desire to share her private impressions. "Auntie, he's one of the entourage, and I know I can trust him. He's a very solid gentleman, and I have yet to hear him complain."

Lavinia laughed. "You're right. I don't think he'll complain to your ears, Eliza. He's rather smitten, I'd say."

"Oh, balderdash! We hardly know each other."

"It has nothing to do with how long you've been acquainted, my dear. Lightning strikes without the least warning."

Eliza rose and swept an India shawl over her shoulders. Her simple dress of dark green muslin might not be warm enough if the rain had brought the cold with it. But she soon realized she wouldn't need it. Downstairs, the scents of boiled beef and onion met her, along with the blaze from a fire in the fireplace. The heat had evicted the damp, and she was grateful for the comfort. The private parlor offered cozy warmth as well, but just as they were about to sit down at the table, there was a commotion by the front door.

Eliza watched as the landlord and the captain hurried forward as a young man stormed inside, quickly dragging a young damsel behind him. They were both wet through, and the girl didn't look older than sixteen. Eliza and Lavinia ran to offer their assistance to the lady. It was easy to see that she was a lady due to the elegant cut of her cloak and her expensive silk bonnet, kid gloves and kid boots.

She stumbled inside, clinging to the young man's arm. She cried, "Thomas!" and then fainted on the floor.

Eliza got onto her knees and lifted the girl's head onto her lap. "Oh, dear, she's going to catch a chest cold if she doesn't get out of these wet clothes."

Lavinia fished a vinaigrette out of her reticule and unscrewed the top. Eliza wafted the strong odor under the girl's nose, and she came to, her cornflower blue eyes dazed. "Where . . . ?"

"Dearest sis, you had one of your spells," the young man said loudly, also kneeling beside her. He pulled her up and carried her to a chair.

"What is going on here?" Captain Hawkins demanded. "Were you set upon by footpads?"

The young man named Thomas shook his head. "No . . . our coach broke down not far from here. I'm escorting my sister to live with my grandmother in Yorkshire."

Eliza stared at him suspiciously, sensing he wasn't speaking the whole truth. His brown hair flopped in a wet wave over his right eye, and his neck cloth hung like a dishrag under his wilted collar. Damp spots marred the crispness of his coat, and he looked altogether despondent, like a dog that had to spend the day in the rain.

His sister didn't look much better, but color had returned to her cheeks, and she glanced around the taproom with curiosity. The landlord, smoking a clay pipe, was staring with great calm as if these types of upheavals occurred frequently at his inn.

"I'm Mr. Thomas Moffitt, and this is Valerie . . . er, Moffitt—also. We're from, er, Ipswich, and as I said, I'm escorting—"

"You seem rather young to traipse across England with your sister alone," the captain said. "Where are your chaperone and your servants?"

"They are unfortunately stuck in the coach. I. . .we, left them behind to fetch help. I'm sorry to be a bother, but mishaps are the reason we're here at this point in time," he added rather stiffly, Eliza thought. He had a haunted look that did support his story, but shouldn't the coachman have been the one to fetch help?

As if reading her thoughts, he said, "My servants are too old to venture forward in the dark."

"Hmm, sounds as if you're in dire need of support," she replied. "Why would your parents let you travel alone with only decrepit servants as escorts? To be blunt, I find that wholly irresponsible of you, sir."

"Yes . . . *ahem,* Father is . . . well, sickly, and my mother never travels."

"Surely, you have some older male relative who could shoulder the responsibility of your transport?" Captain Hawkins sounded incredulous, and Eliza saw anger flash in his eyes. "I find it highly irresponsible—"

"'Tis too late for recriminations," Eliza pointed out. "They are already en route, and we have to help them. Miss Moffitt looks quite done in."

The captain grumbled, but gave her a nod of consent.

Eliza took the young woman's soft hand, and it lay cold

and motionless in hers. "Let's go upstairs and find some dry clothes for you, and then some warm food. Tomorrow, we'll find out how your own attire has fared in the rain."

Eliza expected some kind of response, but none came forth. She led the young lady upstairs, noticing the quiet crying and the red button nose that peeked from the poke bonnet. She handed Miss Moffitt her own handkerchief. "There. Don't be upset; we'll deal with the situation tomorrow, and the comfort of food and warmth will aid you to see the situation more favorably. The men will assure your servants are brought back here tonight."

"Thank you," the young woman said, her voice trembling. She heaved a deep sigh of despair. "This will surely be the end of me," she whispered.

"What? You must be exaggerating. It's only a slight mishap that can be set to rights, Miss Moffitt." She pulled the reluctant girl into her room. "Let's see if any of my dresses fit you. We don't differ much in height."

Another sigh escaped. "My pelisse and my bonnet are surely ruined now."

"Nonsense. My maid Lucy has magical hands with distressed clothes." She shot a glance at Lucy who preened momentarily as she was folding a petticoat. Lucy studied Miss Moffitt and pulled out a pale yellow muslin empire-style gown with a matching spencer.

"This might fit the young lady." She also found clean stockings and a petticoat that had few frills to mar the straight line of the delicate dress.

Miss Moffitt kept dabbing at her eyes with her handkerchief, and Lucy untied the damp ribbons under the girl's chin and pulled off the bonnet. The blond curls lay damp and flattened underneath, and Eliza helped her pull off the wet pelisse. "I'm surprised you didn't pack a heavier cloak for unfortunate weather."

"There was no time," Miss Moffitt mumbled. "No time at all."

"Did you receive an urgent message from your grandmother?" Eliza pried gently, feeling sorry for the young girl.

Miss Moffitt shook her head, but didn't come forth with an explanation. Eliza exchanged a knowing look with Lucy and she sensed that Mr. Moffitt's story had big holes in it, and that the truth was much more dire. *I don't need to be saddled with more problems,* she thought, but it was out of the question to abandon this young lady in need.

"I will not judge you, Miss Moffitt, if you need to explain something to me," she said kindly, but the young woman stared stubbornly at the floor.

She replied with another deep sigh, and Eliza grew out of patience with her. Within minutes, Lucy had toweled Miss Moffitt dry behind a screen and dressed her in Eliza's dress, which fit reasonably. The damp locks started to dry, and shimmered with gold threads. Miss Moffitt was quite beautiful with her rosebud mouth, oval face, creamy complexion, and gleaming curls.

"You look much improved, Miss Moffitt," Eliza said and set down her quill. While the girl had dressed, she'd written down the startling events. "You must be famished, which will be remedied posthaste."

"Please call me Valerie, and even if I haven't said much, rest assured that I'm very grateful for what you've done for me, Miss . . . ?"

"Lytton. But you can call me Eliza. All this formality is quite tiring."

Valerie laughed, a sudden loud sound. "Your views are quite unusual, Eliza."

"I'm not used to the formal customs of this country."

As Eliza saw Valerie's curiosity flare, she explained about her years in Egypt.

"How daring! I would never care to live in foreign parts; I would wither away with longing for home."

"Well, Egypt *was* home to me as long as my father was alive."

Valerie's blue eyes clouded over with concern. "I'm sorry to hear he's no longer with us. I don't know what I would do if . . ." She let the words peter out as if the very thought overwhelmed her.

"Let's repair downstairs for our meal. It has been awaiting our attention."

"I don't know. I'm really not that hungry," Valerie said with some agitation. "My nerves are in turmoil, and my stomach in knots."

"I assured you we would help you take care of your problem, Valerie. Captain Hawkins is a very capable gentleman, and your brother seems to care about remedying the situation."

"I don't have a brother," Valerie blurted out, and then clapped her hands to her mouth, and turned red.

THREE

They halted on the landing above the stairs. "Will you repeat that, Valerie, or did I hear you wrong?" Eliza asked. "Is Mr. Moffitt your brother or not?"

Valerie looked like a trapped doe. Her eyes darted around the walls as if seeking a way out. "What I meant is, I don't have a brother who's very experienced with these kinds of problems," she said, her voice weak and unconvincing. "Thomas is too indecisive."

Eliza knew she was lying, but suspected she would get no further explanation if she pushed the issue. The truth would come out sooner or later, and the situation might be worse than she anticipated. She gripped Valerie's arm and steered her toward the stairs. "Let's join the gentlemen."

Valerie only nodded, obviously relieved that Eliza refrained from asking more questions.

"I warn you, Valerie," Eliza said, "if you're telling me untruths, we shall get to the bottom of the issue."

Valerie's face fell again, but Eliza wanted to put her on notice that she would not be bamboozled.

"I'm not a liar," the younger woman replied, suddenly haughty.

Eliza did not reply, and when they arrived downstairs, she found the captain wearing a grim expression. "Did you retrieve the servants and find out what was wrong with their coach, Captain?"

He pulled Eliza aside in the taproom. "I did. There are no servants, and the *carriage*, which is not a coach but a sporting curricle, has lost a wheel. They have no luggage, and the young man refuses to elucidate on the story. I'll have to take him severely to task before we leave tomorrow."

Eliza shook her head in exasperation. "I'm certain they eloped. We have a serious problem on our hands."

"Of all the shabby things," he yelled, and Valerie stared at him wide-eyed from across the room. "I daresay we could leave them to their fate, but I don't trust that young whippersnapper to take care of the young lady properly." He muttered under his breath. "I shall give him the sharp side of my tongue."

"He deserves it, but I suspect it won't make a difference at this point." She returned to Miss Moffitt, or whatever her name was. "Your servants must have run off with your luggage, Valerie."

The younger woman paled visibly and her face crumpled. Eliza led her into the private parlor where their dinners stood cooling on the table. She made her young charge sit down and handed her a napkin. "There were no servants accompanying you," Eliza said. "I don't understand how you could go haring off into the countryside with no chaperone and no luggage."

Valerie cried, deep sobs heaving her shoulders. Wearing a hangdog expression, Mr. Moffitt joined them in the room, as did Lavinia and the captain. A pall hung over them all. The greenhorn looked unsure and miserable, and his shirt points had wilted even more. His innocent face was pale and creased with distress.

"I . . . *ahem* . . . I *love* Valerie," he blurted out, pushing his hands through his damp hair.

"It's commendable that you love your *sister,*" the captain said, his voice cutting, "but I have to point out that you've failed in your duties, young man. You have acted with a total lack of decorum and circumspection."

"Just tell them the truth," Valerie said, her voice muffled by a handkerchief. Her eyes had turned red-rimmed and puffy.

Everyone's eyes turned toward the wretch. He stepped from one foot to the other, evidently tossing about ideas of what to say. "I, well, we, have presented ourselves under false pretenses. Valerie, isn't . . . er, my real sister."

The captain looked thunderous. "*Who* is she, then?"

"My beloved," the young man blurted out. He was now wringing his hands in despair.

"That much I've gathered," the captain said. "Tell me, what is her real name?"

"Er . . . well . . ."

"Valerie is my real name," the young woman said, still hiding behind the handkerchief. "Valerie Snodgrass. My family hails from Surrey, and if my father catches us he will *kill* Thomas." Her voice rose to a hysterical note. "He *hates* Thomas."

"By Jupiter, you're heading to Gretna Green in Scotland, aren't you?" the captain asked.

"It's the only way we can get married—over the anvil," Thomas said, obviously breathless with distress. "We love each other!" As if to prove his point, he fell to his knees next to Valerie's chair and looked adoringly into her eyes. She returned his gaze and touched his hand gently. A low moan passed her lips as if she were unable to take any more tension.

"Father is vehemently opposed to the union," she

reiterated when she could find her voice. New sobs poured forth into her handkerchief.

"He disapproves of Mr. Moffitt? I'm shocked," the captain said with severe cynicism, his arms crossed across his chest.

Valerie nodded. "Yes."

"I don't have the funds to support Valerie in the style to which she's accustomed, but she says she doesn't care," Thomas explained, again pushing a nervous hand through his hair. He looked more disheveled with every move. "As I said, *we love each other.* Surely there's no higher sentiment."

The captain smiled coolly. "I daresay, but do you have anything to compare your feelings with? From my perspective, you're rather inexperienced, and perhaps—foolhardy."

Thomas looked murderous for a moment, but the sentiment passed quickly. "I'm not that young," he claimed haughtily.

"Perhaps," the captain allowed, "but your actions are those of a greenhorn, so now is the time to finally grow up. You must return posthaste to your home; I shall hire a local woman to chaperone you, Miss Snodgrass, and servants to protect you. I can't believe you threw yourself onto the road without any kind of planning! No change of clothes, and probably no funds. How would you survive all the way to Scotland?"

"I have a brother in Northampton, and we would throw ourselves upon his mercy for a day of rest before continuing on," Thomas replied, his stance unsure.

"Meanwhile, you would just starve?" The captain sounded incredulous.

Thomas grew red around the collar, and stared stubbornly at the floor.

"We would rather starve than return to Surrey!" Valerie cried. "You don't know my father. He's an ogre. He will prevent me from happiness if he catches us. He has always prevented any chance of happiness I ever had." Her voice rose dramatically. "And he'll shoot Thomas through the heart."

"He's probably on his way even as we speak," Eliza pointed out as she placed a firm hand on Valerie's shoulder. "You should know better than to throw yourselves into the jaws of the unknown. Nothing good comes out of elopement. There's no happiness in tying the knot clandestinely, far away from your family, and without your sire's blessing. It spawns more hostility, nothing else."

Valerie clung to her arm, her expression filled with melodrama. "You must not abandon us, Miss Lytton. If you do, I will wither away with grief, I vow I will."

"Collect yourself, Valerie."

The captain looked thunderous, and Eliza exchanged an entreating glance with him.

"You'll have to protect us from my father's wrath," Valerie went on, her hands clasped to her heart. Her red-rimmed eyes brimmed over once more.

"We have no intention of acting as your saviors," the captain shouted. "If your father appears, well, so much the better."

Thomas put up his hands as if to soothe any ruffled feathers. "Don't take on so, Captain Hawkins. We don't intend to become a burden on you in any way. Valerie is distraught, but I shall contrive to take care of her."

Eliza motioned to the captain to follow her back to the taproom as Lavinia urged the rest of the company to sit down around the table. Eliza closed the door behind her, and the close proximity of the captain made her heart beat faster. His anger was palpable, and his eyes blazed.

"We can't put our mission to the side just to assist these idiots," he said under his breath.

"I realize it's an unforeseen circumstance, but I could not in good conscience abandon the young lady to the mercies of this world. She's lived a sheltered life, and I would worry about her among the ruffians and vagabonds that roam the roads."

He rubbed his chin in thought. "The moonling will be unable to protect her. He doesn't even have a pistol or any kind of weapon to protect them both from harm."

"They are in a romantic haze and have acted without thought. Consequences were far from their mind. They would just ride north in perfect weather, and reach that desired destination—Gretna Green. Trivial things such as rain and food, and arranging for shelter did not enter their minds."

He stared at her long and hard. "You have a good heart, Miss Lytton."

"I would hope so. If I had found myself in similar circumstances, I would pray someone would help me along the way. Not that I would ever elope."

"What do you suggest we do?"

"We'll have to escort them back to Surrey."

He sighed heavily and grimaced, but she could sense his capitulation. "Very well," he said. "It will throw you off your schedule, but if you don't mind that, I suppose it's the only solution."

She nodded. "Unfortunately, I don't see another solution—"

"Unless we hire someone to help them," he filled in.

"Wouldn't you worry about the safety of the young

couple? I would, and if anything happened to Valerie, I would blame myself."

"'Tis an unfortunate matter." He righted the cuffs of his blue coat, and shrugged as if defeated. "Let us inform them about our decision."

As she turned to move back into the room, he placed a restraining hand upon her arm. "You're a remarkable woman, Miss Lytton. Remarkable."

She noted that he was on the verge of saying something else, but he held his breath, halting the words before they could emerge. She glanced at his hand that felt warm and comforting through the material of her gown. The pull to step closer to him came over her, but she restrained herself in the last moment.

His eyes grew deeper, darker, and something sparked between them. The force of their attraction made her speechless.

He pulled away as if burned by an unexpected fire. "I . . . well, we should return inside before everyone wonders what became of us," he said, his voice gruff.

She nodded mutely, and she found that her hands were trembling as she opened the door. Valerie was still crying into her handkerchief, and Thomas looked both defiant and crestfallen. Lavinia was eating dinner as if nothing had happened. Nothing seemed to ruffle her, or make her lose her appetite.

"We've decided to turn back and deliver you to the bosom of your families. We'll make up a suitable story to prevent any scandal," Eliza said.

Valerie wailed. "*No,* please don't send me back. I will throw myself off the nearest bridge; I swear I will if you do."

Thomas fell to his knees and cradled one of her hands

in his. "Don't give me such a fright, my sweet. I won't be able to sleep a wink after such a dreadful utterance."

"Nonsense," the captain said severely. "Get up from the floor and stay away from Miss Snodgrass."

Thomas obeyed, slinking to the back of the room like a whipped dog.

"You cannot send me back, Miss Lytton," Valerie said, her voice rising into another wail.

Eliza sat down next to the young woman. "Now, tell me everything! Don't leave out anything, and don't offer me any falsehoods."

FOUR

Valerie blew her nose in an unladylike fashion, and a dazed look came over her face. "I saw this elopement as an answer to all of my prayers. I live with my father who is, well, very fond of the bottle. He always has been. My mother succumbed to inflammation of the lungs when I was young, and my father's sister stepped in to raise me." Her voice broke. "Aunt Elizabeth had no desire to raise a child, but she had no choice as she's penniless. My father has rather browbeaten her over the years, I'm afraid, and she is bitter because he hasn't helped her out of her financial straits. He is, well, a wealthy man, and my portion is rather grand. He thinks Thomas is a fortune hunter of the worst kind even though he's known him for years."

Eliza thought of her own father's pressure for her to marry Melvin Homer, so she found it easy to sympathize with the young miss. She glanced at Thomas who cowered on a chair in the corner, looking miserable, and sensed that he wasn't the calculating type even if it was obvious he had taken this great risk of running away with an heiress. He was too guileless to harbor anything but tender love in his heart for Valerie. Yet something gnawed at the back of Eliza's mind, but she couldn't grasp it.

"My father will punish me in the worst way if he gets wind of this," Valerie said. "He'll lock me up in one of the remote guest bedchambers and feed me bread and water for *weeks*!"

"Surely that's an exaggeration, Miss Snodgrass," the captain said, derision lacing his voice.

"You don't know him," she protested into her handkerchief.

"Treating you thus is incomprehensible. He can't be such an ogre," the captain continued.

"Yes, he is! The reason being, he's not my real father. I inherited all of my mother's money, and he's trying to get his hands on my funds." Valerie's tears grew profuse once more.

"He cannot if you're the legal heir," the captain said and folded his arms over his middle. His eyes had narrowed with suspicion.

"Out of spite, he'll try to stop me from marrying anyone," Valerie said and threw herself down on her knees. "Please don't force us to go back. I can't abide the thought, and Thomas and I belong together."

"Don't fall into histrionics," Eliza said and, gesturing, urged Valerie to stand. "You're overwrought. You need a good cup of tea and a soft bed. Things will look much better in the morning."

Valerie clung to her arm. "You have to promise me, Miss Lytton."

"I can't promise anything. We'll speak about it later and make a decision."

The captain addressed Thomas, "And what about you, young puppy? What is your story?"

Thomas emerged with new vigor in his step. "I've known Valerie all of my life. My father is a squire near Valerie's birthplace, Chaldon, in Surrey. However, father never was very good at managing the estate, and I'm afraid the whole family suffers the consequences. We are rather poor, alas."

"Hmm, if he's that stricken, how is it possible for you to drive as fine a rig as a curricle? And your matched bays are prime flesh."

"I borrowed the equipage from a friend of mine, Lord Wilsey. We went to school together. Father hopes I'll do better through my connections than he ever has, but I'm afraid progress is hard to make without funds."

"But you would have funds if you marry Miss Snodgrass," the captain pointed out. "She's quite a catch, isn't she?"

Thomas nodded mutely, his face growing redder by the minute. "I see that you're painting me with the same brush as her father. I'm not a fortune hunter," he shouted. "I love Valerie and I can't help that she's plump in the pocket."

"No reason to get upset, I'm only trying to investigate the matter. Believe me, young sirrah, we did not expect you to fall into our laps with your myriad problems."

Eliza put a finger across her lips as she saw that the captain's ire was rising.

"I *will* throw myself off a bridge—"

"That is an ill-advised notion, Miss Snodgrass, and if you insist on speaking such flummery, I shall wash my hands of you," Eliza said with steel in her voice. "I'm quite out of patience with the both of you, and I suggest that you withdraw to your bedchambers." She turned to Valerie. "Lucy will watch over you all night."

Valerie clasped Eliza's hand with fervor. "Thank you. I know I can count on you to help me."

Eliza pried loose the tear-wet fingers. "I haven't promised anything."

Valerie's bottom lip trembled. "And my father . . . beats me. I *will not* return to him. My back will be green and blue."

Eliza and the captain exchanged grim looks. These young people presented more of a problem than she had ever thought possible, and she sensed that Valerie would be true to her word.

"Go to bed," Eliza said once more. "We shall talk further tomorrow."

Lavinia led the distraught woman out of the room, and Thomas followed sheepishly. As he closed the door behind him, Eliza turned to the captain. "I daresay we have a greater difficulty than we expected." She sighed and sank down on one of the chairs by the table. The food was congealing on her plate, and she picked at it with her fork, but had no appetite.

The captain sat down opposite her and ate some of the cold stew and potatoes on his plate. "I have a suspicion that this problem will blossom into something much more dire."

"I don't know if I have the heart to send Valerie back to her father if he is such an ogre."

His eyes widened. "You suggest that we allow them to complete their elopement? That would be against every propriety, and the scandal would reach far and wide."

"I doubt that Valerie or Mr. Moffitt have moved in fashionable circles. They are innocent of the ways of the world, but brave enough to swim against the currents."

"Brave? They are senseless," the captain said, setting his jaw with disapproval.

She looked into his stormy eyes and felt that delicious attraction once more, but why would it appear at an awkward moment like this? Feelings had no respect for the problems looming ahead.

"Are you wholly set against aiding them to complete their trip to Gretna Green?" she asked, knowing his answer.

He nodded. "It's against everything that is decent."

She smiled. "Where is your sense of romance, your sense of adventure? Did you never enter a lark in your younger days?"

He relaxed and an answering smile lit his eyes. "I'm not that old, Miss Lytton." He leaned back in his chair. "I might have made a mad dash for the border in my younger years, but—"

"But now you're old and a curmudgeon."

He nodded, chuckling. "Yes. At eight-and-twenty I have developed high moral—and possibly prejudicial—standards. No more the young-buck-about-town, but I committed a few devilries in my time."

"'Tis staid and boring from now on?" She toyed with her fork as their eyes sent silent messages across the table.

"Definitely," he said. "I'm a monument of decorum."

She pursed her lips in thought. "Somehow I don't believe it, Captain. You're as eager for adventure as you ever were, and that's why you accepted this position."

He crossed his leg over the other and looked at her speculatively. "It could be that we're cut from the same cloth, Miss Lytton. You sallied forth with alacrity on this trip, and travel is in your blood."

She nodded. "Yes, I like challenges and a change of scenery. Too long in the same place, I grow restless."

"You're an unusual woman, Miss Lytton. Few ladies have expanded their world as you have."

"I'm grateful to have had that opportunity. I believe my father would have appreciated your uncomplicated approach to life."

"I deal with problems as they arrive, not dwell on them. Sometimes you have to make quick decisions." He tore a chunk of bread and spread butter over the uneven surface.

"And now we have to deal with this problem."

He nodded. "Trust me, we shall find the best solution. The adventurous part of me is ready to escort the young couple to Scotland, while the staid curmudgeon says 'absolutely not.' Miss Snodgrass has to return to her father however much she resents it. She's too young to know what's best for her."

"Mr. Moffitt does not strike me as someone who has the gumption to elope. He's a rather ineffectual young man."

"Desperation makes us do strange things. 'Tis likely Miss Snodgrass forced him into the situation if she was frantic to leave her father. He sounds despicable, and I don't have any previous knowledge of him. Miss Snodgrass evidently never had a Season in London, or she would've been a catch with her substantial portion."

"Yes, that's fact. She's barely out of the schoolroom, so I'm not surprised she hasn't had a Season. She's very comely and could pick any gentleman of her choosing, but she chooses this greenhorn."

"Love is incomprehensible, isn't it?" He lifted his claret glass and stared at her over the rim. "Tell me, Miss Lytton, have you ever been struck with love?"

"No, never," she replied quickly—too quickly perhaps. She looked away from his probing gaze. "Have you?"

He sipped gently and set the glass back down. He sighed. "Am I to open my bleeding wounds in front of you?"

"It's no more than right. You started the discussion with your suggestive question, Captain."

"I have some wounds, yes. I was betrothed to marry Miss Agatha Dillon when I returned from the war." He hesitated. "I didn't come back a hero, rather a shadow of my former self. I caught an infection in the wounds and almost died from it. She didn't have enough love in her heart to stand by me during my illness, and she married a local squire who had more in the way of funds, and at that time—health. It's entirely possible she had toyed with the idea of marrying him before I came home. I was absent for long periods during the campaigns, and it's likely she couldn't wait, or couldn't resist the man's charming ways."

He sounded bitter as he uttered that last statement, but he forced a smile.

"You've sworn off love forever?"

He nodded. "It's likely, but I realize she didn't feel the depth of emotion that I did. Who can blame her? She may have been helpless in the tide of emotion for this other fellow. An act of fate, perhaps."

"I admire your tolerance, Captain."

"It may have helped me develop a more mature view of romantic love. I doubt I'll ever be a victim of severe infatuation, such as these young turtledoves."

She laughed and poured some claret for herself into an empty glass. "Yes, I'd say they are in the throes of a turbulent sea. When they step out of it, they will wonder how they could get caught up in such a storm."

"You take a more sedate view on romance, Miss Lytton."

"Yes. With time comes life experience, but I'm inexperienced in love."

He glanced at her, a devilish glint reaching his eyes. "I've poured out my confession, now it's your turn, Miss Lytton. Surely you must have had admirers in Egypt and beyond."

"The community of compatriots is small in Egypt, and

my father and I led a limited social life. I was, however, invited to myriad dinner parties, where inevitably I encountered young men, but no one who touched my heart." She put down the glass. The wine was rising to her head quickly, as she'd barely eaten. "I don't think about it much."

"Surely you're going to marry someday. You're a lovely woman, combined with intelligence."

"Well, thank you, Captain!" She laughed.

"'Tis not a joke."

"Then I came across Mr. Homer, who had grand hopes for a union. My father favored the suit, but I cannot see myself tied to that man in any manner. In fact, just thinking about him makes me shudder."

"Not to worry. I believe you've given him a strong enough rejection that he won't bother you again. If he does, he's a coxcomb of the first order."

"Yes . . . but he has lofty aspirations, and he saw my funds as the means to establish his goals."

"I shall protect you, Miss Lytton. Since you've been abroad, I predict you'll take society by storm once you enter fully. Everyone will be curious about you. The gentlemen will fall at your feet."

"You're very kind, but I have no intention of entering the society whirl. It's insubstantial but at the same time rigid. One faux pas and you're considered an outcast. I have no patience for such narrow-mindedness. Besides, I would have to learn all the niceties to fit in."

"Are you saying you don't know the dances?"

"That's one area in which I lack."

He stood suddenly and bowed before her. "Let me teach you the most daring of the dances, then, the newfangled waltz. The patronesses of Almack's have frowned upon it, but I have no objection. Before my accident, I was rather fond of dancing."

He held out his arm to her, and she accepted as a bubble of laughter burst from her lips. "You surprise me, Captain."

"Because of my foot injury?"

"No . . . I considered you a rather cautious gentleman."

He took her hand in his and placed his other arm around her back. "I may have hidden depths. I might surprise you. Now, put your hand on my shoulder, and I'll guide you around the floor."

"Are you going to provide the singing, too?" She obeyed him with some reluctance as his proximity made her lose her reasoning. His hand felt warm against hers. Her heart had jumped to her throat as he touched her, and she swallowed, but it didn't slow her racing heartbeat.

"I'm sorry to say my voice is worse than a frog's. Now move, one . . . two . . . three." He showed her the steps, only slightly awkward with his damaged foot. She noticed that he was surprisingly light on his feet.

"I don't share your view that frogs possess inferior voices, Captain."

He twirled her around the floor, and she followed, almost sensing the music in her mind. "Very well, worse than a creaking door, then," he said.

She laughed. "That *is* unfortunate, and I don't have any oil in my reticule. I have to say you have a good sense of rhythm, though."

"And you follow wonderfully, though I suspect you're more comfortable in a leading position."

"It depends on the situations at hand. I'm content to follow you in the dance; it's quite exhilarating."

He gave her a mighty twirl, and she whooped with laughter. When she'd caught her breath, she found herself bent back over his arm and she felt deliciously helpless. A dizzy sensation of wine bubbled through her blood, rising to her head.

"You're going to wake up the entire inn," he said, laughter lacing his own voice. He lowered his head and gently touched his lips to hers. She lost every sense of time and place, now aware only of the softness of his mouth on hers. He grew more demanding, and she knew she should fight his daring advance, but she couldn't. She couldn't find an ounce of strength to stop him, and part of her didn't want to. Her mouth opened under his, and she responded to his kiss, drowning in its sweetness.

When he finally released her, she caught her breath and stared into his dark, passionate eyes. She sensed his longing, which responded to hers, something he must read in her eyes. When she could find her footing, she moved out of his arms.

"I . . . well, I never expected," she whispered and touched her lips.

"I'm sorry," he said, taking a step toward her, but she moved away. "I don't know what came over me, Miss Lytton. I only wanted to show you the dance that is all the rage in London."

"Thank you," she mumbled. Her face blazing with embarrassment, she looked for her reticule and remembered it was in her bedchamber upstairs.

He stood irresolute in the middle of the room. "You must judge me as a complete scoundrel," he said, his voice low with concern.

"I . . . no, but it was—the kiss was unexpected," she said. "We'd better forget this ever happened if you want to stay in my employ."

"Of course I do. I acted like an oaf, and I would fully understand if you don't want to ever see me again."

"No—no," she said, holding up her hand to stop any further words from him.

"Miss Lytton—"

"Just don't tell anyone, or my reputation will be tarnished. Not that I care much about that as I know my own sterling qualities, but there's no need to alarm Lavinia or the servants."

"I fully understand. I don't have any plans to force my attention on you further, and I'm grateful for your tolerance."

She turned toward him and smiled. "Kissing is not a crime."

"You're right on that score, Miss Lytton, yet I'm concerned—"

"Evidently not concerned enough to stop the assault on my senses," she scoffed gently.

He spread out his hands as if searching for something that would change his past actions. "I don't know what came over me. You bewitched me."

"So the blame is all mine?" She went and stood in front of him and crossed her arms over her chest. Straightening her back, she met his gaze fearlessly.

He thought about her challenge, a smile playing over his lips. "Yes," he said finally. "Your vivacity and the allure of your lips so close to mine made me lose my head."

"Now you're piling injury upon injury."

"If you're not careful, I might kiss you again," he murmured. He stepped closer but she moved away, heading toward the door.

"I never thought of you as a rogue, Captain, but I find that impressions can be deceptive."

"Truly, I'm not normally like this," he defended himself.

"The whole atmosphere of this evening addled my brain—and the claret, of course."

"Whatever you blame it on, I expect you to be in control of your senses, Captain. And your actions. I will let this slip by, but any encore will be frowned upon."

He nodded. "I assure you it shan't happen again, Miss Lytton."

She left the warm parlor, closing the door behind her. The passage was drafty and cold, and she hurried toward her chamber. She sensed that the captain was not trustworthy when it came to the matters of the heart. He would take advantage of her if she spent any more time alone with him. Part of her was thrilled at the idea, but the more sober part said he had nothing to offer except a clever tongue and a handsome physique.

But perhaps she had something to offer him.

FIVE

When Eliza woke up in the morning, her head ached and her limbs were heavy as if she'd not slept at all. She thought of the situation at hand and realized they hadn't quite decided what to do with the young elopers.

She would have a good talk with Valerie before they went down to breakfast. She dragged herself out of bed and Lucy looked at her with disapproval. "The water is ready for your sponge bath, Miss Lytton. I pulled out your heavy green traveling ensemble even if the weather seems fine this morning." She fluttered around the room like a nervous hen, picking up garments. "Do you want breakfast sent up?"

"No, Lucy, and don't fret over me. If the weather deteriorates, I shall cower in the coach with you."

"I daresay it's the best way to travel."

Eliza made her ablutions and sat patiently as Lucy fashioned her curls into a chignon with delicate tendrils framing her face. Her maid's touch was brisk and heavy-handed, but Eliza's mind was on other things and she didn't pay much attention to Lucy's ministrations.

She couldn't get the memory of her dizzy waltz with the captain out of her mind. She relived the force of his mouth on hers, and the weakness she'd felt in his arms. He had taken advantage of her, but she hadn't minded.

In fact, she'd encouraged him by staying in his presence until she couldn't stretch it out any longer. She wondered if he were plagued with the memory of last night as well.

Leo Hawkins had finished tying his neck cloth and when he was satisfied with the folds, he shrugged on his blue coat and adjusted the simple fob chain across his middle. He had slept soundly due to his deep level of exhaustion, but it had taken hours to fall asleep. The memory of Miss Lytton's laughing eyes and the softness of her lips haunted him, and he cursed under his breath. He longed to hold her in his arms again; he longed for companionship, for romance.

But he had no right to be in the throes of these feelings for Miss Lytton and resented his weakness. The stark truth kept staring him in the face. He saw no way to pursue this connection with her, as he had nothing to offer her. From now on he had to maintain his distance, or he would be singed by fire. *Stay away from the flames of passion or you're bound to burn,* he told himself.

With another curse and a sigh, he brushed his hair and went downstairs after packing his simple belongings into his valise. As an officer, he'd learned to live simply and he liked it. The rigors of military camp had taught him to sleep anywhere and to pack up and move quickly if necessary. It was a certain sense of liberation, and he'd chafed under the restrictions that his injury had put upon him.

He was not about to put himself at risk to becoming a prisoner of his emotions. He'd better push away the disturbing thoughts of Miss Lytton, he thought. It would take a lot of discipline, but he could accomplish it. The years as an officer had taught him lots of discipline.

He pulled on his top boots and went downstairs. Today was a new day, yesterday long forgotten.

He almost collided with Miss Lytton on the landing, and his heart made a mad somersault, damn it all. Her mouth looked just as inviting as it had yesterday. "Good morning," he greeted briskly. "I hope you slept well, Miss Lytton."

She nodded. "Yes, thank you."

He wondered if she was lying. The dark shadows under her eyes spoke of a restless night. "Glad to hear it," he replied.

Her gaze searched his, and he glanced away. "And you, Captain?"

"Despite the rather rough aspect of the mattress, I slept well," he lied. He indicated that she should walk down the stairs ahead of him, and she did, her head held high. He sensed they had reached a silent agreement with their brisk formality. This is how it would stay for the rest of his employment, he thought, and set his jaw.

In the private parlor Lavinia was drinking coffee and chatting with Miss Snodgrass, who still wore Eliza's gown. Valerie threw a frightened glance at the captain, and one of pleading at Eliza, but Eliza steeled herself. There was no easy solution to the problem at hand, and it looked as if they would be saddled with the young couple for the rest of the journey.

As Eliza sat down to a plate of eggs and kippers, and hot coffee, Valerie came to her chair and fell onto her knees. "I beg of you—" she began.

Eliza's patience snapped. "From now on, keep to your feet when addressing me, Valerie. I won't cotton to any histrionics on your part, and if you are to go to Scotland with Mr. Moffitt, you'll obey my slightest command."

Valerie clasped her hand ecstatically. "Dear Miss Lytton, thank you!"

"I said *if* you are to go to Scotland. I must have windmills in my head to even consider such a foreign notion." She pulled away from the cloying clasp and pointed at Valerie's chair. "Return to your seat, please."

Valerie obeyed, radiant.

"Where is Mr. Moffitt this morning?" the captain asked as he viewed the young woman.

"Oh, he sleeps long hours," Valerie said with a dismissive wave of her hand. "I daresay he's still in the land of oblivion."

The captain pushed his chair back and marched toward the door. "He's a nincompoop of the first order," he said to the room at large. "I'm not about to change my schedule because of him."

He came back five minutes later, his expression thunderous. "The man sleeps like the dead, but I roused him. Cold water on the face will do the trick."

Eliza chuckled. "How much water did you actually use?"

"Half a pitcher. Almost choked him," he replied and set to eating his cooling breakfast with gusto. "He'll be altering his habits quickly if I have any say about it."

The firmness of his voice amused Eliza. His military training would be useful in this instance.

The sleepy youth joined them twenty minutes later, his neck cloth askew, and his shirt points still sadly wilted. In fact, he looked as if he'd been dragged through a hedge backwards. His Byron curls that had been pomaded yesterday had lost their luster, and now lay like a wilted floor mop on his head. He wore an anxious expression as he sidled into the room.

"Did anyone catch up with us?" he asked, his voice subdued. He sent a frightened glance toward the door.

The captain shook his head. "Not yet, but I daresay they are not far behind us."

"Then everything is doomed," Mr. Moffitt said morosely.

"We decided to bring you along—for now. At least Miss Snodgrass will be chaperoned, and we can contrive a plausible story, should we face confrontation. Her reputation won't be in complete ruin."

"Thank you!" Mr. Moffitt acted as if he wanted to fall to his knees, too, but Eliza waved him away. "Hurry up and take some sustenance, Mr. Moffitt. We don't want to be delayed, and I'm quite out of patience with you."

He slunk to his seat and his thin arms darted out to ladle some food from the platters onto his plate. By the tall mound of cold eggs, Eliza knew he didn't lack an appetite. Whatever Valerie lacked in that department, he made up for with obvious delight.

Eliza and the captain exchanged amused glances, but her amusement mingled with a wave of frustration at this added burden. She would have to deal with it, and she genuinely wished to save Valerie from her ogre of a father.

They set out an hour later, the landlord waving on the front step. The party had brought him profit, and he'd made sure they got the best posting horses.

It would be a long day, but at least the sun was brightening the greenery around them, and the sky seemed bluer than ever before. A few cottony clouds floated across the sky, but no threat of rain hung upon the horizon. The day would be simply perfect if it weren't for

Valerie sitting in a corner of the coach sniffing into her handkerchief and sighing.

"Surely you ought to be happy about our decision, Valerie," Eliza said in a firm voice. "There's no need to shed any more tears."

"They are tears of relief," Valerie said, her tones muffled by that much-abused handkerchief.

"Then they ought to dry up shortly. A smile is much more attractive, and much less melodramatic."

Valerie gave her a sullen look. The moodiness of the young woman bothered Eliza. "Buck up, Valerie. Look on the bright side."

"Very . . . well," Valerie said with a theatrical sigh. "I'm grateful to you and the captain." She gave another heavy sigh. "He's rather a handsome fellow, isn't he?"

"I haven't looked too closely," Eliza said defensively. "He's in my employ, nothing else."

"If it weren't for that limp, he would be perfect, and I'd say he looks at you very fondly."

"He's a satisfactory employee and a kind man. I have nothing to say against him. Not that I'm prone to gossip as it is. I find it a very destructive pastime."

Valerie nodded. "It ruins lives. It's rather rampant in my village, and has done a great deal of harm . . ."

She didn't elaborate, and Eliza wondered if she hinted at her own life, or someone else's.

"It saddens me that you haven't had a female family member to guide you. No aunts, no older cousins?"

"I do, but Father has frightened them away. No one ever visits any longer, and he has expected me to care for the household, which I can't begin to manage. I have little experience in that area, and the servants have been less than helpful. They resent anything I say, and my father has done nothing to improve the situation with them. It has been quite intolerable for a long time now." Her lips started trembling anew.

Eliza put up her hand as if to stem the flow. "Desist, do. I have no patience with watering pots."

Valerie hiccupped once and blew her nose hard, but she wore a stoic expression when she emerged from her handkerchief, and her eyes were dry.

"It surprises me you haven't had any other suitors, Valerie. You're quite fetching and you have an ample portion. Mr. Moffitt isn't exactly a man of the world even though he aspires to become one. I could see you make a much more fortunate match."

"Thomas is nice . . . well, easily managed. He's uncomplicated, so unlike my father, and I'm quite fond of him."

"Fond? You mean to tell me that your true feeling is fondness? To take the enormous step of marrying someone you ought to be sure of your love for one another first."

Valerie looked out the window, her expression mutinous. "I made my decision. Thomas will make an excellent husband, and I wish nothing else, or no one else." She took a deep breath. "That is—" She never finished the sentence.

Aunt Lavinia tut-tutted in her corner, and Lucy pretended she wasn't listening as she stared out the window. "On top of everything, you'll have a rushed, clandestine wedding, which won't leave any pleasant memories behind," Lavinia said. "It's a sad start to anyone's married life."

Valerie gave her a cool glance. "Be that as it may, it's better than staying with my father, and as I told you, Thomas will be a good husband."

"He's a popinjay," Lavinia said mercilessly. "He can barely put one foot in front of the other without tripping."

"That's very unkind of you, Miss Lytton," Valerie said to the older woman.

"But true nevertheless. You're about to take the most momentous step in your life, and your sole reason for it is to escape from your previous situation."

"I *am* fond of him," Valerie said with a show of temper.

Eliza looked out the window where Mr. Moffitt was riding with the captain. He still looked bedraggled with his wrinkled coat, pale complexion, and worried expression. He'd pushed his beaver hat low over his brow, and he tried to keep up with the captain's superior mount.

The captain looked handsome as he sat straight and proud in the saddle. As if he felt her eyes upon him, he turned his head and stared straight at her. Her heart leaped and she broke the contact immediately. How had this happened? She couldn't explain their uncanny connection, but it was there. Her cheeks burned and she promised herself she wouldn't look at him again.

Leo had felt her attention like a charge, and he was surprised at the intensity of her gaze and his own reaction to it. He cleared his throat, flicking the reins, and the horse surged forward. He longed to stretch out in a wild gallop across the countryside, but that wasn't part of his duties. The bright sunlight glanced off everything around him, creating an almost painful brilliance. After yesterday's rain, the grass shone greener than ever, and the trees swayed gently in the southern breeze. The air smelled of molding leaves and flowers in bloom. He hadn't felt this alive since before the accident, and the pain in his foot had improved.

This was life—the open country, the ever-changing vistas.

He shaded his eyes with his hand and looked down the winding lane. Everything was quiet, and he saw no other equipages on the road. It was still early. They had left the inn to take advantage of the glorious weather.

The young whippersnapper rode up beside him. He couldn't see the beauty all around him. He threw a furtive glance over his shoulder past the carriage.

"Captain, I believe we need to hurry, or the party following us will catch up."

"What are you afraid of, Moffitt? Will her father call you out?"

"In all likelihood he'll shoot me on sight," Mr. Moffitt said with great trepidation. "He has a terrible temper."

"And that would be within his rights to do," Leo said bracingly. "In his shoes, I would be tempted, too. You're doing Miss Snodgrass a disservice, and you'll look back on these events with regret."

Mr. Moffitt's horse snorted as if agreeing with Leo. "I have no other choice, do I? There's no gainsaying Valerie when she sets her mind to something."

"I thought you love each other so much you can't be parted," Leo said and urged his mount off the road. He watched the coach lumber past, the oval of Miss Lytton's face visible in the window. He tipped his hat to her, and she turned away from him. That's how it was going to be, then, he thought, some of his former happiness evaporating.

But she acted correctly. He had no business wishing she had smiled and waved at him. This was no more than a paid assignment, and he had to keep reminding himself of it.

"I hope Miss Lytton keeps Valerie hidden for the rest of the trip. It would be the safest thing for us."

"There's no reason why a search party would suspect us of having a connection with you. They won't look at us twice, and your curricle is back in Walford. When they discover that, they'll think you are traveling post—or by common stagecoach as you're low in funds."

Mr. Moffitt looked very uncomfortable. He inserted a grubby finger under his neck cloth as if it were too tight. "Perhaps they'll follow the stagecoach and search it. That will give us some more time."

"Perhaps. You made a daring move and now you have to live with the consequences."

The young man moaned under his breath. "Devil take it, what induced me—" He stopped himself before he had finished the sentence and threw Leo a furtive glance.

"I sense there's more to this story. You haven't told us everything, and if you want my protection, you'll have to make a clean breast of things."

"There's nothing else. I fear the consequences, and I never expected to carry this heavy a burden upon my shoulders. I don't know how I'll contrive to make Valerie happy. She's the sweetest woman alive, but underneath she has a will of steel."

"I daresay she'll lead you in a merry dance, young man."

"Damnation," came the tortured reply.

"You're too young to be leg-shackled, my friend. You need a few years upon the town to sow your wild oats."

"Yes . . . but, well, I'm committed to Valerie, y'know. I always honor my promises."

"That is commendable. This adventure will make you mature very fast."

"Captain, I'll have you know I am a grown man," the youth said haughtily. He straightened in the saddle, looking slightly less bedraggled.

Leo chuckled to himself and remembered his days of innocent youth. Every day was a new adventure to explore, and every young lady a conquest. He'd had boundless energy in those days, and he'd never lacked it until the accident. But he could feel his energy return, as the sap flows in the trees in spring.

They arrived at an inn, The Hawk and Arrow, in the small hamlet of Farnham, for their noon meal. Miss Lytton got out of the coach and stretched. She beckoned him closer.

"Arrange the food to be sent outside, if you please, Captain. I'm going to sit under that oak," she said and pointed toward a small hill topped with a giant tree. "Some ham and bread with cheese is plenty for me."

Lavinia winked at him and followed her niece up the slope to the welcome shade of the tree. Valerie stayed in the coach with Lucy. Leo went inside and ordered the food from a serving wench who carried a large smoked ham in her sturdy arms. "And a pint of ale for me and the young man," he said. He sat at the long wooden table and waited for his order to be filled. Mr. Moffitt joined him shortly. "I'm famished, Captain."

The captain laughed. "Nothing wrong with your appetite, eh?"

The youth shook his head. "Where's Valerie?"

"There's no reason for her to be seen around here," Leo replied, and threw a cautious glance at an old gentleman nodding by the sooty fireplace. "We'll take out some food to the coach."

The maid served them the ale, and then carried a basket full of food outside. Leo finished his ale and went back outside. He joined the ladies on the hill, and Miss Lytton invited him to sit on their blanket. "There's plenty of bread and ham," she offered.

Grateful to get off his feet, he sat down. He surveyed the food: thick slices of ham, a round loaf of bread that Miss Lytton was tearing into pieces, a fruit compote in a bowl, a wedge of plum cake, and a flask of lemonade. Delicacies, indeed, when one's stomach was grumbling, he thought. He received a hunk of bread from Miss Lytton's hand, and their fingertips touched, making him acutely aware of her presence.

He shot her a glance, but she didn't return it. She handed him a slice of ham and he joined it to the bread and ate. After he'd swallowed, he said, "Food always tastes better outdoors. Why is that?"

"Perhaps it's the company," Lavinia replied, and he regretted his question as it led into a treacherous area he wanted to avoid.

"The birds and the butterflies, of course," he said smoothly. "Not to forget the squirrels." *Saved.* He pointed to one that had climbed onto a long branch above and was staring at them, probably hoping that some food would be left behind.

"This is the perfect picnic spot," Miss Lytton said with a sigh of pleasure. "So quiet and serene."

He nodded. "Yes. You can see the road but also the hills and valleys in the distance. We still have a long way to go, and the countryside will only get more beautiful as we travel into the mountains."

Miss Lytton laughed. "You sound so wistful, Captain. There must be a poetic streak hiding within."

He shook his head and laughed. "No, I'm afraid not.

The Muses passed me by completely. Perhaps you are overcome with odes that have to be written down, Miss Lytton?"

Her laughter filled the air. "No. We're in the same predicament, it seems, but I enjoy writing in my journal."

He caught her glance, and that special spark flared between them. She glanced away instantly, and he wished the older woman wasn't present. But then again, Lavinia was the perfect barrier to any dalliance. He'd promised himself he would stay away from Miss Lytton, but she pulled him inexorably. It had been like this since the moment he first laid eyes on her.

He finished his simple meal as quickly as he could. "I'll be waiting for you by the stables, Miss Lytton." With a bow, he left them alone.

"He's so handsome," Lavinia said with a sigh. "You could do a great deal worse, Eliza. But I know your father wouldn't approve of such a match. He never liked military men, did he?"

Eliza shook her head. "No, he didn't, but I believe he would've looked past the uniform to the individual." She thought of Melvin Homer, her father's choice for her, and shuddered. "Father spent years with me, yet he could not read my heart. That he would think that Mr. Homer and I would suit is an atrocious miscalculation."

"You're right on that score," Lavinia said and struggled up from the blanket. "I'm glad I'm too old to have to ponder eligible suitors."

SIX

The journey continued, and that night everyone slept in deep exhaustion. The weather had cooperated, and by the end of the day they had made up for lost time. They had reached the inn at Setterworth on the border to Leicestershire, as planned, and after a meal, everyone had retired to their rooms.

Eliza wrote in her journal:

> *Our travel is going well despite the addition of two elopers for whom I feel responsible. Young people so in love and it makes me wonder if I'm ever going to find that connection with another. I have to admit I find Captain Hawkins so very attractive and interesting—indeed, relaxed. He's keen to make sure I'm always comfortable, and no one ever paid that kind of attention to my well-being. I find that soothing, and I find that I long for more.*

She blushed as she put down her quill. It was true that she longed for more attention, and that she wanted to see where it would lead. But she was unsure how to go about it.

* * *

The following morning, Jimmy the coachman stepped into the taproom and caught Leo's attention. "Cap'ain, sir."

"Yes, Jimmy." Leo noticed the troubled look on Jimmy's face.

"Sum'un 'as destroyed one of the shafts on the coach."

"What—?" Leo followed the coachman outside with a curse under his breath. "What happened?"

"Dunno, Cap'ain. When I woke up this mornin' and went out to do me business, I saw that the shaft 'ad been smashed."

"How odd." Leo surveyed the damage and found that the wood had truly been splintered right at the area where it attached to the horse. "It looks as if it were done with an axe." This was no accident.

"There's a wood shed be'ind the stables, Cap'ain. Sum'un was per'aps lookin' for valuables to filch, and when they couldn't find them, they broke the shaft."

"Why would they unleash such a fury?" Leo had no answer to that. "We'll have to find a carpenter who can fashion another one until it can be rebuilt properly."

"Devil take it, Cap'ain, it'll take a few 'ours." Jimmy scratched his head under the woolen hat.

"Well, however long it takes, we can't continue until it has been done."

"Aye."

"I'll talk to the landlord. He'll know of a local carpenter." Before going back inside, Leo went to look for an axe in the woodshed and found one lying on the ground next to the stump they used for splitting the logs. He could not tell whether it had been used to break the shaft, but in all likelihood this had been the tool.

Leo returned to the inn and wondered what to tell Miss Lytton. The truth, no doubt. He hadn't been able to protect them from this misdeed, but who would've thought vandals abounded in the area?

He spoke with the owner of the establishment who promised to send one of the grooms over to Mr. Hull, who did excellent work—for a price.

Leo smiled coolly. "That doesn't surprise me," he said. "But carry on. I'd like to be gone by midday at the latest."

"I'm surprised this 'appened, Captain," the landlord said. "We don't often see vagabonds and ruffians in these parts. I'll send for the constable as well."

"Thank you," Leo said. He went to break the news to the ladies, who had just finished their breakfast in the private parlor at the back.

"Good morning, Miss Lytton and Lavinia, Miss Snodgrass. I expect you had a peaceful night." He addressed Miss Snodgrass. "All except you, perhaps."

She sighed theatrically, and he hurried to continue before she could open her mouth. "I have something to report. There has been a mishap." He told them the details and Miss Lytton's eyes widened.

"Who would want to break—?"

"Any villain, Miss Lytton," he explained. "They saw your carriage—one of fine quality, I might add—and decided to see what they could find within to steal."

"How very crude," Miss Lytton said. "How uncivilized!" Her eyes blazed with anger. "They didn't find anything because we didn't leave anything behind."

"A very wise decision, Miss Lytton." He explained how long it would take to mend the shaft, and she had to resign herself to the delay. "I daresay anything is possible when you travel. You leave yourself open to both good and bad things."

"At least no one was injured," Lavinia pointed out.

The whole morning was lost to a frustrating wait, but

at least they'd found someone who could fashion the piece they needed. The carpenter discovered something on the ground as he worked. It was small gold fob, nondescript, yet elegant with engraved leafy swirls. Leo turned it over in his hand. The vandals must've stolen it from the owner of the fob before they got to the coach, or the man who'd destroyed the shaft had lost it while laboring. Vandals did not wear gold fobs, he thought.

But why hadn't anyone heard the man—or men—as they worked the hatchet? He couldn't quite reconcile the facts.

Miss Lytton approached him. "You look thoughtful, Captain, quite grim, in fact. What is worrying you?"

"I've been pondering why this happened, and why someone didn't hear anything in the night. The stable hands sleep right above the stables. That's close to where the coach was left for the night."

She nodded thoughtfully. "Yes, I agree. You think it has anything to do with Miss Snodgrass and Mr. Moffitt? Then again, no one knows they are with us."

"Their relatives would not attack your coach; they would attack *us*, rather, or me." He glanced down the road, which was empty. "I suspect we won't be alone for very long. With these kinds of mishaps, the people pursuing the young lovers will overtake us soon."

Distress crossed her normally calm features. "I'm not wholly convinced it was the right thing to take them along, no matter how cruel Mr. Snodgrass is. We've stepped into responsibility that we know little about."

He touched her arm gently. "You're a very capable woman, and I have no doubt that you're able to salvage the situation. The truth is that we're protecting Miss Snodgrass and I don't care what anyone else says."

She breathed out slowly. "Thank you for your support,

Captain. I find that you surprise me with your depth of dedication. It's more than I ever expected, and I admire your aplomb and calm authority."

His face brightened in a smile. "Thank you, Miss Lytton. Those words have made this trip with its challenges very worthwhile."

She blushed and looked away. "But that's all," she said. "Don't let the compliments go to your head."

"Never!" He glanced at the small gold fob again, knowing something was wrong. "I believe it's important that we leave as soon as possible. I don't like that strangers lurk around your coach at night."

Eliza nodded. "I agree."

The trip continued, and nothing untoward happened that day. A shower in the afternoon drove them to seek shelter in a copse of trees along the road, but the rest of the day was uneventful. The day's delays caused them to fail to reach their goal, and they were forced to spend the night at a small inn north of Leicester that had inferior beds and a landlord who served lumpy potato soup as the main fare.

Miss Lytton, however, did not complain. She got up the next morning with a smile on her face, and Leo admired her fortitude. He had slept terribly on the hard mattress, and he'd listened with half an ear for movements outside. His head sat like a leaden weight on his shoulders.

He returned her smile. "If I didn't know better, I'd say you'd slept the entire night on a feather bed."

"I pretended I did," she said with another smile, and sat down at the rough table where a large bowl of porridge stood, surrounded by smaller bowls and spoons, and a pitcher of milk. The porridge had turned glutinous, and as she ladled it out, the glob stuck to her spoon.

"Dear me," she said, not daunted in the least.

"It tastes no better than it looks," he said, "but you have to break your fast somehow. Perhaps the bread and butter are easier."

She sent a dubious glance at the rough rye bread slices and shook her head. "I don't dare to try. I might crack a tooth."

He nodded. "There's always a chance of that." He enjoyed looking at her graceful movements. "Tell me, what did you eat while in the desert of Egypt?"

"Lots of flat bread and dates, smoked meat that was tough as shoe leather, all kinds of fruit, and various grains that were cooked every day with spices. My habits are simple, and I've slept on harder ground than the lumpy mattress upstairs. One of my fondest memories involves the hard bottom of a boat and the bounty of stars. We traveled down the Nile by boat to a village near the excavation sites. The sky in Egypt is indescribable, so dark and velvety at night. The millions of stars are brighter than anywhere else—unforgettable. I got the sense of a universe that is unfathomable, yet almost at my fingertips if I just stretched high enough."

He smiled. "That's beautiful. I can picture it."

"I got so lost in the stars that I never really felt the hard boat under my back. I could've spent every night lost like that, but duty called eventually. My father had no patience with the stars. He was a very practical man, and he wanted to accomplish so much before he died."

"He lost a lot of beautiful moments by not paying attention."

"Do you ever gaze at heavenly bodies, Captain?" She chewed on the tough porridge and swallowed.

"I have at times. I've lain by the Atlantic Ocean staring at the brilliant canopy above. The overwhelming beauty has touched me many times. I believe there's so much more to discover about this world, and the next."

"Yes, I suspect we know very little, but for those who so wish, there's plenty to explore."

"You're an unusual woman, Miss Lytton. You never fail to intrigue me."

"In the area of research my father did, you find that our time is just a small pearl on an endless string of what went on before, and what is about to come."

"You're right, and some knowledge is lost already. We can catch only a glimpse of the greatness of the ancient Egyptian civilization."

"Yes, and with the simple tools they had, they created a lot of beauty. Father had an ancient artifact or two that the Egyptian government gave him for cataloguing myriad finds."

She valiantly ate some more porridge, and then put her spoon down with a thud. "I think it's time to wake the others. We have no time to lose after the delay yesterday."

Leo went outside and breathed deeply of the morning air. Wraiths of mist hung over the meadows around the inn and shrouded the trees in mystery. In the distance, horses were grazing in a field. Everything was so peaceful even the birds sounded subdued. He suspected they would come to life once the sun penetrated the mist.

He went to inspect the coach. To his utter outrage, he discovered that someone had painted great red swirls all over one side of the body of the vehicle.

"Hell and damnation!" he shouted and kicked a tussock of grass. "Why didn't I put out guards? Who would've thought!"

He couldn't believe this had happened and he dreaded telling Miss Lytton. He didn't have to. She had followed him outside and stood speechless beside him as they surveyed the damaged coach.

"I'm sorry you had to see this, Miss Lytton. I have failed in my duties to protect your property."

"You had no idea this would happen, Captain."

"No, but I knew what happened yesterday, and I should've posted an all-night guard just in case something else occurred—as a precaution. Someone is following us." He touched the paint gingerly with his fingertip and found that it was still wet. "I'm going to have this taken care of."

He asked the stable hands to help clean off the paint, which they did with turpentine-moistened rags. Not all of it came off, and the smeared paint cast a pink tone to the black surface underneath. No one had seen anything untoward, and Leo grew more concerned. This was vandalism at its most insidious.

He glanced at his employer who could not hide her disappointment even if she tried.

"I promise you, Miss Lytton, that this won't happen again. From now on, we're going to keep a close eye on the coach at night, and everything else as well. No more nasty surprises."

She nodded, a puzzled look on her face. "Who dislikes me so much they're willing to stay up at night so that they can wreak havoc with my possessions? I don't have any enemies."

"Did your father have competitors in his field, people who aspired to reap all the glory? Perhaps they are searching for the material your father entrusted to you, but why would they vandalize your property? That is plain vindictive."

"Yes. Father had no enemies that I know of. He was a peaceful man, and was never driven by the idea of rewards at the end of his work. He loved that old civilization and that's what motivated him to discover more. There were others who only did the research for the possible fame they might gain, but never Father."

"I see. We'll exclude envious fellow researchers for now."

"Besides, they are mostly still in Egypt. I'm the only one who has returned."

"It's mystifying," Leo said and rubbed his chin. "The paint speaks of dislike and anger."

"Yes. Vindictiveness." She leaned against the stone wall of a well in the stable yard. "I'm quite flummoxed." She glanced toward the road. "If we see someone with red under his fingernails, we know who the culprit is."

"Yes, but he or they might be long gone."

"He lost that fob as well. I suspect the perpetrator is the same."

She sent him a sideways glance. "I don't know how this is possible. I have nothing really of value except my father's findings, and his writings. The tablet he worked on deciphering is safely in Cairo. He had a cast made from it, from which my uncle will work to decipher the rest. I brought two artifacts from Egypt that might serve as a lure to villains, but they are not here. Besides, who would even think of following me? I don't know very many people in England."

"It is a mystery, but I suspect we'll find out soon enough. I also imagine that he or they will strike again."

She looked unhappy. "I'm sure you're right, and it bothers me no end. All I wanted to do when we set out was to travel peacefully to the North Country, and on the second day of our journey we got saddled with problems not even of our own making." She gurgled with sudden laughter. "The whole business is absurd."

"One thing we do know: you have no enemies."

She nodded, dragging a finger along the cleaned surface of her coach. It came away with a pink tinge. "No, but the person who did this must harbor a grudge against me."

"Do you suspect anyone?"

"The only person I know who might have gotten offended by my forthright manner is Mr. Homer, the man my father hoped I would marry."

Leo thought back to the encounter outside Miss Lytton's house in London. Homer had seemed respectable enough, but sometimes the façade could be deceptive. He had appeared angry, but had concealed it well.

"It's preposterous to think that Mr. Homer would go through all this trouble to avenge himself. A young greenhorn might follow us, perhaps, but Mr. Homer is of middle years and rather staid. His mother would never let him leave her side for any number of days just to pursue me."

"It is rather far-fetched, but perhaps he counted on your financial support. Who knows how long he's been counting on this union to come to a close. Your father might have mentioned something, and Mr. Homer never married, waiting patiently for you to come back. He had expectations." He touched her shoulder. "I'm sorry—"

"Don't commiserate, Captain," she said, turning toward him. "These events won't bring me to my knees."

His hand fell off at her abrupt turn. She stood so close he could see the bright warmth in her eyes, and the fearlessness. He was grateful for her strength.

"You're a lioness, Miss Lytton, straight off the plains of Africa."

"Hmm, come to think of it," she said, staring at a pink

smudge on her finger, "I always wanted to see the lions in the wild, but never had the chance."

"Perhaps one day. I would like to take you there," he blurted out, instantly regretting his words.

She stared at him intently. "That is very kind of you, Captain, but I don't see an opportunity for that."

"Of course not. I don't know what came over me—a thoughtless comment, no more."

She smiled. "I can easily see you riding an elephant, Captain. You're rather a fearless man and an adventurer at heart."

He chuckled. "I accept your compliment. You make me feel manly and strong."

She laughed out loud at that. "Look at us. We ought to be outraged over this last debacle, and all we can do is stand here and laugh."

"And talk about elephants."

Lavinia soon joined them, dragging a sleepy Valerie with her. They both stared wide-eyed at the coach. "What happened?"

"Perhaps you can enlighten us, Valerie," Leo said. "I daresay this is more than some silly prank."

Valerie cringed behind Lavinia as if loath to look at the coach. Miss Lytton stared at her, but the young woman turned her gaze away, turning up her stubborn chin.

"Valerie, please look at me," Miss Lytton said. "Do you know anything about this?"

The young woman shook her head mutely, her face hidden by the wide brim of her poke bonnet.

"Why do I sense that you're lying?" Miss Lytton asked, her voice severe.

"I'm not lying, Miss Lytton," Valerie said, looking up at

last, her eyes flashing. "Why would I be the one involved in every mishap? It's excessively unfair."

"I didn't imply you're involved. I only asked a simple question and you reply with disproportionate anger."

"I feel persecuted, and I'm innocent," Valerie said, her whole body trembling, and her face crumpling in a fit of tears.

"Dear me," Lavinia said and handed the young woman a handkerchief. "Here we go again."

"I'm quite exasperated with your tantrums, Valerie. You'd better dry your eyes, or I might consider leaving you right on this doorstep." Miss Lytton pointed toward the inn and the rough front door. It was not a place at which to be stranded. "From now on, act with poise and decorum, and I don't want to hear another word of complaint about the lumpy mattress or the state of the food we're served." Miss Lytton indicated the inn anew. "Now go eat some porridge. It'll be the only fare you'll have until we arrive at our destination this evening."

Valerie strangled a wail, and turned beet red. Leo sensed her fury and wondered where the bedraggled waif they'd rescued on the first night had gone. Miss Lytton stared at her with narrowed eyes, and the young woman finally tromped off to the inn. How much porridge she would eat was anyone's guess.

SEVEN

The coach set off with the captain and Mr. Moffitt in tow. The tension inside the carriage was high after Valerie's rebellion, and Eliza sighed inwardly. Everyone's suppressed tempers did not suggest a tranquil trip through the sunny landscape. She exchanged a pained glance with her aunt, and they both looked at the young woman who sat ramrod straight in the corner, a wounded expression on her face.

Eliza promised herself that if Valerie's attitude didn't change, she would free herself of the young woman's company. Drat the girl and the greenhorn tied to her apron strings! Eliza was hard pressed to see any happiness in the future of that duo. Their relationship was surely cursed from the day Valerie and Thomas clapped eyes on each other.

"It's the strangest thing that someone would paint your carriage, Eliza," said Aunt Lavinia. "It seems almost like a curse."

Eliza laughed. "Curse? I don't believe in curses."

"Neither do I, and I daresay it was a prank perpetrated by some local youths." She turned to Valerie. "Do you have any thoughts on the matter?"

"Only that it was cowardly and unnecessary. If someone

holds a grudge, why not vent it in public? After all, you were present at the inn."

"You're right on that score," Eliza said with a sigh. "I'm no wiser, but this should be the end of it."

Late that evening, after an uneventful drive, they stopped at a large posting inn, the Bird and Hand in Chesterfield. Everyone was tired, but the evening was beautiful with a light breeze and a setting sun that colored the sky in dazzling pinks and oranges. Spring could not be more glorious, Eliza thought and inhaled deeply as she got out of the coach. She shook out her green traveling dress and readjusted her hat and pelisse. Her legs felt wooden, and she longed for a short walk to stretch the tightness out of her body.

"Lavinia, please take care of Valerie until I get back. I'm going to walk down the lane for ten minutes to ease my stiffness."

"I would like to accompany you, but I'm floundering with thirst. I shall go in search of some lemonade, and I'll take Valerie in hand. She won't say no to some refreshments, and Lucy will have your cases brought to your room."

Eliza started walking, enjoying every moment of the summer evening. She heard steps behind her and turned her head, finding the captain catching up with her. He fell into an easy step beside her, his limp barely noticeable.

"I'm here to protect you—part of my assignment, if you recall."

She smiled. "No need to sound defensive. I wasn't going to rebuff you, even if it might be the best thing."

"Why? I'm concerned for your safety. Even in these mellow woods you might come across footpads. I won't take that risk."

"Your concern warms me, Captain, but I'm perfectly safe. I know how to swing my umbrella if need be, and my kicks are rather sharp."

He laughed. "I don't wish to come within your range, should your ire arise."

"Egypt is full of beggars and pickpockets. I developed eyes in my neck while I was living there."

"You're a most unusual woman, Miss Lytton."

"You've said that upon occasion. But you must've met many interesting people abroad during the campaigns."

"Yes, I did, but we had no time to develop new friendships as the army was on the move. I rarely had a quiet moment, but every day of the campaign in the Peninsula brought new challenges. I was never bored, and yes, we encountered some lovely Spanish señoritas. They are spirited and outspoken, not unlike you."

"The English misses are tied too tightly to convention, and perhaps the gloomy weather has something to do with their spirit."

"Tonight is a rare moment of beauty," he said enigmatically.

"Yes . . . the weather is certainly cooperating."

"Tell me, Miss Lytton, will you stay in England, or do you long for a sunnier climate?"

"I haven't given it much thought. I have to put order to my affairs, and when that's done, a new life begins. I might help Uncle Claude with the research, but I don't have the burning interest that he has, or my father had."

"You might take up embroidery or watercolors," he teased.

She narrowed her eyes. "I'd rather join my aunt on her walks through the lake country."

He didn't reply, and she noticed that he looked thoughtful. Finally, he said, "I hope you have sturdy walking boots." His eyes twinkled. "Perhaps you can build palaces, or government buildings, open up a shipyard, or become the next ruler of England."

"You're jesting, of course, but I admit I enjoy challenges. Architecture has always fascinated me, and ships are amazing, intricate works of art, and I like to rule the roost," she said matter-of-factly.

He threw his head back and laughed. "You have a perfect answer to everything, Miss Lytton."

She nodded, unable to look at his attractive, smiling face. She longed to stick her hand in his, or feel his arms around her, but she had to fight the yearning. She kept her attention on the sandy lane before her, and listened to the birds in the trees, and the crickets in the grass. The sun was now a red line over the treetops, and dusk was slowly creeping in. They had walked farther than she thought.

"I think we'd better return to the inn," she said.

"Yes . . . but I've enjoyed this short foray into the Derbyshire countryside." She sensed he was about to add something, but held back. His voice grew sharper. "I'll arrange for surveillance of the coach tonight."

"Do you believe Valerie's father will catch up with us?"

"He, or whoever makes up the search party, must be traveling slowly. If they rode, versus traveling by coach, they would've come upon us already."

"Yes. I'm not sure anyone is following us. Valerie is not the forlorn waif she portrayed on the night we first encountered her, and Mr. Moffitt seems helpless against her charms."

"The mystery shall be revealed as we go along, I'm sure. They are spoiled children, and even if we're tempted to abandon them, we cannot."

"Yes, but my patience is sorely tried, Captain."

"If we can find a side saddle, you can ride with me tomorrow, breathe the fresh air and admire the vistas. Lavinia is more than able to keep a tight rein on the damsel."

"You and I might get lost in discussions, Captain, and lose track of the coach."

"What better way to get lost, Miss Lytton? I'm sure the horses will toddle along behind the carriage."

"Is this an invitation?" she asked, her heartbeat escalating.

He thought for a moment. "Yes, I daresay it is, but there's no calculation on my part to remove you from your company, only a sincere wish to ease the tedium of the journey."

"I accept," she said, and threw a glance at him in the gathering gloom. Something rustled in the grass beside the lane, and she instinctively stepped sideways, bumping against his solid torso. "Oh, dear," she said.

He caught her before she could fall, and held her steady. His warmth burned through the sleeves of her dress and made her skin come alive under his touch. She held her breath, staring into his dark, enigmatic eyes. A muscle worked in his jaw, but otherwise his face revealed no expression. The pull to stand on her toes and kiss him tormented her, and she struggled with the longing. He stood stock-still, only holding her, staring.

She regained her footing and slowly stepped back. He let go of his grip, and smiled. "You want to build palaces, but you're afraid of mice."

"Mice? It could've been an adder ready to strike."

"Doing it too brown, Miss Lytton. Admit it, you're afraid of mice."

"Very well," she conceded, filling with aggravation.

She stepped quickly down the lane toward the noisy inn. "I don't like the furry creatures."

He chuckled behind her, and she felt weak with tension.

"Honesty is a virtue," he said.

"There's no reason to tease me, Captain." She hurried faster down the lane, and had soon left him behind, as he could not maintain the quick pace. She regretted her action, but she didn't trust herself with him any longer. In fact, she didn't trust her own emotions.

"Miss Lytton," he called out after her, but she ignored him. She almost ran to the sanctuary of the brightly lit inn.

As she stepped inside, everything was pandemonium. Four young children were running everywhere, and a matron of ample girth wearing a huge mobcap and a woolen cloak sat on a wooden settle with an infant clasped in her arms. An older gentleman stood talking to the landlord, and the children ran in loops around him.

Another gentleman, this one dressed in a flawless blue coat and shiny Hessian boots, stood at the counter where a large ale barrel rested on its side. He held a tankard of ale to his lips, and his blue gaze played over the scene. His blond hair was curled and pomaded, and his long fingers bedecked with a multitude of rings.

"Miss Lytton, I presume," the landlord said and bowed.

She nodded to him, but had no desire to yell to be heard over the noise.

He indicated that she should step toward the back where an open door beckoned her. The children crossed her path, laughing and chasing each other, and she fled. The blond gentleman bowed to her as she passed him. He looked intriguing, but she read the subtle lines of dissipation on his face and decided he would not be someone she'd like to know better.

Lavinia sat inside the private parlor with Valerie, and they threw curious glances at Eliza as she stepped inside and closed the door.

"What infernal ruckus," Lavinia said. "A schoolroom of youngsters descended upon us. They are tearing up the taproom, and their parents aren't disciplining them in any way. I'm quite distraught at all the noise; it's giving me a headache." She pressed her stubby fingertips to her temples and sighed. "A cup of strong coffee might be just the thing."

Valerie was picking at a bowl of cherries and eyed a plate of strawberry tarts set before her. Her lemonade glass was empty. There was no sign of Mr. Moffitt, and Eliza was grateful for that reprieve. She sank down on a chair, her head still filled with images of Captain Hawkins holding her. She could still feel the slight pressure left by his hands on her arms. It would not do, she thought, as her heart raced. These are silly, romantic notions, and I have no desire for dalliance.

A harried barmaid brought in a basket of bread and bowls of oxtail soup. Then came a platter of sliced veal and mashed turnips, green peas, and a dish of potatoes. Eliza's stomach growled, and she wondered where the captain was.

Leo surveyed the location of the coach as the breeze was picking up, tossing tufts of hay into the air.

He made sure the coach had been parked as close to the stables as possible. He would pay to have a guard on duty all night, and chose two of the sharpest stable hands to do the duty. They were pleased to make the extra money, but expressed the opinion that Leo had windmills in his head. He didn't argue the point.

"If someone does damage to the coach tonight, it'll rest on your shoulders," he threatened.

They looked confident enough, and Leo went back to the inn, where he wondered if there would be any empty beds left after the huge family milling in the taproom had been settled. He eyed the stranger at the bar, and decided that a tankard of ale would be just the thing.

"Good evening," he greeted the stranger. "I'm Captain Hawkins."

"Theodore Findlay."

"The Findlays of Bath?" Leo eyed the blond-haired gentleman, younger than himself by perhaps five years.

The stranger nodded. "Yes. Traveling to Yorkshire. A hunt, y'know. And you? Sold out, have you?" He viewed Leo's civilian clothes and obvious limp.

"Yes, your powers of observation are keen."

Findlay laughed. He was already slightly foxed. "I've been doing nothing but stare at these plaguey thimble-wits all evening. It's very much of a bore, and I've vowed to never be saddled with that many children." He indicated the four lined up at a table shoveling potatoes into their mouths. "Why they don't have a nursemaid, I don't know."

"Perhaps they can't afford it."

"Then show some restraint in the marital chamber," Findlay said in disgust. "Damned idiots."

"Some people like children." Leo raised the tankard to his lips, disliking the man more by the minute.

Findlay shuddered. "I'm not made to be a father. Give me the turf, the hells, and the hunt, and I'm happy."

Leo looked at the cheerful children and realized he wanted some. He wouldn't mind a family with the right woman—if he could find someone who would consent to marry him. "The gambling and the turf get deuced boring in the long run. You realize at some age that you want life to continue long into the future. That's why we have children—to see a future for ourselves—in them."

Findlay laughed, an altogether unpleasant laugh. "Pure selfishness when it comes down to it? Never thought of it that way, but you'll turn up your toes like the rest of us, and then what do you care?"

Leo chuckled. "And here I am, thinking I'm immortal." He viewed the younger man's elegant clothing. "Spending the night or just changing horses?"

"No, I think I'll spend the night. There's a young woman here who caught my interest."

Leo felt a flash of intense jealousy as he thought it might be Miss Lytton.

"The haughty blond damsel. I would like to see her humbled a notch or two."

Miss Snodgrass? Leo gave the man a narrow stare. He liked the man less and less for every word he uttered. "She's spoken for," he said.

"You're warning me off? She gave me a saucy enough wink when she walked by, and I sense a rather free and spirited young woman behind that prim façade. Fancied a sampling for myself."

Leo moved so close he could feel the man's breath in his face.

"Step back, sir," Findlay said, surprised.

If it weren't for the other guests, Leo would've gripped Findlay's lapels and twisted, and he would have planted him a facer. "You heard me. She's not available. You stay away from her."

Findlay shrugged. "Very well. No skin off my nose. She's just another simpering miss, and I prefer my women more mature—such as the other one, the short one with fire in her eyes."

Again that knife of jealousy twisted in Leo's middle. He longed to wring the man's neck, but something told him that Findlay was trying to raise his ire beyond the point of no return. Why, he didn't know, but Leo had no problem with self-control. "The women are under my protection, and if you so much as tweak a hair on their heads, you shall answer to me."

Findlay laughed. "At least you're taking your position seriously."

Leo nodded curtly and stepped away. Boiling, he went to join the ladies in the private parlor, and found that a plate had been set aside for him. Only then did he realize how hungry he was.

EIGHT

The next morning Leo got up with the rooster and went to check on the coach. The morning was crisp, dew resting on every blade of grass and every flower. Mist hung over the meadows, and the sun was warming up the world. The hens pecked inside the chicken coop by the stables, and the horses chomped and snorted within their stalls.

His nerves tightened as he surveyed the coach and found to his relief that nothing had happened. He found that one of his sentries had fallen asleep sitting in the driver's seat, and he went to poke him with a stick. The man's slouch hat fell off, and he jerked awake, staring wildly around him.

"What . . . when . . . don't ye dare!" He raised a blunderbuss as if to shoot, then he recognized Leo. "Oh, it's you, sir. Sorry."

"It's me, and I caught you sleeping."

"Just forty winks, sir." The stable hand set down the blunderbuss and came off the coach as if drunk, but Leo realized he wasn't quite awake yet. "It was real quiet, sir. Not a twig moved all night."

"That's good," Leo said, relieved, yet wondering if the man had slept all night. He looked inside the coach and found nothing untoward. And when he glanced underneath, he found nothing out of order. Any misdeed had been foiled, and perhaps they'd left the villain behind at Setterworth. He ordered the groom to have the coach ready for travel in one hour.

He returned to the inn and the landlord served him some hot coffee. "Lovely mornin', ain't it?" the man commented, sounding tired. "The birds shrieked sumthin' arful outside me window at dawn. 'Tis enough to drive a body insane."

"I can't recall I heard the birds until I stepped outside." He sipped the coffee, leaning on the wooden counter, which was sticky with old ale. "By the way, do you know the gent who drank ale here at the counter last night?"

"Mr. Findlay?" The proprietor rubbed his stubbled chin, and shrugged his heavy shoulders. "'E told me 'e was bored, and was lookin' for some sport. Not much of that in these parts, unless ye 'ave friends."

"Still here?"

"Aye, I reckon that 'un will sleep late. A man about town likes the dark hours better than daylight."

Leo wondered if Findlay had any connection to the past defilement of the coach, but he doubted it. Miss Lytton had not recognized him, and he'd seemed mostly interested in Miss Snodgrass. It was just a coincidence that the man happened to be here at the same time as they.

An hour later Miss Lytton stepped downstairs looking fresh and bright as a new penny. She wore a pearl gray traveling habit trimmed with bright red braiding, and a matching hat that supported two red ostrich feathers that curled over her forehead.

"You look beautiful this morning, Miss Lytton."

She smiled and mouthed a thank you. "Captain, you're up early as usual. Did you have a good night's sleep?"

He nodded. "I did, but I have to admit some worry about the coach lurked at the back of my mind, giving me nightmares. I found out, however, that it's safe. Nothing untoward happened last night."

"Thank God for that," she said with a smile of relief. She looked out the window toward the stables as if concluding that all was well, and then sat down at one of the tables in the taproom. She soon enjoyed a cup of coffee and fresh crumpets that came from the kitchen in the back. She offered him one, but he declined.

"If we push hard today, we'll make up for lost time," he said. "We are not advancing as quickly as we could."

"We're not pinched for time. Uncle Claude is expecting us, but he doesn't know the exact day of arrival. We still have to deal with the young couple."

Leo nodded, annoyed as he thought of their awkward charges. "If we're fortunate, they'll decide to run away," he grumbled.

"That's very uncharitable of you, Captain. They won't run away as they don't have any funds with which to support themselves. We have to take them to Gretna Green, which is not that far from Carlisle, near where Uncle Claude lives."

"I'm trying to shirk my duty."

"For a military man, that is unusual," she teased.

"I daresay my patience runs thin when I'm faced with such immaturity as they display."

She brushed some crumbs off her cuff. "Yes, I suppose you bypassed those stages in life, or you don't remember. I, however, recall those awkward between times."

He nodded. "You're too kind, Miss Lytton. You make me feel quite inadequate."

She laughed. "Liar."

He was going to rebuke her when commotion on the

stairs brought his attention to Lavinia and Valerie appearing together. Valerie looked as if still half asleep, and she wore a sullen expression.

Lavinia, however, looked sprightly. "I'm ready for some ham and eggs," she told the landlord. "Bring a pot of strong tea, too, please."

Valerie sat down at the table, and Miss Lytton offered her a crumpet, which she accepted with reluctance. She picked it apart on a plate and ate minuscule pieces. Her hands trembled and Leo noticed her tense shoulders.

"Where's Mr. Moffitt?" he asked.

"Not down yet," Lavinia replied and stared toward the kitchen.

"I'd better light a fire under him, then," Leo said and walked up the stairs to the bedchambers above. He almost ran into Theodore Findlay on the landing. The man bowed stiffly, his eyes bloodshot. He may have looked tired but he was a picture of elegance even this early. His neck cloth lay in flawless folds, and his waistcoat of watered silk and coat of blue superfine sat perfectly creascless on his muscular body. His boots shone with newly applied blacking, and his hair had been arranged to perfection.

"Good morning," Leo greeted.

"Is it that good?" Findlay replied. "I would like to wring the neck of the rooster and have him for breakfast."

"I wouldn't if I were you. I suspect the landlord is not a very forgiving man, and would not take kindly to such an act. Looks like he has a handy pair of fives."

Findlay only laughed and bounded downstairs. Leo went in search of young Mr. Moffitt and found him sleeping with his head under the pillow and the heavy quilt tossed to the floor. He shook the greenhorn's shoulder and only got a grumble in reply.

"If you don't get up now, Moffitt, we shall leave without you."

"That . . . would . . . *ahem,* be a blessing," came the muffled reply, a response that made Leo uneasy.

"You have thirty seconds to get out of bed." Leo pulled the pillow away from the young man's head.

Thomas Moffitt struggled up and sat on the edge of the mattress. He groaned and clutched his head as if he'd drunk too much on the previous night.

"Where did you get the brandy?" Leo asked. "You retired early."

"It's not brandy. I'm plagued with headaches, and last night I spent tossing and turning, trying to find a solution to my current dilemma."

"Yes, any gentleman with a code of honor would be disturbed with current events. At least I'm glad to hear that you have a conscience."

Moffitt groaned, his head still in his hands. "Dear God," he whispered. "Why . . . why . . . why?"

"What are you talking about, Moffitt?"

"Don't mind me, Captain. Give me a few minutes to gather my wits. I'll join you downstairs shortly."

Leo had to be content with that. Suspicion had risen within him, and he sensed there would be lots of problems to face before the mission to bring the couple to Gretna Green could be accomplished. Mayhap it would never happen. The groom didn't seem overly keen on the idea, and Valerie had changed from the blushing, anxious bride to sullen reticence. He couldn't fathom what had happened between them.

Downstairs, Mr. Findlay had engaged Miss Lytton in conversation and everyone was laughing at some witticism he'd uttered. Leo cursed him under his breath, knowing they would all be better off if they left the inn right away.

He knew the man had only one goal, to further his own schemes.

Valerie had begun to glow with pleasure at the man's attention. Findlay leaned against the door frame between the taproom and a side chamber. He cradled a tankard of ale in one hand and gesticulated with the other as if making a point.

". . . and there I was, running as fast as I could as her father was aiming a pistol at my back. This only for an ode that I had composed to her beauty." Findlay turned to Valerie. "She could not hold a candle to you, Miss Snodgrass. I could wax quite lyrical gazing into your blue eyes."

Valerie simpered and looked down at the table.

"That won't happen, Mr. Findlay," Miss Lytton said with some asperity. "As you see, Miss Snodgrass is amply chaperoned, and any further blandishments will fall short. In fact, they will be frowned upon."

Findlay clapped a hand to his heart. "You're stabbing me, Miss Lytton. Have you no heart, no romantic lode of gold in you?"

"I daresay I'm a practical person."

"Too practical, perhaps?"

Miss Lytton laughed. "You're incorrigible, Mr. Findlay. I have a great nose for untruths and flowery balderdash, and I'm not easily taken in. You, Mr. Findlay, have sharpened your talent for finding the most useful phrases to seduce the ladies."

"I'll take that as a compliment, Miss Lytton."

"You may take it as you will; we're going to continue on our journey." She stood, her back straight, her face full of purpose.

Leo admired her immensely, and he was grateful that she'd seen through Mr. Findlay's slippery words. Valerie looked reluctant to leave, and Mr. Findlay stared at her with narrowed eyes. Leo made a shooing motion with his hands toward her. "Miss Snodgrass, the coach is waiting."

She gave Findlay a small smile, and he bowed, but reluctantly, as if loath to take his eyes off her even for a moment. Miss Lytton brought the young girl outside and Lavinia followed suit. Lucy had already packed away the boxes with Sir Walter's papers in the coach, and the valises had been stowed away.

While waiting for Mr. Moffitt, Leo ate some bread and ham, washing it all down with coffee. Mr. Findlay followed his every movement with his eyes, as if trying to decipher the plans for the day. Leo stared back, chewing. As he finished he said, "I realize you might consider flirting with Miss Snodgrass a great sport, but I assure you that nothing will come of it, and to get to her, you'll have to come to me first." The veiled threat hung in the air, and he gave Findlay no room to speak.

"Moffitt, there you are at last." The young man came downstairs, still as bedraggled as a wet dog. He looked no better than a scarecrow in his stained and wrinkled coat, and he hadn't seen a clean shirt since before the trip. It was clear he'd had no time to pack any change of clothes. "I'll have to lend you a fresh shirt tomorrow."

"Why would you do that?" Mr. Findlay asked, full of curiosity. "Did the young man fail to bring his valet along for the trip?"

Thomas Moffitt gave Mr. Findlay a murderous stare. "Deuced brazen comment coming from a stranger," he blurted out. "No one asked you to speak."

"Hurry up to eat something before we leave, or take it with you," Leo intervened before tempers could flare brighter.

"I'm not hungry, and this *gentleman* ruined any appetite I might have had," Moffitt said, furious.

"Well, no time to nurse grudges. Let's go," Leo said and almost pulled the young man out of the building. "You're acting like a bear with a sore head. What got into you, young popinjay?"

Moffitt sighed. "'Tis too early in the morning to encounter such conceited fribbles. I resent—"

"That's neither here nor there. You have to concentrate on the trouble at hand. You have to contemplate how you're going to take care of your young wife after the ceremony. I won't be here to aid you. Time to grow up."

Mr. Moffitt moaned, his face paling. "Oh, my head!" He rubbed his temples and slouched forward, walking like a hunchback toward the stables.

Leo felt a stab of pity for the cawker, but Moffitt had chosen this road for himself, and had been fortunate to encounter helpful people along the way.

"Get yourself under control, Moffitt. You're not a damsel in distress."

That got him to straighten up and focus on the object at hand, to get onto his horse. He managed, his teeth clenched. He gave the coach a sullen stare, and Leo knew without a shadow of a doubt that Mr. Moffitt didn't want to go any farther. He would have a serious talk with him that evening.

Eliza did not ride with them; evidently she was guarding Miss Snodgrass.

As they paused at a hedge tavern to slake their thirst with lemonade and ale, Leo took a short walk around the premises. He came across Mr. Moffitt and Valerie on the road outside the tall hedge that bordered it. They were having a heated discussion.

"You never told me that—" Moffitt cried, his voice tortured with emotion.

"You never asked, you maggot wit," she shouted back. "Do I have to explain everything to you? Grow up, Thomas. I'm getting excessively tired of listening to your moral tirades."

He pressed his face close to hers. "You're behaving—"

She stomped her foot. "You have no right to lecture me, Thomas Moffitt. You're worse than my father with your speeches. I believed you were my ally, my friend."

"I am," he shouted, and then halted abruptly as he noticed Leo's presence.

"I daresay your rose-tinted adventure is already seeing some wear," Leo said.

They both fell silent, staring at him with confusion. Valerie had lost none of her hostility.

"I suspect we made a huge mistake when we decided to aid the two of you," Leo continued, angry with the young couple. "You'll have to make a clean breast of everything if I'm to take another step north with you."

"Clean breast?" Mr. Moffitt asked. "We have nothing to hide."

"Well, you're not the loving turtledoves one would expect in a situation like this."

"I have known Thomas most of my life," Valerie said haughtily, as if that explained everything.

"You do treat him like an abused younger brother, Miss Snodgrass, and I'm surprised to witness your arrogance in this matter of the heart. You claimed to love him beyond words."

"You don't know anything," she said in a voice full of accusation. She gave him a challenging stare. "What *do* you know of matters of the heart? You don't even have the gumption to approach Miss Lytton even if it's clear for everyone to see that you have a *tendre* for her."

"It's simple. She's my employer, and I adhere to the moral code of a gentleman."

"How stuffy!" A world of contempt laced her voice.

If he were to be honest with himself, perhaps she was right, he thought. But his actions were not under scrutiny. "There's no reason to turn this discussion away from yourself, Miss Snodgrass. I shall have the truth, sooner or later."

Miss Lytton came through the gate in the hedge. "There you are. Isn't it time to leave? Valerie, you sneaked away from my aunt's care, and I'm not surprised t o find you here with Mr. Moffitt—and Captain Hawkins." She quieted and glanced from one to the other. "I pray everything is well?"

Leo longed to accuse the young people in front of Miss Lytton, but he didn't want to place any burden on her shoulders. She would blame herself if this plan to escort the lovers to Gretna Green went askew. "Everything is well," he said, and offered his arm to her. "I shall speak with you later, Mr. Moffitt." He smiled down at Miss Lytton's face. "Let me escort you back to the coach."

"You're trying to pull the wool over my eyes," she accused, her eyes sharp.

"I'm dealing with the frustrations of the trip," he replied, evading her gaze. "I want this to be pleasant for you, not trying and distasteful. It's my job to lighten the burdens of this journey."

"I thought that was the duty of the horses," she said lightly.

"It is. I daresay we've brought more problems onto us than we planned, but never fear, everything will be taken care of."

She looked as if she wanted to press him, but only heaved a deep sigh. "Very well. I trust you, Captain."

"Please call me Leo—at least when we're alone. Captain is so formal, and since I'm in your employ, you're entitled to call me by my given name."

"Leo? I like that. Is it short for Leonard?"

"No, but by some quirk of my mother, I was named Leo Nigel Edward Hawkins."

She laughed. "Regal, indeed. And I'm Eliza Mary Lavinia. My mother's name was Mary."

"Eliza is very lovely, just like you."

The moment, as if bathed in light, was perfect as they gazed at each other, but Lavinia interrupted the magic. "I declare, the girl runs away as soon as I turn my eyes!"

Leo laughed. "I daresay she runs faster than you, Lavinia."

"Saucy minx!"

"She's safely behind us," Eliza said, pointing at the couple walking along the road toward them.

"Safe might not be the right word here, but definitely behind us," Leo interjected. "And not going anywhere else if I have any say in the matter. I'll see to the horses. We must reach our planned destination tonight. We don't have that far to go."

"Thank you—Leo, you're a great support to me," Eliza said and squeezed his arm. "Despite our mishaps, I know I can trust you."

His chest swelled with pride. "It's a great pleasure working for you, Miss Lytt—Eliza."

Lavinia gave them a searching glance as she heard him address Eliza with such familiarity. Clearly, she didn't want to ask any questions and went to scold Valerie and Mr. Moffitt. Leo heaved a deep sigh of relief that she hadn't raised any questions that he really couldn't answer.

Eliza gave him a knowing look, and he felt as if he were sinking too deep into unknown waters. He needed to get a grip on his emotions before he drowned.

NINE

When they arrived at the coach to continue on their journey, Eliza got a terrible shock. She noticed as she was about to climb into the coach that someone had scratched the door with a knife, two deep gouges to be exact. She turned to Lucy who had finished stowing the boxes into the coach. "Did you see this before? How long have you been here?"

Lucy came outside and stared at the ruined door. "Miss Lytton, I was not aware of any damage when I arrived, but I don't recall looking at the outside of the door as it stood open."

The captain joined them and swore under his breath. "I apologize for not keeping an eye on things," he said between gritted teeth. "I thought we were safe in the middle of the day. This is the outside of enough! I inspected the coach at the crack of dawn this morning, and all was in perfect order. I don't understand how this could've happened during a short break."

He immediately rounded up the stable hands and Jimmy, the coachman. No one had any answers to his curt questions, and no one had seen anything suspicious around the coach.

"Miss Lucy is the only 'un wot came back 'ere afore you," Jimmy said. "Then there wus a stranger, the gent changing 'orses, but 'e's already gone orf." He clawed at his hat. "I wus busy with the tackle, Captain."

"I see." Leo turned to Eliza, and she had a sinking feeling in her stomach. "It looks as if someone slunk up to the coach when no one was looking and gouged it," he said.

"I'm angry with myself for not keeping a closer look on things."

"Don't blame yourself, Leo. You can't be everywhere at once." She glanced at the young couple. "With them in tow, you have more than one responsibility. We took them on voluntarily—or, I did." She rubbed her hand over the damage. "Quite vicious, don't you agree, but nothing that can't be repaired in due course." She clapped her hands to get everyone's attention. "We have to move on, but I implore you to help me by keeping your eyes open so that this mystery can be solved."

They went to take their seats in the coach or climb into saddles. Leo pulled Eliza aside. "I'll have to think about this, but theoretically anyone except you, Lavinia, and myself could've done it, but who would hold such a grudge against you?"

She chewed on her bottom lip as if running through the list of people in her mind. "I trust Jimmy, and I doubt Lucy—"

"How long has she been working for you?"

"Since I came back to England. Lavinia insisted that I should have a proper maid, and Mrs. Brown found Lucy. I trust Mrs. Brown's judgment, but I'm rather disappointed with Lucy. She's moody and opinionated, but she works diligently, and knows all the details of proper conduct. I frequently annoy her with my careless attitude about the niceties of fashion."

"What about Mr. Findlay?"

"A chance encounter with a stranger? I doubt he holds any kind of grudge toward me."

"Yes, I'm clutching at straws. He's selfish, and I suspect he would be vindictive if crossed, but it's unlikely we'll ever see him again. Probably looking for a new adventure. He might have considered Miss Snodgrass fair game, but I put an end to that."

"You're a great support, Leo," she said with a sigh. "I don't know what I would do without you." She gazed at the door once more. "Such viciousness!"

Jimmy stared down at them from the box. "The team is ready to go, Miss Lytton."

Leo touched her shoulder. "Don't worry. Nothing more will come out of this, mark my words."

She nodded, feeling better, yet knowing he couldn't protect them all on his own. Everything had started going wrong when they agreed to help the young couple to reach Gretna Green.

The weather stopped cooperating after the midday meal and the gray clouds gathered into a heavy, endless canopy. Water drizzled steadily and as it turned into a relentless downpour, they decided to seek shelter at the nearest inn.

The Striped Cat in Bronfield was a small establishment without posting stables, and they would have to let the horses rest before they could continue. The leaden skies didn't promise any improvement in the weather.

After letting everyone out at the front door of the inn, Jimmy pulled the coach down to the barn that stood near the road. Leo rode up behind him. The barn was a ramshackle building, part of the roof missing, and moss growing on the unpainted walls. The coach would not fit inside, so Jimmy pulled alongside and set the brake. He released the horses from the shafts and led the tired animals into the barn that smelled of dust and old hay.

Inside, Leo took the saddle off Gambler and wiped him down. He glanced over at the coachman. "Jimmy, don't be shy in your reply, but who do you think is doing evil mischief on the coach?"

"I don't rightly know, Cap'ain." He put down the currying brush. "I think that Mr. 'Omer is involved."

"But he isn't here, Jimmy."

"'E will be, ye mark me words." He picked up the brush and continued to curry the horse. "'Im and 'is mother were pullin' in to the posting inn when we left this mornin'. 'E may 'ave traveled with us right along."

Leo frowned. "He did? I never saw him." He muttered to himself, "Just what we need—a jealous suitor."

"Never liked that man. 'E arrived at the Conduit Street house as if 'e owned it when 'e first came to visit Miss Lytton." Jimmy shook his head. "A sore loser, that 'un."

Leo nodded. "I can see that, but why does he try—?"

"Can't bear the truth, Cap'ain. Ye mark me words, 'e'll try to convince Miss Lytton that she's made a 'uge mistake when she jilted 'im."

Leo laughed. "The man's an idiot." He led Gambler to one of the stalls and forked a mound of hay before him.

"Aye, I agree, but ye didn't 'ear me sayin' so, Cap'ain."

"Jimmy, I'm quite deaf. I shall keep watch myself tonight, and if you don't mind, you can sleep inside the coach. The seats are quite comfortable."

"Better 'an the 'ayloft, I gather."

Leo chuckled. "Yes, unless you have a soft bosom as a pillow."

Jimmy's eyes gleamed. "It 'appens, but not on this trip—not the way things are goin'."

Leo nodded and washed his hands in a water trough by the door. "Yes, we have a mystery, and it'll take our combined efforts to capture the villain. I'll not give up until we know who has perpetrated the ill deeds."

"Aye, I'll plant 'im a facer meself," Jimmy growled. He pushed his rain-dampened hat back. "Looks as if this weather will continue through the night."

Loath to agree with the coachman, Leo had to nod. "Yes, the rain is persistent, and it'll create delays for us. On the bright side, it may deter our villain."

"Depends on 'ow set 'e's on mischief," Jimmy replied. "'E might think 'e's safe from spyin' eyes in weather like this."

"I'll keep watch from the barn." He gave Jimmy a quick glance. "I hope you're a light sleeper just in case I need your help to capture the villain."

"Aye," Jimmy said, and pushed his hat back down over his eyes. "I am, and I'm rarin' for a fight. 'As been a long time."

Leo went into the inn where the guests sat crammed along a wooden bench in front of a burned and pitted tabletop. A large pot held a grayish-looking soup that didn't smell bad even if it looked unappetizing, and round loaves of rough bread had been put straight on the table with a knife sticking out of one of them.

A pot of butter made greasy rings on the table as the guests moved it around. Everyone ate from the wooden bowls in silence, and no one had the strength to complain. Leo was grateful for that. He ladled soup into a bowl for himself, and he suspected the pieces of meat were rabbit. Disks of carrot and slim potato slices swam with the meat, and he closed his eyes for a moment before taking the first taste. Not bad, except that the stock was somewhat watery.

"The horses are well cared for, and Jimmy will keep an eye on the coach," Leo said to Eliza. "I'll join him tonight."

He ate with great appetite, and the landlord brought in a basket of cherries from the garden outside. "First crop is as sweet as sugar," he claimed.

He wasn't lying, Leo thought as he grabbed a handful of the fruit as dessert. Eliza liked them very well, if her smile was any indication. He admired her for her aplomb. Nothing seemed to be able to crush her good spirits, and he was grateful for that, too. She had the right to blame him for failing to take care of her property, but she never did. Guilt had been eating at him all day.

He was also grateful that there was no sign of Mr. Findlay. At least he didn't have the temerity to show himself here and complicate things.

Sleep was encroaching after dinner, and he decided to take a nap in the chair by the fireplace. Tonight he'd have to stay awake, and he needed to steal whatever sleep he could before then. The fire in the fireplace crackled and the flames leaped in invitation. The room was pleasantly warm, and he longed to stretch out his stiff legs, but there was no room. His foot ached, but he dismissed the weakness, and aimed his leg toward the warming fire.

Leaning his head against the back of the wing chair, he closed his eyes. Through narrow slits he could see Eliza read a thin leather-bound book nearby. She concentrated with a frown between her fine eyebrows. Valerie had gone upstairs with Lavinia, and Mr. Moffitt was slouched over a tankard of ale at the dinner table, clearly lost in a sea of turbulent thoughts.

Leo hoped he would keep to himself for the time

being. The beer might put him to sleep, and Leo wouldn't have to listen to the greenhorn whining.

He drifted off into a delicious wave of sleep, and dreamed that he was holding Eliza close in a dance, every curve of her pressing against him. She was so close he could feel her every breath, and stars lit her eyes with promise. He heard a loud, drawn-out moan, filled with distress.

Another moan filled the air, jerking Leo out of his sleep. He sat up, shaking his head, and found that the moans were real. Mr. Moffitt sat at the table, his face flattened against the tabletop. Every so often, he flinched and moaned, and Leo was about to bark out an order when the door opened.

The rain poured outside, and out of the immense darkness stepped a middle-aged man swathed in a dark cloak shiny with rain. He had a beaver hat pushed low over his forehead, but Leo had no problem recognizing Melvin Homer. Close to his side clung a female, also swept in a voluminous cloak. His mother.

Eliza emitted a small cry as she stood, dropping her book to the floor. "Mr. Homer! What are you doing here?"

The man turned to her and gave her a cold look.

"Mr. Homer, are you following me?" Anger glittered in her eyes, and her shoulders had stiffened.

"Miss Lytton." He took off his hat and bowed. "No, I'm not following you, but I'm glad I caught up with you. What I witness here shocks me. It's not seemly that you should travel all over England with only servants to look after you." He gave Leo a disdainful glance. "And I'm appalled to see that he's already wormed his way into your graces. You should not be sitting here unchaperoned with a man who has God only knows what kinds of designs on your future. It's obvious I need to oversee that you arrive safely at your uncle's house. He would approve of my concern."

"Of all the—" Eliza spat. "Mr. Homer, I've asked you not to meddle, and I'm perfectly safe."

Mr. Homer threw a glance around the soot-darkened walls and ceiling. "Seems that your escort has been unable to secure suitable lodgings for you, m'dear. I've arrived in the nick of time, it seems."

"If it is so distasteful, then what are you doing here, Mr. Homer?" Leo asked, fuming.

"Offering my aid to Miss Lytton." He swept the room with one hand. "This is completely beyond the pale."

"Nonsense!" Eliza said "We called a halt to our travel when it began to rain in earnest. And I assure you, my servants are loyal. They do what I ask of them."

"That's well and good, Miss Lytton, but I doubt your experience in these matters. The world is full of ruffians and other people who desire to take advantage of you."

"Balderdash! I'm quite out of temper with you, Mr. Homer." Eliza put her hands on her hips and addressed the pale woman at his side. "Mrs. Homer, I'm surprised you let your son haul you around the country in the rain. It's very unfeeling of him, and I'm quite annoyed at your appearance here."

"Oh, Miss Lytton," the woman said breathlessly, "we don't want you to make the mistake of your life."

"Mistake? All I'm doing is traveling to my uncle's residence in Cumbria."

Mrs. Homer shook off the hood of her cloak, revealing a black poke bonnet with a lacy frill that covered most of her gray curls. She wore a dark gray gown with long sleeves and a high collar under the heavy cloak. She sat down with a sigh. The landlord stepped warily around her as if expecting her to lash out, but all she asked for was a cup of weak tea.

Leo saw the exasperation in every line of Eliza's face. He went to her side. "Do you want me to deal with them?" he whispered. "You could seek the shelter of your bedchamber."

Eliza shook her head. "No, I'll have to make it clear to Mr. Homer that he's not welcome at my table," she whispered, her eyes blazing. "I'll tell him myself."

She stepped closer to the undesirable man. "What brings you here to the heart of Derbyshire, Mr. Homer? I distinctly remember your telling me once in London that you abhor traveling, that it interferes with your digestion."

He looked down his beaky nose at her as he untied the cloak at his neck and threw it aside, right on the landlord, in fact, who dropped the tea, splattering it all over the floor. "I haven't slept a wink since you left, m'dear—all for worrying about you."

"Piffle, you're a sound sleeper—you told me so the day you spent hours regaling me with the story of your early life."

"You fell asleep, Miss Lytton," he said with ice in his voice. "I'm surprised you would remember."

"I may have nodded off," she said, "but I still heard you droning on."

"Such unkind words are uncalled for, Miss Lytton." Mr. Homer gave her a cold look. "I resent—"

Eliza raised her voice. "You don't hear anything stated politely. Any kindness is wasted on you, Mr. Homer." She stepped very close to him so that he had to retreat, this time stepping on the landlord's toes. Suppressed curses erupted from that worthy's mouth.

"Mr. Homer, I demand that you stay away from me

and my party from now on. We have nothing more to talk about, and if you think you can worm your way into my graces, you're wholly misinformed."

"Dear me, such unladylike tones," he said, clearly peevish now. "What right—?"

"You heard what Miss Lytton said," Leo reiterated and stepped forward.

Mr. Homer gave him a scathing look and Eliza left the room with a swish of her skirt.

"How dare you throw yourself into the conversation, Captain? Stay in your place. No one asked for a servant's opinion," Mr. Homer said, elbowing the landlord as he tried to pass.

"I protect Miss Lytton's best interests, and it's clear to everyone in this room that she has no desire to speak with you."

Mr. Homer looked around the room, finding only Mr. Moffitt, still asleep, the landlord, Mrs. Homer, and a drunken farmer muttering in a corner. "I don't put any score on their opinion."

"But the problem here is that you show no respect for Miss Lytton's wishes. She doesn't want to speak with you."

"She's just obstinate. Her father left instructions that we should marry, and I'm only following his orders. She does herself a great disservice to act against his wishes. I'm here to rectify that, once she's willing to listen. She should be grateful that I have the determination for the both of us to do the right thing."

"Miss Lytton is of age, Mr. Homer. She respected her father, I'm sure, but nowhere is it stated that she's forced to marry you."

"Forced?" Mr. Homer's eyebrows flew up. "She should consider herself fortunate that I'm willing to consider *her* as my wife. As it is, it'll disturb the equilibrium in the comfortable life my mother and I have created for us, but Miss Lytton will have to find a way to accustom herself to our habits. She'll do quite a bit of fetch and carry for my mother, which is natural." He gave his parent a fond smile, and she returned it weakly. "I daresay it's quite a challenge for my mother to accept Miss Lytton into our family, but she's willing to sacrifice herself."

Leo couldn't believe he was hearing these words, and he swore to himself he'd do anything to protect Eliza from this vulture.

"She'll have to follow orders," Mr. Homer continued.

"Surely you must have servants to fetch and carry." Leo spoke more forcefully than was necessary.

"Servants are expensive these days."

"You would treat Miss Lytton as an unpaid servant after she becomes Mrs. Homer?"

"I'm sure she would be grateful to find a husband. After all, she's quite on the shelf, isn't she?"

"You're out of your mind, Mr. Homer. If Miss Lytton were to have a Season in London, she would be an enormous success. She's immensely attractive and vivacious, and a lady who knows what she wants."

Mr. Homer gave him a suspicious glance. "You sound besotted, Captain. Don't think you can rise above your station and hope to gain Miss Lytton's interest. That would be excessively preposterous of you."

"I certainly wouldn't make her fetch and carry for me," Leo said icily.

"You have to keep a short rein on the servants, or they'll think they're worth something," Mr. Homer said to his mother.

Leo was even more shocked. "I beg your pardon." He stepped so close he could feel the other man's breath on his face. "I warn you. If you so much as say another distressing word to Miss Lytton, I'll call you out. I suggest that you leave just as soon as you can arrange for fresh horses—"

"We're not leaving in the rain," he said haughtily.

"When the sun rises, then. I want you to be gone by the time she comes downstairs tomorrow morning. If you're still here, you'll taste the sharp side of my tongue, and more."

"Hmph! You're taking on airs, Captain. Pride always goes before the fall."

"Well, then you should've fallen a long time ago, Mr. Homer. My threat is serious, and I know you're the last man Miss Lytton would ever dream of marrying."

"Rubbish!"

"She's said as much a number of times."

"What she says doesn't matter," Mr. Homer said with a snort. "Women have no say."

"What *I* say matters, Mr. Homer. I'll have you know I'm an expert marksman, and my threat is real."

The older man paled, and Mrs. Homer wailed. "Be careful, Melvin. The man is a lunatic." She sobbed in a theatrical fashion and covered her face with her hands. "I could not *bear* to lose you, Melvin!"

"Mother!" He looked outraged. "I'm not helpless on the dueling field."

"It's illegal, Melvin. I would die of palpitations if you ever stepped onto that field. You know how weak my heart is already."

"Desist, Mother." Mr. Homer's voice seethed with suppressed rage. "I won't have you showing me in such a weak light in front of these people. If need be, I'll put this nincompoop into his place. He shan't ruin my chances with Miss Lytton."

Leo felt the itch in his hand to slap the man and get the challenge underway, but he knew Eliza would be unhappy at such a development. There was no need to fight Mr. Homer. Leo only had to ignore him, and the wind would go out of his sails. "I don't find it necessary to repeat myself, Mr. Homer. Since you don't hear what I say, you shall find out the hard way that Miss Lytton has absolutely no plans to follow her father's wishes. If Sir Walter saw you now, he would no doubt turn in his grave."

"Never! He highly approved of me—a scholar of the first order."

"Yes, be that as it may, but then I have to say he was a poor judge of character."

The barb went deep, and Mr. Homer paled with fury. Leo stared at him.

For one tense moment, Leo thought he would be the one to be called out, but Mr. Homer jerked away, turning his back on Leo.

Leo bowed to Mrs. Homer. "Have a pleasant night." Knowing she wouldn't, he turned toward the front door.

TEN

The next morning arrived, still overcast and damp. Leo awakened at dawn. He felt frozen even though he'd bundled up in horse blankets in the barn. He sat on a mound of hay leaning against the doorjamb. Nothing had happened in the night, and he'd slept with fits and starts. Jimmy, the coachman, came out of the carriage and stretched himself. His back arched, and his joints cracked. His hair looked worse than ever, long and scraggly, and he pushed his hat back onto the snarled mess. Throwing a shrewd glance at Leo, he said, "I 'ad a more comfortable bed than yerself, Cap'ain. I 'eard nothin'. Did you?"

"No. I think everyone stayed out of the rain last night, including our villain."

"Or 'e knew we kept watch." Jimmy shook out his wrinkled caped coat and stretched once again. "Perhaps it wus that barmy gent wot arrived late last night and demanded to 'ave the best stalls fer 'is 'orses."

"Mr. Homer? I wouldn't put it past him, but if he hopes to win Miss Lytton's approval, he won't vandalize her equipment."

"Ye never know with 'im. A strange 'un. I'd say 'e 'as a vicious streak, a viper with fangs."

Bone tired, Leo got up from the hay and stretched his

aching back. His foot throbbed, but as he walked around, the stiffness eased and the pain subsided. He studied every detail of the coach, and found nothing untoward.

When he'd washed his face in a basin that one of the landlord's daughters had carried down to the barn, he combed his hair and brushed down his coat. It was wrinkled, but wearable. At this point he didn't overly worry about his appearance, as Miss Lytton's safety mattered more than anything else.

He stepped into the taproom and to his surprise found Mr. Findlay eating a large plate of eggs and bread with strips of bacon. He looked rested and abominably cheerful. He must have arrived earlier in the evening and gone straight to bed.

"Good morning, Captain Hawkins."

Leo muttered a greeting, but he had no desire to fall into a conversation with a man he didn't trust. What was this, a gathering of all the people who could make his work more difficult?

"Where's Miss Lytton?" Findlay gulped down some coffee without a concern in the world. He had dressed with care and obviously knew he looked handsome with his neck cloth perfectly folded and his coat wrinkle free.

"None of your concern, Findlay." Leo stopped at the table and looked down on him. "How come you're here? Are you following us?"

"Absolutely not! I'm recovering from my ride in the rain yesterday—just as you're doing. I'm free to stop and rest my feet anywhere I want."

Leo gritted his teeth. "For the third time, stay away from Miss Snodgrass and Miss Lytton. If you don't, you'll have to answer to me. I'm not going to warn you again."

"You do have a terrible temper; it's something you need to work on to overcome, my friend."

"Findlay, your words mean nothing to me, but you'd be much better off quiet."

"I see. I just have to listen to your chastisements and meekly accept them?"

Leo took a deep breath. "That's correct. Don't get my gall up, Findlay. I have no quarrel with you—yet."

Findlay laughed and forked some more egg into his mouth. "I shall endeavor to rub you the right way from now on."

"That is if we meet again. I hope not. Good day, Mr. Findlay." Leo gave him a curt bow and continued upstairs where he found Mr. Moffitt curled up and cocooned in his blankets in the same room as Mr. Homer. Shortage of beds, Leo thought. He shook the young man's shoulder, loath to awaken the other man.

Mr. Homer slept straight on his back, his hands clasped as if in prayer on the coverlet, and a black cloth covering his eyes. His nightcap teetered over one eye.

"Psst, get up, Thomas! Time to rise and go on."

Mr. Moffitt gave him a bleary stare. "What—?"

"Get out of bed this instant. You have something to explain. Don't think I forgot about last night."

"Arrgh, Captain . . ." Mr. Moffitt groaned. He swung his legs over the side of the bed and gave Leo a cautious glance. "It'll have to wait. I can't think right now."

"Clear your head with some cold water, young man!" Leo stormed out of the room, his patience completely at an end. And it was no later than seven in the morning. He marched outside and breathed deeply of the fresh air. Kicking some clumps of grass, he tried to find his inner calm. He wondered if Eliza had spent a peaceful night.

* * *

Out of sheer exhaustion, Eliza had slept right through. She rose feeling much more cheerful than when she went to bed. She knew that unpleasant encounters would occur later as Mr. Homer and his mother were still present, but she felt capable of handling any problems cropping up.

She dressed in a cheerful red habit with black braiding and frog closures across the tight jacket. Over her shoulders she flung a colorful shawl from India and waited patiently as Lucy knotted the hat ribbons under her chin.

"I'm surprised you'd wear such bright colors, Miss Lytton," Lucy said with a downward twist of her mouth.

"I like some bright color on a gloomy day like today, Lucy," she replied lightly, and then swore to herself that she would find a more cheerful abigail when she returned to London.

"I find this journey distasteful, Miss Lytton. It bothers me that we would aid the young couple to elope. 'Tis immoral."

Eliza gave her a long stare. "Immoral? It would be worse to leave them vulnerable to the dangers of the world. I'm surprised at your *narrow* views, Lucy." Eliza pulled at the short jacket and adjusted the brim of her hat.

Lucy blanched but kept silent.

"The young couple is my responsibility, not yours, Lucy."

The maid gave a stiff nod, and Eliza sensed that anger boiled close to the surface. The maid might be jealous of the young, dashing couple. Lucy had failed to snare a husband, a fact that didn't surprise Eliza. If Lucy had completely forgotten how to smile, she would not attract anyone.

She went to the door, and behind her she heard Lucy whisper, "immoral, indeed."

Eliza braced herself, expecting to run into Mr. Homer and his mother, but to her surprise she found Mr. Findlay in solitude with his plate of eggs. He buttered his toast and gave her a wide, predatory smile.

"Miss Lytton! What a view for tired eyes. I'm overcome with admiration for your beauty, and your eyes sparkle as only they do after a good night's sleep."

"Thank you, Mr. Findlay," she replied. She sat as far away from him as she could. "I daresay you were caught by the rain as well?"

"Yes, I was drenched. My coat is still drying upstairs. It was a most hellacious storm, but my spirits are high. No need to dwell on past mishaps." He glanced toward the stairs. "And Miss Snodgrass? Is she still in the land of Nod?"

"I surmise as much," she replied crisply. "Tell me, Mr. Findlay, this must be pure tedium to you, this sedate country pace. You seem sadly out of place here."

"I enjoy a break in my habits at times. I've been invited to a hunting box in Yorkshire, but the weather has slowed me down."

"I see." She watched as the landlord brought in a pot of coffee and a plate of strawberry tarts for her. They were freshly made, filling the air with the aroma of hot pastry and sweet berries. She thanked him. Wishing she could enjoy these treats in peace and quiet, she ignored Mr. Findlay's close scrutiny.

"I never really noticed how utterly lovely you are, Miss Lytton," he said just as the door opened and Leo stepped inside.

Eliza's heart fluttered as she saw Leo, but he looked murderous as he stared at Mr. Findlay. "Do you recall what I said earlier, Findlay?" His voice could've cut a block of ice in half.

Mr. Findlay shrugged, concentrating only on his food.

Leo threw a glance at Eliza and seemed to decide he could not pursue the current conversation. He bowed to Eliza and smiled. "Did you enjoy a peaceful night, Miss Lytton?"

She nodded. "Thank you, very much." She glanced toward the window and mouthed the word *coach?*

"All is quiet, Miss Lytton. This has to be the most peaceful spot in Derbyshire, and I doubt nothing much changes here." His eyes warmed, and she felt that strange flutter again. She lost herself in his gaze, and forgot her train of thought.

Mr. Findlay laughed, pushing them out of their fascination with each other. "I understand why you warned me off, Captain. You have a personal stake in the matter. It's clear for anyone to see that you're besotted with Miss Lytton."

Anger flashed across Leo's face, and she was afraid that he would explode, but he only gave Mr. Findlay a disdainful glance, and she admired his patience. He turned back to her. "Jimmy is getting the coach ready."

"Lucy has all the boxes organized upstairs. She's like a mother hen with her chicks."

"I'll ask the landlord to help her with them. I'd like to get an early start."

"I heard my aunt scold Miss Snodgrass earlier, so they should be down any minute."

"I suggest we pack a hamper for the midday meal, Miss Lytton. I'd like to press on. No need to linger on the road."

"And to avoid any stops where we might encounter undesirable people." Eliza threw a glance at Mr. Findlay.

"Exactly. No time to lose."

Mr. Findlay laughed derisively. "No time to lose, eh?"

Those words became very important as Valerie and Lavinia stepped downstairs. Mr. Findlay flew up and offered his seat to Valerie, who simpered and fluttered her eyelashes at him. She sat down on the chair and her eyes glittered with excitement.

The captain pressed his lips together with annoyance and went outside to oversee the rest of the arrangements.

"Valerie, I suggest that you gather your wits and partake of some breakfast before we leave," Lavinia said firmly. "I don't want any complaints later." She glanced around the room. "It looks as if we're the last people to rise this morning." She turned to Eliza. "My back bothered me last night. I found it difficult to wake up this morning."

"We're not the last," Valerie said. "Thomas is bound to be the tardiest riser." She smiled once more at Mr. Findlay. In fact, I don't see him anywhere. What a bore he is, don't you agree?"

"I daresay *you* don't have to worry your lovely head about other people's habits," Mr. Findlay said. "Mr. Moffitt has to take responsibility for his duties, or perhaps you need to find yourself another protector."

"Mr. Findlay," Eliza said, "I find your suggestion distasteful, and I suggest that you busy yourself with your breakfast and nothing else."

The landlord brought more eggs and newly fried rashers of ham, toast, and strawberry tarts. Valerie gathered two of those onto her plate, and gingerly sipped some tea.

"Miss Lytton," Mr. Findlay said in wounded tones, "you mortally wound me."

"Nonsense," Eliza said, her ire rising by the minute. She glanced at Valerie, who couldn't stop smiling—the minx! "You sorely lack respect, Mr. Findlay. Miss Snodgrass is none of your concern, nor is anyone else in this party."

"I'd like to place myself at your service. Since we're traveling the same road, I can help—"

"Mr. Findlay, how blunt do I have to be? We don't desire your company." Eliza stood and removed Valerie's plate and set it beside her. "Valerie, I desire you to sit by me this instant."

Valerie made a moue, but obeyed without objections. Mr. Findlay shook his head, but acted as if nothing had happened. He finished his breakfast and washed it all down with a tankard of ale.

Mr. Moffitt came downstairs, even more bedraggled than last night, and Eliza remembered that she had to confront the young people before they went any farther north. Somehow she'd begun to feel as if she were harboring foxes in the hen house, and she didn't like it.

"Ah!" cried Mr. Findlay. "The moonling has joined the living." He got up from the table and executed an exaggerated bow. "Mr. Moffitt, I would like to give you the name of my tailor."

Mr. Moffitt's face fell even farther. He looked unreasonably unkempt with his hair lank and two days' growth of beard on his face. His eyes held a haunted expression as if he'd fought with ghosts all night.

"You're about in your head, Mr. Findlay, and I don't want to become involved in a conversation with you. It's too early to cross swords," Mr. Moffitt said with as much dignity as he could muster.

Eliza silently applauded him. She longed to leave before Mr. Homer and his mother joined the dismal party. She urged Valerie to finish her breakfast so that she could take her seat in the coach. With some luck on their side, they could shake off these unpleasant people.

Valerie gave her fiancé a sullen look, and Mr. Moffitt refused to look at her. When they'd ended their meal,

Eliza urged them outside. When Leo saw them coming, he met them halfway. He gripped Mr. Moffitt's arm and confronted him.

"Before we take another step, you'll have to confess what you meant by your argument in the road last night." He turned to Valerie. "We don't accept any lies, and I believe you two are trying to bamboozle us. Honestly, you don't seem to be a couple in the throes of passion."

Valerie and Mr. Moffitt exchanged a tense glance, and Eliza sensed that the young man was weakening. He looked very uncomfortable, and kept shifting his weight from one foot to the other, as was his wont when pressured.

"It's just that we—"

"Don't, Thomas!" Valerie spoke with a firmness Eliza had not known she possessed. "You promised . . . You can't abandon me now, not when we're on the verge of succeeding. You can't wish for failure."

"What are you talking about?" Leo demanded. "I'm tired of your games, and I want the truth."

"We have told you the truth, Captain," Valerie said with great force. She leaned forward with the effort of convincing him. "We are to be married in Gretna Green, and you can't stop us."

"I can if I decide it's the right choice to make. So far you've succeeded in playing us all for fools, but we are no fools." He turned to Mr. Moffitt. "Before we take another step, I want you to tell me the truth."

"She's speaking the truth," Mr. Moffitt said in a whiny voice. "I promised to, I *swore* to her that I would take her to Gretna Green, and you've been so kind as to aid us upon this unfortunate journey." He lowered his voice. "The mishaps have inspired in me a doubt that we're doing the right thing."

"You idiot!" Valerie shouted. "Thomas, how can you doubt the perfection of this union?"

Mr. Moffitt gave her a long, searching stare, and Eliza knew a great piece of the puzzle was missing. "I wanted to move ahead on this journey to get rid of some undesirable people in our wake, but now I'm beginning to suspect that we shouldn't move until you tell us the whole story."

Valerie pulled at Mr. Moffitt's arm. "I abhor their suspicion. I have no desire to be a victim of their interrogation, and I suggest that we go along with Mr. Findlay. He'll be kind enough to take us to Gretna Green."

Eliza shook her head in wonder and exchanged a glance with Leo. He laughed as if disbelieving his ears.

"That would be an excellent idea," Leo said, and Eliza would have responded the same way to Valerie's suggestion. "He can travel faster, and he's—"

"No!" cried Mr. Moffitt. "I won't have anything to do with that here-and-therian. It's unpleasant enough that I have to clap eyes on him at all, but to travel in his company would be pure agony."

"You're such a nincompoop," Valerie said scathingly.

"And you're a spoiled child," he retaliated. "How I ever thought . . ." His voice petered out as he looked at the captain cautiously.

Leo held out his arm to Eliza. "Let me escort you to the coach while these children sort out their differences."

Eliza took his arm. "Thank you." She whispered as they moved away. "Are you serious about the threat?"

"Absolutely. They managed somehow before they met us, and I feel ill-used." He smiled into her eyes. "Were we ever that young?"

"They are only immature," she said, "and I sense there's a wholly different story behind their flight from Surrey."

"I think you're right." They glanced back toward the arguing couple and found that Mr. Homer stood on the stoop in front of the main entrance of the inn.

"This journey has become riddled with more obstacles than I ever dreamed possible." She squared her shoulders. "Perhaps it's about time I divulge the untold part of my reason for hiring you, Captain Hawkins. If you recall, the advertisement offered potential employment of a more delicate nature."

His eyes filled with curiosity, and he studied her face for more clues. Not that he would ever discover the depth of her attraction, but she sensed that he trusted her.

"You're a woman of many surprises," he said.

"I don't strive to be." She sighed. "There's a letter my father wrote to me before he died. He had planned for my future, you see, but as you realize by now, he was far more interested in books than the real world. I know he had my best interests at heart, and that he loved me dearly, but he had no understanding of me as the individual that I am."

She hesitated, and he urged her. "Go on."

"I'm a woman capable of forming my own opinions, and I have my own feelings." She took a deep breath and held it.

"Of course. That's what makes you so . . . so *alive.*"

"To gain my full inheritance I have to marry. I now ask you, Captain Hawkins, will you do me a great favor. Will you marry me?"

ELEVEN

"*What?* Are you completely gone out of your mind?" He couldn't believe he'd heard her right.

She blushed, and she pressed her fingertips to her cheeks. He'd never seen her so embarrassed. "I'm serious, Leo, and I'm sorry if I shocked you."

"Er . . ." He cleared his throat noisily. "Usually it's the gentleman's role to propose, and to be asked in this manner . . ."

Tears glittering in her eyes, she said, "You *are* shocked, aren't you?"

"We're no better than they are," he said, tossing his head in the young couple's direction. He didn't know how to take the proposal. He was both elated and aghast at her assumption that he would accept her offer.

"What do you mean?"

"You had an ulterior motive for hiring me," he said, "just as they have an ulterior motive on this journey."

"Truth is, I wasn't going to ask you, Leo. I don't have any desire to wed, but I'm overwhelmed, and I need your help."

She threw a worried glance at Mr. Homer still standing on the stoop. He followed her gaze and noticed the venom in Mr. Homer's eyes as he watched. She shuddered and turned away, walking around the coach so that the man couldn't see her. Leo followed, for once at a loss for words.

"I don't know what to say, Eliza. I know you're serious and that you need your inheritance to live and someone to look after you, but this is very outlandish." He tried to gather his thoughts and make some sense out of them. The overwhelming realization was that he had to say no. If he listened to his heart and his feelings, he wanted to leap at the chance to wed her, but blocking them stood the gray sentinels of duty and pride.

He sighed and braced his back against the coach door. Jimmy, as he sensed the tension in the air, slunk into the barn to give them privacy.

She gave Leo a long stare. "I sense that you're going to reject me."

He sighed. "You put me in a difficult spot, Eliza. Part of me is flattered beyond anything, but I'll have to be reasonable. I have nothing to offer you, no standing to speak of, no steady employment that would secure our future, no . . . er, funds. Everyone would call me a fortune hunter. You're well aware of this."

"Is that all?" she scoffed. "I don't see that as a real obstacle to the union."

"*I* am the obstacle, Eliza. I can't bend this view, and part of me holds a romantic notion that marriage should be based on mutual love."

Silence stretched unbelievably heavy between them, and Eliza refused to look at him.

"I can't enter this business arrangement, Eliza, but I promise to protect you from the likes of Mr. Homer. He won't be a threat as long as I'm here, and he can't force you to marry him."

"Thank you, but you won't always be at my side," she said in a strangled voice, and fished in her reticule for a handkerchief. He found his first and pressed it into her trembling hand.

"Take this, Eliza." He touched her hand as she accepted the piece of cloth. "I assure you once more, I'm very flattered by your offer. You'll find the perfect gentleman to marry you one day, someone who can give you everything that you wish, and who will love you unconditionally."

Her voice breaking, she said, "I'm devastated. I spoke out of turn, and I feel excessively foolish now."

"Don't take on so," he said, wanting to add the word *dearest,* but that was out of the question.

She placed her gloved hand on his arm. "Please don't bandy about the contents of this conversation."

He could only stare at her. "I never would! By the code of a gentleman, I will not spread vile rumors. Never have, and I won't start now."

She nodded, hiding her face in his handkerchief. He pulled down the folded coach step and helped her step inside. "I'll find Lavinia and the food basket. We'll soon be on the road."

He went back to the inn and encountered Miss Snodgrass and Mr. Moffitt arguing with Mr. Findlay. Turning a deaf ear, he passed them in the taproom and saw Mr. Homer and his mother through the open door to the coffee room. They stared at him with deep disapproval, but he ignored them as well.

Lavinia was supervising the packing of the food basket, and Leo was glad to see two bottles of claret sticking out of the top. The landlord's wife was folding a white cloth around a plum cake, and loaves of bread were cooling on the windowsill. Despite the insignificance of the inn, they delivered a good fare.

Lavinia smiled at him. "We're just about finished, and

Jimmy is helping Lucy to bring down our articles." She glanced behind him. "Where's Eliza?"

"Waiting in the coach. I daresay we'll give the unpleasant people in the taproom the slip, and the young elopers have found themselves a new champion."

Lavinia put her hands on her hips. "I'm loath to admit it, but I'm glad to be rid of that responsibility. Miss Snodgrass lost her sense of gratitude very early on, and I, for one, grew tired—"

"Say no more, Lavinia. We are as unencumbered as we were starting out on this journey, and we'll make up for lost time."

The landlord smiled as Leo handed over a generous sum for the food. "Come, Lavinia, let's go before the young couple change their minds."

Lavinia chuckled and followed him out of the inn. The landlord followed, carrying the basket.

"*That man*, Mr. Homer, looked at me as if he wanted to burn a hole in my back," Lavinia said. "He's a scorned suitor, and I daresay he's a sore loser."

Leo nodded. "Let's make haste. I want to forget all that has happened since we left London."

Lavinia slapped him on the arm. "Is it that horrendous, Captain Hawkins? I'd say you're getting along swimmingly with my niece."

Leo could not deny that, but he didn't dare to look Lavinia in the eye. "Yes, I'm very pleased with my employment, and Miss Lytton is a delight to work for, so I don't have any complaints in that area."

"It sounds so dry, Captain. Can't you speak with some feeling about my niece's sterling qualities?"

"What kind of expression are you looking for, Lavinia?"

"Ha! You are one slippery fellow, Captain. I've noticed

the way you look at her when she's not watching, but I understand if you don't want to confess."

"There's nothing to confess." He set his jaw, annoyed at her probing. The morning had started horribly, and if he had to witness Eliza moping about, it would be very difficult to keep the employment. The whole business had turned awkward, and if he'd known what the discreet words in the advertisement meant, he would've never applied for the position.

Lavinia pursed her lips in thought as they approached the coach. "This journey is like none I've ever made before, and I've never seen Eliza so beleaguered."

"As I told her, I'm here to protect you both, and I take my duty very seriously."

She smiled up at him. "Thank you."

He rode behind the coach that day, pondering Eliza's words. How he desired to meet someone like her, but someone who cared about him, not just someone who wished him to help her reach a financial goal. Or that she would desire him for the services he might provide.

It began to drizzle, but he didn't care about the deteriorating weather. The coach lumbered on, and behind them, there were no signs of the Homers or of the young couple. Perhaps they were traveling a roundabout way, or had decided to spend a day or two at the inn to rest. He was glad to be rid of them, but he suspected they hadn't seen the last of them.

At midday they broke off the trip to have their picnic meal in a broken-down barn beside the road. It was dry, and they found a rough wooden bench that someone had left inside. Eliza got out of the coach, and he noticed her heavy spirits. His heart ached, and he longed to sweep her into his arms and make her smile again, but he braced himself against the desire. He had to remain strong, or everyone would end up suffering more. Besides, Eliza's relatives would never bless their union.

He remained separated from her with the excuse to check on the horses and the coach. Chewing on a thick wedge of bread and a slice of ham, he viewed the old damage to the carriage. The mystery made his blood boil anew, but he had no further ideas on how to find the culprit. All morning he'd been preoccupied with the thoughts of Eliza's proposal, but this was more important, wasn't it? If he couldn't solve this problem, he would've failed in his duties.

He threw a glance over his shoulder at Eliza where she sat, and caught her staring at him. She averted her glance quickly, but he sensed her turmoil. He didn't want to know what was going through her mind.

Eliza had never felt more foolish. A gently bred lady would never act as she had earlier in the morning, and she felt the brunt of Leo's revulsion. He must be appalled at her action, but it was too late to take back her words now. She would never be able to look him in the eye without blushing, but she'd been desperate. Since they'd left the inn, she realized she'd acted in haste. Mr. Homer would never be a real threat, not as long as she held firm in her rejection of him.

Still, the dilemma existed. How would she gain her inheritance without a marriage contract? What in the world had propelled her father to put such a stipulation on her future? He hadn't trusted her to handle the management of the funds. She didn't understand that he would've been so blind. She'd helped him in all other matters, yet, he'd never allowed her to learn estate management. He'd said it was the duty of a gentleman to care for his wife and family.

Well, there wasn't anyone but her, she thought angrily. Lavinia had her own funds, and her uncle didn't need her, nor did any of her more distant relatives. As it were, she'd had to fight with the solicitor who handled Father's affairs to receive anything.

She gazed surreptitiously at the captain. He would be a fine husband, she thought. She'd never suspected he would reject her offer. She even went so far as to admit she had developed deep feelings for him, but she pushed them back and tried to slam the door on them, but they keep seeping through the cracks of her heart, like water. Excitement could not be contained, but it had turned into sadness. Every pore of her emitted sorrow, but she tried to keep up a friendly conversation.

"We should arrive at Claude's in a day or two at the latest," Lavinia said in a comforting voice. "I, for one, will be glad to be out of the rain." She looked through the big hole in the barn wall. "Looks as if the clouds are growing heavier once more."

"They are," Eliza whispered.

"You look like someone who sold all the eggs and lost the money. I don't know what's gotten into you, Eliza."

"Nothing, Aunt. I'm concentrating on planning for the future. I won't stay long at Uncle Claude's as I have obligations in London."

"I wish you would have a regular Season, m'dear. You need to find a suitable husband, grow a family. 'Tis not right that you should be all alone in the world."

Eliza smiled. "You're exaggerating, surely. I have you, and I'm never at a loss for friends."

Lavinia threw a glance at the captain as she drank

some wine. "What are you going to do about him? Keep him in your employ?"

"He is very useful, but no, when we return to London, he'll have other duties, I'm sure."

"You get along very well, I've noticed, and despite his injured foot, he's a very capable fellow."

Eliza nodded. "A gentleman through and through, but a stubborn one. He's a man of rigid codes."

"As can be expected from a military man, m'dear. I like someone who's dependable, and I'm certain he's well-liked among his cronies."

"Aunt Lavinia, where's this discussion going?" Eliza asked suspiciously. "You speak as if you have to impress me with his sterling qualities. You don't; I'm already aware of them."

"I'm delighted to hear it, m'dear. Despite his lack of funds, he's rather a catch."

Eliza blushed and cursed herself under her breath. "Then some fortunate young woman will recognize that and snap him up."

"I thought—"

"No need to worry your head over it, Aunt," Eliza interrupted.

"Well!" Lavinia drank the last of her wine as if needing to fortify herself.

"Sorry if I bit your head off," Eliza said. "I'm quite out of temper since I clapped eyes on Mr. Homer and his mother."

Lavinia burst into laughter. "Don't let that nincompoop rattle your composure, dear. Don't give him that satisfaction."

"I shan't talk to him ever again, Aunt. If I see him, I'll ignore him."

Lavinia nodded. "Yes. There's no reason to speak with him as he doesn't listen."

Eliza sighed. "Just mentioning his name puts a pall on my day." She glanced toward the coach. "Lucy looks very bored. She won't move from the carriage even to stretch her legs."

"That sourpuss should be replaced just as soon as you get the chance, m'dear."

"Yes. I only hired her because Mrs. Brown recommended her. Lucy has an excellent work record, but she's the first face I see in the morning, and her sour demeanor puts a damper on my day. It would put anyone off their food."

"We could've foisted her on the young couple," Lavinia said, "but that would've been cruel to both parties."

Eliza laughed. "How right you are."

"I'm glad you still have your humor tucked away somewhere," Lavinia said with an unladylike burp. She stood and brushed the crumbs from her skirt. "It's time to get on with it."

Eliza followed her cue and a sparrow flew into the barn and fearlessly attacked the bread crumbs on the dusty ground.

"Look at that fellow, Eliza. He doesn't hesitate to take an opportunity when it comes along."

I wish the captain were a bit more opportunistic, Eliza thought, yet she knew she had proposed to him for the wrong reasons. Failure loomed high on the horizon, but she tried to push away the feeling of defeat and cheer up—not the easiest thing in the world at this juncture.

That evening, as the shadows lengthened, they arrived at the Anvil and Hammer in Longsmith. The posting inn was a respectable one with lots of movement at the stables, hostlers running back and forth to care for the new arrivals, and guests resting weary bodies on benches outside. Inside, the private parlors had been taken, and the coffee room was already full with guests waiting to be fed. The air smelled of fried meat and potatoes, onions, and the tang of boiled cauliflower.

Eliza's stomach squeezed with hunger, and she decided the taproom was as good a room as any for a hearty meal. The scrubbed wooden table and the benches in front of it offered rest for the tired party, and the captain made sure she and Lavinia received the best spot by a window that looked upon the stable yard.

Dogs barked outside, the sound mixing with creaking coach springs and the restless clomping of horses. The setting sun cast a rosy glow over the treetops on the horizon, and the birds darted from tree to tree looking for a suitable branch to offer them rest.

"A beautiful evening, to be sure," she said to her aunt.

Lavinia nodded. "Yes, this is quite comfortable despite the comings and goings of so many people. I'm famished."

A young maid brought them lemonade and bowls of beef vegetable soup with bread. The captain must have ordered the food. Eliza sought him with her eyes and found him in a cluster of men at the bar. He hoisted a tankard of ale to her and smiled.

His gaze asked her if she liked the food, and she nodded to him in approval. She loved his concern and his eagerness to make sure they were always taken care of in the best manner. He gave her a sense of comfort, of support, and it came naturally for him. She knew he enjoyed caring for their well-being, and every day, his traits endeared themselves more to her. She sighed. Her paying any attention to his sterling character was pure folly. She looked out the window, forcing herself to pay attention to other things but him.

When the maid brought a rack of lamb and potatoes swimming in butter, however, he joined them. "I took the liberty of ordering this excellent fare so that you didn't have to bestir yourselves," he said as he sat down opposite.

"Thank you," Eliza mumbled.

"You know exactly what I like, Captain," said Lavinia as she started in on the lamb. "Nothing like a good meal after a long day."

"I agree with that," he replied. He turned to Eliza. "Are you of a similar opinion?"

"Silly question," she replied. "Hunger is the best spice."

She felt his eyes on her, and she focused on the food. She wasn't quite ready to face him yet after her horrendous faux pas earlier in the day.

"Are you going to post guards by the coach tonight?"

"I will. However, I daresay no one could approach the vehicle without being seen. The stables are overrun with hostlers, and I suspect they keep an eye on the animals at night. I noticed there's some high-bred horseflesh in those stables, and Jimmy will sleep in the coach as he did last night."

"You must be exhausted from your surveillance, Captain." Lavinia wiped her butter-stained fingers on her napkin. She offered him bread from the basket beside her, and he accepted a slice.

"Yes, but the mystery keeps me on high alert. I wish to find out who perpetrated those rascally deeds."

"We may never know," Lavinia said. She drank deeply of the cool lemonade. "Ahh, this is delicious."

"I don't give up easily," the captain said. "Whoever tries to disturb your peace is a villain of the first order and should be punished."

"But we're alone now that the young elopers left, and I trust everyone in our party."

Eliza evaluated everyone in her mind, knowing her servants could be trusted—at least she thought they could be, but how much did she know of their background? She hired them when she had returned from Egypt. Mrs. Brown had recommended everyone, and she trusted Mrs. Brown's judgment.

"I shan't remain suspicious of everyone around me," she said. "It'll ruin the trip to keep an eye on the servants' every move."

"That's true," Lavinia said. "They're all good people, including Lucy, though I can't abide her surly demeanor. She's a miserable harpy."

Eliza did not pursue that thread of conversation. Lucy was all of the above, but not important in the greater scheme of things.

They finished their meal in silence, and the maid returned to carry away the empty platters. She brought a teapot and cups, and Eliza enjoyed the golden liquid. It brought solace to her nerves, and for the first time that day she could relax. She heaved a great sigh of relief, and felt the tension of her failure draining away. Yet, she could never take back the proposal, and things were never going to be the same with the captain. After this trip, however, he would be nothing but a memory.

She glanced out the window, her peace shattering as she recognized Mr. Homer's coach. The teacup fell from her hand, splashing hot tea all over the table and the front of her pelisse. "We have company," she said, her anger rising.

"Mr. Homer?" Leo asked and leaned forward to glance out the window.

"None other. They must've stopped at every inn to

inquire about our whereabouts," Eliza said. "He's only doing this to annoy me."

Leo's eyes burned with anger. "I shall call him out."

"*No!* Before it comes to that, I shall discharge you from your post. I won't have anyone's blood on my conscience." Eliza stood. "I'm going to have a word with him."

"Sit down," Lavinia demanded, but Eliza was already halfway to the door. Leo followed her, and she turned a fierce eye on him. "Don't involve yourself, or I'll have to fire you."

His jaw was set, but he gave her a curt nod. "Very well; you're my employer."

Eliza wished they'd met under different circumstances, but she had to push such thoughts away as she needed all of her strength to deal with Mr. Homer. She walked down the path toward them and heard the door slam behind her. She glanced over her shoulder and found that the captain had followed her.

The Homers were getting out of the carriage when she stepped forward. "I asked you to stay away from me, Mr. Homer," she blurted out.

He feigned innocence. "Oh, there you are, Miss Lytton. Fancy we should meet again."

"You're following me on purpose."

"It's always good to know there are friends watching over you," he said lightly. "Mother and I are making a valiant effort to make sure no harm comes to you on your journey."

She could barely speak for the anger choking her. "Of all the thick-headed people, you surely take the prize, Mr. Homer. I made it clear I don't need your escort, and I don't want it. I'm extremely upset by your appearance here."

He shrugged, all of her angry words washing off him.

"We have a right to stay where we can find a comfortable bed," he said.

Eliza turned to Leo and spoke under her breath. "We're leaving *now.* Make sure Jimmy procures fresh horses and I want the coach ready in half an hour." She pulled him by the arm toward the stables. "The nerve of that man!"

Leo's expression was grim. "He's behind our troubles, but I can't prove it now. I will, though."

"I'll wait in the taproom with Lavinia, and when everything is ready, please fetch us."

He nodded and went to fulfill her orders. Eliza returned to the inn, fuming. Lavinia looked upset, her lips pursed with disapproval. "I can't get rid of them," Eliza said and sank down on the bench. "But we're leaving. I don't care if we have to stay at a hedge tavern tonight as long it's at a different location."

Lavinia nodded. "The Homers are most annoying people, and Mr. Homer is beyond arrogant to think he has authority over you just because of some old friendship with your father. I think Walter was about in his head to cultivate that friendship."

Eliza nodded. "You're right on that score."

When they got outside, they witnessed Mr. Homer struggling with a heavy human burden that waved feeble arms. A black cloak fluttered in the breeze.

"Miss Lytton," he cried, "*my mother,* please help me." He staggered under the burden, and set it down on a bench by the stables. Eliza recognized Mrs. Homer, her face pale, and her body trembling. Her poke bonnet was askew on her gray locks, and her nose looked red and swollen as if she'd been crying.

Eliza couldn't very well reject the plea, and she hurried forward. "What's the matter?"

"I don't know," Mr. Homer said breathlessly. "Mother

had a turn. She fainted, trembling all the while, and now she doesn't recognize me." He gave her terrified look.

Eliza found her vinaigrette in the reticule hanging from her wrist and stuck it under Mrs. Homer's nose. The old woman's eyelids quivered and she opened her pale blue eyes. They failed to focus for a moment, but as she caught sight of Eliza, her gaze sharpened.

"You!" Her voice shook with accusation. She struggled up on one elbow.

"Mrs. Homer, you had a fainting spell. Are you feeling better now?" Eliza asked.

The older woman sank back down onto the bench. More people had gathered to offer assistance, but Mr. Homer waved them off as he obviously worried about privacy. Mrs. Homer's hand hung limp over the side of the bench.

"I suggest that some sturdy stable hands carry her inside," Lavinia said at Eliza's side. "You don't want to make a spectacle of yourselves."

He nodded. "Could you help me? I don't want to spend the evening alone with mother just in case something happens."

The captain joined them shortly. He wore a thunderous expression. "What is going on here?"

TWELVE

"Mrs. Homer had a bad turn," Eliza explained.

"I'm sorry to hear that, but how convenient," Leo replied, his voice scathing. He turned to Mr. Homer. "It's beyond my comprehension how you can take your mother on a lengthy trip like this when she's feeling poorly." He glanced toward their coach. "And I'm surprised that you didn't bring attendants—not even one maidservant."

"We left in haste, and—" Mr. Homer halted himself, but Eliza knew he'd almost brought up the matter of the cost of bringing extra mouths to feed and house.

"Very inconsiderate of you, Mr. Homer," Leo went on. "An act of desperation, I take it."

Mr. Homer gave him a dark glance, his mouth set into a thin line. He busied himself with arranging the folds of his mother's cloak until two stable hands arrived to help carry Mrs. Homer inside. She was soon deposited on a settle in the coffee room that had emptied of guests, and Eliza stood uncertainly by the door.

"We should send for the doctor," Lavinia said.

Leo replied, "I'm certain he won't find anything wrong with her, but I daresay we have to go through the charade."

Eliza stared at him. "Are you implying that Mr. Homer has been planning this show all along?"

"It wouldn't surprise me. He's a calculating man, and perhaps he noticed that we aimed to leave before he could get his clutches back into you, so he invented something that would pull on your sense of duty." He gave her a long look. "Fact is, you don't have any responsibility for Mrs. Homer's well-being."

She nodded. "I know, but I don't want to act uncivil, or I'll regret it all day."

Leo sighed. "It's clear that he knows your sense of duty well. I daresay our early departure has been postponed."

"Yes, for the time being. Until the doctor has given his verdict. If I were ill, I wouldn't want to lack female attendance."

He nodded. "I understand. It's just another display of your vast heart, Eliza, and for that I can only admire you."

She blushed. "Thank you." She sat down in a wing chair and waited patiently for the doctor to arrive. He took his time, and as it turned out, Mr. Moffitt, Miss Snodgrass, and Mr. Findlay arrived before him, adding more burden to Eliza's already burdened morning.

Mr. Moffitt looked thunderous, but Mr. Findlay seemed to be in fine fettle, as did Miss Snodgrass. With gestures and coy smiles, they flirted recklessly as they walked up the path to the door, and Eliza wondered about the outcome of this new romantic twist.

"It looks as if Valerie's affections have moved in a different direction," Lavinia said with a grim smile. "She's a saucy minx, that one, and I now fully understand her father's concerns." She looked at Eliza, a serious expression on her face. "Perhaps we should write to him? We need to discover his address, but I might be able to milk that out of Mr. Moffitt. He looks mighty tired of the whole business."

"Yes. . . it's about time that someone takes Valerie in hand. Or perhaps her father wants to wash his hands of her, and encouraged this dash to Gretna Green. How she bamboozled us from the start!"

"Yes. I don't want to deal with them as well. My patience is quite worn as it is." Eliza looked longingly at the blue sky and the open road beyond, but she knew it would be some time before she faced that freedom.

Valerie saw them first as she stepped into the taproom. She went red with indignation, but the expression soon gave way to an ingratiating smile. "The Misses Lytton. Fancy encountering you again. I thought you would be all the way in Cumbria by now."

"I thought *you* would be well on your way to your destination of choice, Valerie," Lavinia said.

Valerie tittered. "The border will always be there, won't it?" she said. "I'm enjoying this trip more than I ever imagined."

"By the looks of Mr. Moffitt, he's not enjoying himself half as much," Lavinia said dampeningly. "He doesn't look so much lovelorn as lost."

"Oh, him! He's always in a pucker about something. He's turned into a picture of propriety and every word is laced with censure. He's become a complete bore."

"At least he takes his responsibility seriously, which does him credit," Eliza said. "He's more mature than I thought." *He's doubtlessly several notches higher on the rungs of sensibility than that coxcomb, Mr. Findlay,* she thought uncharitably. "Valerie, I have to point out to you that I think it would be a mistake to marry someone you consider a complete bore." She glanced at Mr. Moffitt and wondered if he realized she was trying to do him a good turn.

He looked more morose than ever as he slouched over one of the tables in the taproom, drinking ale. Eliza wondered where he'd found the money to pay for it.

Valerie made a moue. "Any conversation with you, Miss Lytton, is ultimately very disappointing." With a swish of skirts, she joined Mr. Moffitt at the table and badgered him to order her a plate of cherry tarts. He did obey, without enthusiasm.

Mr. Findlay leaned one elbow on the counter that held two kegs of ale. He drank from a foaming tankard, his eyes dancing with the excitement of the chase, and his stance nonchalant. Eliza suspected that Valerie was very close or had already fallen for his superficial charm.

She closed her eyes to shut them out, and the doctor arrived twenty minutes later. He pronounced that Mrs. Homer would be right as a trivet if she rested for a day. Nothing wrong with her except the strain of the trip, he explained to Mr. Homer.

"We should be able to continue," Eliza said under her breath to Lavinia. She glanced at Mrs. Homer, who looked much better.

There was no sign of the captain, and she went outside to look for him. He was talking to a florid-faced gentleman in a gig, and Jimmy was busy with a leather harness that needed some reinforcements.

Leo noticed her, and said good-bye to the gentleman. "I saw who arrived earlier," he said, his voice filled with disgust. "I don't know how to get rid of them unless we travel in the opposite direction."

"They should not dictate our movements," she said. "Let's set out in half an hour. We're already considerably delayed."

They heard a shout from Jimmy, who was walking by

the coach. "Odd's fish! There are more scratches on the door."

Leo and Eliza hurried across the yard, and she was dismayed to discover more damage to her coach. Fury rose within her, and she wanted to lash out at someone.

"Devil take it," Leo swore. "How did this happen?" He glanced inside the coach, but Lucy was no longer there. The boxes stood in a neat pile on the floor beside her seat, evidently untouched.

"Where is she?"

"Went to, er . . . to the privy some time ago," Jimmy said, his voice laced with embarrassment. "'Aven't seen 'er since."

Eliza looked at the boxes, counting them, and found them all there. "Strange. Lucy has guarded my articles faithfully, and for a moment she chooses to leave them, and meanwhile, someone finds the time to scratch my coach." She glanced around the stable yard. "Surely someone must've seen who did this?"

Leo went in pursuit of answers, and Lucy returned shortly, her face pale. She curtsied. "I'm sorry, Miss Lytton, but my stomach—" She bit her bottom lip as if embarrassed.

"Not to worry, Lucy. Everything is still here, but did you witness any stranger lurking around the carriage?"

Lucy shook her head, instantly sullen. "No."

"Are you sure?"

"You can't blame me for—" Lucy broke down and started crying. She fumbled for a handkerchief.

"I'm not blaming you for anything, Lucy. We're looking for clues, that's all." She studied the gouges on the door. "Someone hates me, and I don't know why. I haven't been in England long enough to have enemies."

Lucy kept snuffling into her handkerchief. "The captain hasn't been able to protect you, miss, and I'm highly suspicious of him." She looked at Eliza with red-rimmed eyes. "After all, isn't he the one who arrives at the coach first in the morning? Isn't it he who checks on it last?"

"He and Jimmy, yes, but I'm astounded that you would throw blame in his direction, Lucy."

"I don't like saying this, Miss Lytton, but he's a fortune hunter, no doubt about it."

"Pshaw. I don't know how you gathered that impression, Lucy. Captain Hawkins is wholly trustworthy and comes with great recommendations."

"Those you saw," Lucy muttered, her expression still sullen.

"What are you implying?" Eliza asked sharply. "That the recommendations are false?"

"There's that, of course," Lucy said airily. "He can walk; why did he sell out? He could've gone back to his post."

"Possibly, but it's clear to see he's incapable of walking very far, and I daresay he's often in great pain."

"They ride, don't they? I'm convinced he was ordered to leave, and now he's preying on unsuspecting females."

Uneasiness took hold of Eliza, but she couldn't believe her maid's suspicions. "It's clear to see that you don't like him, so you would be prone to think the worst of him."

"Well, he hasn't been able to find any other employment, has he? They might have looked into his past."

"Nonsense, Lucy. He was recuperating from his injury, and this is his first assignment since the accident."

"That's what he told you, Miss Lytton, and forgive me for saying this, but you have an air of innocence about you. A man of the world would know how to take advantage of you."

Eliza laughed at the absurdity, but Lucy's words dug

into her. Eliza had only trusted her instincts, not researched his past. She'd never had a reason to mistrust him as he'd tackled any problem that cropped up with aplomb. Yet, there had been the times when he'd kissed her and waltzed with her. Attraction had seethed between them, and she'd fought to stay in control. Perhaps he had expected her to fall for his charms? But then, why had he rejected her proposal of marriage? He would have accepted with alacrity.

She looked toward the sky as tears burned in her eyes as she thought of the enormity of her actions. She had *proposed* to him! Had he only pretended to be aghast, to deceive her into believing he would only marry for love, but was only biding his time until he would accept her proposal?

Confusion reigned within her. Part of her laughed at Lucy's assumptions, yet she didn't have enough experience of courtship to know what was real and what wasn't. It was easy to see that Mr. Findlay was playing a game with Valerie, but was she able to see it if the captain was doing the same?

The thoughts made her cringe within. She turned back to Lucy. "Thank you. We'll be leaving shortly, so please keep an eye on the boxes."

The captain joined Eliza in the yard. "No one saw anything untoward," he said. He rubbed his jaw. "It's quite puzzling."

"I'm surprised you can't find any answers, Captain," she said, more sharply than she intended. "Someone is vandalizing my coach in broad daylight and no one has witnessed a thing. I'm quite disgusted with it." Feeling as if her world had fallen apart, she said, "I don't know whom to trust anymore, and I'm tired of this journey. Let's finish it as soon as possible." She turned away abruptly and went back to the inn, even if she had no desire to speak with anyone inside.

Mrs. Homer was sitting up by now, clutching a cup of tea between her hands. Her cheeks had returned to a normal pink hue. Eliza addressed Mr. Homer. "It would behoove you to return to London, Mr. Homer. It's careless to tow your mother around England without concern for her comforts."

"Hmph. She's quite comfortable," he replied, his narrow shoulders stiffening. "I don't do anything she doesn't desire herself. She goes where I go; we're inseparable and proud about it."

Eliza shuddered. "Then it's your responsibility to look after her health, not follow your own dubious desires and pull her along."

"How very outspoken you are, Miss Lytton," Mrs. Homer said, her face twisting with disgust. "I have no complaints."

Eliza longed to speak her opinion about that, but she clamped her mouth shut. She did not want the situation to get out of hand, for Mrs. Homer would have another spell. "I'm glad that you are of a strong constitution, Mrs. Homer," was all she said. They could read into those words what they wished.

Mrs. Homer gave her a sour smile.

"Come, Lavinia, time to leave," Eliza said.

"However much you detest the idea, I will keep an eye on you, Miss Lytton," Mr. Homer called after them as they walked to the door. "I'll never break my promise to your father."

"He promised nothing," Eliza whispered to Lavinia. "It's most unlikely that he knew about Father's will before Father died, unless someone informed him."

"He's trying to pry the door open to your life, m'dear, and he's a very persistent fellow."

"He should know by now that it's the wrong way to approach me." Eliza stood on the front steps taking deep breaths of fresh air. The weather was improving, the sun shining through tattered clouds, and a gentle breeze whisking the dampness out of the air.

The captain was overseeing the progress as the grooms strapped the last of the valises to the coach. Her heart turned over in her chest. He looked so handsome, so familiar to her. She remembered her proposal and cringed once more. He must think she was touched in her upper works. She suspected he longed to leave her company as soon as possible.

"At least he's not badgering me like Mr. Homer," she said out loud.

"Who? The captain?" Lavinia heaved an audible sigh. "It might not be such a bad idea if he did."

"Don't you dare to approach him, Aunt! I recognize that look in your eyes. I would be mortified if you so much as mentioned my name in his presence."

"Silly goose. I think he's quite taken with you."

"Don't you dare meddle! He's not going to receive any favors from me. After all, we don't know much about him, do we?"

Lavinia gave her a long stare. "I'm surprised at you, Eliza. You've never had a reason to mistrust him, and you always trust your instincts."

Eliza rubbed her temple with her fingertips. "My instincts might lead me into a heap of trouble. I'm perhaps too trusting."

"The song is very different than the one you sang before," Lavinia said. "What has come over you, m'dear?"

"Nothing. Don't listen to me, Aunt. I just don't know whom to turn to." She touched Lavinia's arm. "At least I know I can trust you."

THIRTEEN

Lavinia was closer to the truth than she knew when she told Eliza that Leo was smitten. He was sinking rapidly into the depths of love. He had difficulty pushing Eliza's face out of his thoughts. He'd cursed under his breath when he'd witnessed the pain and confusion over the damage done to her coach, and he wanted to protect her at all cost. But he'd failed.

He helped her to take her seat, her small hand innocent in his. He clasped it harder than he thought, and she gave him a shy glance, like a cautious doe peeking out through green foliage. For one wild moment, he longed to sweep her into his arms and swing her around and tell her that she made his heart skip beats every time he laid eyes on her, but he only bowed and assisted her. She looked beautiful in a blue dress and pelisse, a wide-brimmed hat perching on top of her curls, and a lace veil drifting across her face.

He'd been tempted this morning to tell her that he'd hardly slept all night for thinking of her, and he still had more energy than he knew how to spend. He didn't know where it came from. After all the inactivity at home, he could now race to the end of the earth—or so it felt. And his foot didn't ache as much, despite the damp weather. In fact, he hadn't felt this good in a long time, and he attributed it to Miss Lytton, and the freedom of riding across green hills. Even though they had an enemy that kept haunting them, the threat couldn't rob him of his sense of inner well-being.

"We're entering a more hilly terrain now," he said as he folded up the coach step. "We're in the middle of the Dales, and we'll arrive at our destination tomorrow night, I hope, if we drive hard."

"I, for one, am relieved," Lavinia said, pushing at the fingers of her gloves. "This has been a very trying journey."

"Yes . . . but we have prevailed so far, and I admire your fortitude," Leo said with a smile.

Lavinia grinned back. "I like your optimism, Captain. That Mr. Homer should take a page or two out of your book."

"He won't bother us again. I suggest we travel slightly off the main road and find an inn that is less known. Tonight we shall all sleep peacefully."

He gave Eliza a searching glance, but she refused to look at him. Still smarting from his rejection, he thought. He wished he could've given her a different answer, but it was unthinkable. "If you so desire, I shall send a messenger to your uncle about our arrival, Miss Lytton."

She shook her head. "No need to do that. Uncle Claude would forget, anyway. He lives in his own world, bless him. Ancient Egypt and mathematics occupy his mind at all times."

"I see," Leo said, not heartened by the information.

"If he didn't have such kind servants, he would forget to eat," Lavinia explained. "He believes he'll discover the answers to the world's impossible questions if he thinks hard enough. My brother is very kind, but he's not present in a normal sense of the word."

"I take it he never married," Leo said through the open window.

"No . . . no woman in her right mind would have him, but he doesn't seem to mind," Lavinia said. "He and I have that in common. I could not abide any gentleman who offered for me in my youth, and now it's too late."

Leo laughed. "At least you're not afraid to admit your position." He threw a glance at Lucy, whose small mouth held an expression of disapproval, but her eyes were downcast, and her demeanor humble. The maid wore an invisible hide full of thorns. He tried to meet Eliza's gaze one last time before he took to the saddle, but she looked in the opposite direction.

He gripped Gambler's reins from the waiting hostler and swung himself up. As Jimmy got the coach back on the road, Leo rode behind. His exchanges with Eliza had become fraught with tension, and he vowed he would speak about it tonight. There was no reason to hold on to the past, or words that had been spoken. Just as the sun came up every morning to a fresh day, so did they have a new beginning. Each day was a fresh adventure.

The rest of the day passed rather uneventfully, and as the ladies grew tired and spoke of rest, Leo brought them to the hamlet of Wigdon, two miles east of the main road. The Rose and Thorn was a modest but comfortable inn, and they were known for their excellent steak-and-kidney pie. The Dales swelled all around them, rocky crags covered with grass, and scant trees across the landscape.

"I like this," Lavinia said as she viewed the red roses climbing over an arbor leading to the front door of the inn. "How welcoming. I pray they have feather beds."

"I would not expect too much," Leo said as he joined them.

Jimmy had pulled the coach to the stables at the back

of the inn, and Lucy stood with her boxes behind them, waiting patiently.

Leo held the door for the ladies to proceed, and the landlady, Mrs. Melton, welcomed them, obviously delighted to serve Quality. "I shall fetch a pot of tea presently, but ye must first inspect yer rooms, Yer Highnesses," she said. She scuttled up the stairs to a narrow corridor above, and Eliza followed.

She was exhausted and decided to ask for a tray to be sent up to her room. The chamber had a large wooden bed, woven mats on the floor, embroidered pictures on the unpainted walls, and a vase of flowers on the windowsill. Very cozy, Eliza thought, and stood by the open window. A breeze lifted the simple white cotton curtains and touched her face. She waited until Lucy had shaken out some dresses and hung them on hangers.

"When you're done with that, I wish you to have an evening to yourself, Lucy. I can manage on my own."

"But, miss, who will take down your hair?" Lucy looked at a loss, her arms laden with flounced petticoats.

"I know how to wield a brush, Lucy." She sighed. "Sometimes I wish you were less conscientious. You should let down your own hair once in a while."

Lucy gasped. "Are you gone mad, miss?"

"Perhaps." Eliza made a waving movement with her hands.

Lucy looked far from pleased.

"Now leave, Lucy. I see the pitcher is full of water, and the towel is hanging pristine on the rack. I'll be able to wash my face."

"What . . . about . . . later? What about the buttons on your dress?" The abigail put down the petticoats on a chair.

"Sometimes you treat me like a prisoner, Lucy." She

opened the door, and the maid went outside, her face wreathed in disapproval. "Arrange for a tray to be sent up in an hour, please."

Eliza knew a moment of pure happiness. She threw herself onto the bed, finding the mattress tolerably comfortable. Her body ached from bouncing in the carriage all day, but to just lie here and stare at the plastered ceiling was perfect. She snoozed for a few minutes, and when she revived, she pulled off her half boots and took the pins out of her hair. Brushing her wayward curls, she sighed in relief.

The sun slanted orange through her window as she settled on the bed with her journal and ink pot. After sharpening the nib of her goose quill, she dipped it in the ink and started writing. She expressed her chagrin about Mr. Homer and the elopers, and she expressed her gratitude that the trip was almost over. She would miss the captain, she thought.

I've never been more mortified as when the captain declined my proposal, and I don't know what came into me in the first place. I acted in a reckless and abandoned manner, but my heart was crying out to him, and I sense that we would get along famously, were it not for his stubborn pride. I know little about marriage, but I have to surmount the hurdle that faces me—gaining my inheritance. Perhaps I approached him the wrong way, but how could I speak of what is in my heart if he's not confessing his feelings to me? 'Tis unthinkable to broach the subject. I will forever remain mortified as to my wanton behavior, but I don't regret kissing him.

Here she made a pause and put the quill down in its case. She *had* enjoyed his attention a great deal. Is this what love felt like, she wondered? This sweetness, this uncertainty, this admiration for a man's every nuance? She could find no fault with Leo. In fact, her eyes caressed him every time she looked at him.

Perhaps it bothered him no end. There was no telling what was really going on behind that cheerful and calm demeanor.

> *How will I ever face him again without blushing? I've made a cake of myself, and I might regret it for the rest of my life. Oh, I wish I could take back that infamous proposal and see his eyes light up with love again—as they had before I blurted out those fateful words.*

She set down her quill again. She could not see any solution, and even just writing about him brought both agony and elation to her.

She closed her eyes and could see his ready smile and his dear face. Perhaps she had fallen in love for the first time in her life. In parts it was more painful than it was pleasurable, but she could not stop the relentless thoughts revolving around him. They had begun the very first time she clapped eyes on him.

A knock on the door startled her, and she set down her writing implements on the nightstand. "Who is it?"

"Lucy with the tray, miss."

Sighing, Eliza let her in, and the maid put a large tray on the table by the window. If she hoped to stay, Eliza squashed that idea immediately. "Good night, Lucy. I'll see you bright and early in the morning."

Lucy pinched her lips together and left, the door closing with a disapproving thud.

Eliza found a wedge of smoked cheese, potatoes adorned with dill, boiled eggs in aspic, thin slices of ham, a large piece of apple pie with a dish of heavy cream, and a note. Curious, she opened the note and read.

Dear Eliza, I pray you've not succumbed to a sore throat or an attack of gout. Eliza had to laugh at that. *I write because I'm concerned, and I'd like to speak with you if possible this evening. According to your maid, you're on your deathbed, but I know better. I realize it's not appropriate, but if you agree by hanging something on your door handle, I will pay you a brief visit in your room. In that manner you can avoid everyone else, and I promise I won't overstay my welcome.*

To your health, Leo

Eliza's heart lurched as she read the bold scrawl of his signature. He suggested an assignment, however innocent, which in itself was wholly beyond the pale.

She paced the room, thinking about seeing him here, with no prying eyes, and it frightened her. Of course she wouldn't put anything on the door! An absurd suggestion in the first place. How could he?

She paced some more, unable to make a decision. Perhaps he was even now keeping an eye on her room. The idea alarmed yet exhilarated her beyond words. How could she face him? She couldn't. It brought back the memory of all the things they'd said to each other, especially that infamous proposal.

She couldn't face him. Pushing her hands through her hair, she wanted to scream with frustration, but she couldn't do that without drawing attention to herself.

"Drat it all," she cried. Her hunger had disappeared and she stared out the window, now feeling the room as a prison around her.

Perhaps she could slink outside without anyone being the wiser? She rearranged her hair into a chignon at the nape of her neck and put her hat back on. Tying her cloak at her throat, she looked for her gloves but couldn't find them.

Never mind. Tiptoeing to the door, she listened for sound, but all was quiet. Slipping into the corridor, she noticed there was another set of stairs at the very back. To her delight, she found that they led into the backyard, actually into the herb garden. She heard voices within, but she kept walking against the wall until she came to a hedge that bordered the property. Within seconds she had left the inn behind and walked up a dusty lane that curved through the distant hills.

To her right was the village, the white church spires glowing in the last rays of the sun, and to her left, a spinney spread out.

She found a narrow path that led through the trees and followed it. A green silence surrounded her, and she breathed deeply. Her face felt hot from the exertion of walking uphill and from her agitated emotions. She sat down on a moss-covered stump and let the peace of the spot seep into her.

All she had wanted was an evening of peace and quiet, and here she was, her hat askew, her tresses in wild disarray, forced out of her tranquil haven. It wasn't his offer; it was her own agitated state of mind that had pushed her outside. She could breathe here, and she pulled in a long, shivering breath.

Without any warning, tears swam to her eyes, and she cried. A dam had burst in her, and she hadn't realized how much she'd held back. She cried for her father, and for her own unconventional upbringing, and for her mother whom she'd never known well. She cried for her unruly tongue and her forward manner, and she cried for the bout of loneliness that had swept over her.

When all the tears had dried up, she heaved a deep

sigh. Peace had followed release, and she could return to the Rose and Thorn now, much lighter. She got up and brushed off any moss sticking to her cloak. It smelled so good of old wood and damp peaty earth.

She returned to the lane and was surprised to see Leo walking toward her from the distant hills. He was limping more than normal, but his face was set with determination. She debated whether to continue back alone, but he'd already seen her and waved. She worried that the old agitation would come back, but it didn't, so she waited.

"Eliza! I thought you were spending the evening in your room." He came to a halt beside her.

"I was, but I needed some air."

"I did, too. I took a walk, forcing myself to exercise my foot, and then I planned to check for items on your door."

"I didn't put anything out," she said cautiously.

He slowed down. "Does that mean you don't want to talk to me?"

"It depends. I can't very well avoid you now." She looked at him to gauge his reaction, but his expression didn't change. He looked cheerful as ever, but he threw a quick assessing glance at her, probably noting her red nose and eyes.

"You can if you wish," he said. "I don't intend to pressure you, Eliza, but I think we need to clear the air after that . . . er, awkward moment when you—"

She nodded, swallowing hard. "Yes, I daresay that would be appropriate. I spoke in haste, and I've regretted it ever since. I don't blame you if you're appalled."

"I never said that. Your own fear is putting words into my mouth."

"Nevertheless, my action was inexcusable." She felt hot tears try to overflow again, but she forced them back.

"Are you crying?" he asked gently and handed her his handkerchief.

She pushed it away. "Why is it that you're always ready to hand over a clean handkerchief? It's a very annoying trait."

He laughed. "I find that females are prone to tears, and they never carry their own handkerchief, and if they do, it's an inadequate scrap of lace. From a young age I learned to carry large supplies of sensible handkerchiefs."

She smiled through her tears. "If truth be told, it's endearing of you."

He gave her back the article, and this time she accepted. "I abhor watering pots," she said.

"Sometimes it's good to open the gates. Eliza, can you tell me what has you so upset?"

She thought he had a very smooth way of prying. "Everything became too much. Mr. Homer and his mother, Mr. Findlay. The elopers, of course, and I admit I still worry about them, no matter how unpleasant Valerie became in the end. She's at the mercy of two gentlemen, one ruthless, and the other inadequate at protecting her."

He nodded. "Yes, but you have to remember that you don't have a responsibility toward these people."

"I know, but my conscience won't leave me alone."

"Don't tell me you sat in the woods crying over them?" He sounded slightly disgusted.

"No . . . I cried over my own behavior the most." She stopped and touched his lapel. "You have to understand that I didn't try to 'buy' you, Leo."

"Yes," he replied firmly and patted her hand. "I never thought you did. You're only trying to create order to your life. Your father left you with a large burden."

"He didn't mean to. I'm sure he never dreamed that I would reject Mr. Homer."

She twisted the handkerchief between her hands. "I don't know what to do. If we speak frankly, do you know of anyone who might be interested in marrying me as a business arrangement?"

He gave her an incredulous look. "No . . . You would marry just to gain your inheritance?"

"If I want to eat, yes. The sooner this can be arranged, the sooner my life will improve. He has to be a decent man, and I will reward him generously. Perhaps you could help me find such a person?"

"It's unadvisable, Eliza. You'll be miserable with such an arrangement. How will you know he's not going to cheat you in the end? He'll have full control over your fortune."

"I'll have my solicitor draw up papers beforehand, and there's part of the fortune from my mother's side of the family that my husband could never touch. My father managed the trust for me. I'm richly provided for—that is, if I can get to that point." She looked at him. "It takes a burden from my shoulders to speak with you openly, without fear of your response."

"I still think it would be a huge mistake to marry without love. You'll have to live with this person for the rest of your life."

"I wouldn't have to see him very often if we live separate lives."

"Don't you ever dream of love coming into your life, Eliza?" He looked uncomfortable.

She shook her head. "No. If it did come, there would only be some kind of barrier—the gentleman in question might not care for me. I don't want to suffer unwanted emotions, and I certainly wouldn't want to mope after someone who doesn't care about me."

"Yes, I can see your point."

She wondered if he'd sensed that she already suffered from that awkward emotion that had no real outlet, no solution. She could not speak about that to him, not when he had no idea what she felt about him. It wouldn't last for long, she swore to herself. When this journey was over, she would forget him.

"I understand your opinion," he continued, "but I don't agree with you."

Confused, she wondered if he'd read her thoughts. "What?"

"That you would not want to suffer from unrequited love. No one wants that."

"Oh."

"If you don't allow yourself to feel love in this life, you've missed the whole point of living; don't you agree?"

"You mean suffering is all in due course and expected of us?"

"Love is the only thing that gives depth to life. I loved Agatha; she rejected me, but I learned a lot from that relationship that came to naught. I found that I'm capable of feeling deeply, and through that I knew I have something to offer another woman—that is, if I can find someone who can accept my lack of . . . er, standing. That is my burden, but I would never compromise my feelings just to get leg-shackled." He sighed, gazing straight ahead. "I hope to have a family one day."

"I believe you'd be a good father, Leo. You're steady and patient."

He smiled at her. "I'm glad we can talk as friends again. It concerned me that I might've lost you. It has enriched this trip to share my life with you, and that you have understood my dilemma. You accepted me without judgment."

"Well, you can't help your station in life, and you've made the best of it, a rather excellent career, I daresay, until your accident. That can't be taken away from you."

"Thank you," he said simply. "Your kind appraisal warms my heart."

Silence fell between them, and a tension rose that hadn't been there before. It was as if he probed the very depths of her heart without looking at her or speaking to her, and she was doing the same to him. She found a hesitation, a shyness about him, which endeared him even more to her.

"I . . . well, don't know what the future holds in store," she said lamely. "But I'll be brave and meet it directly." She shot him a quick glance. "Are you sure you don't know someone who might—"

"Desist, Eliza! I won't be party to your business arrangement. Perhaps your uncle can help you with that."

Another awkward silence fell, and they had come upon the hedge that lined the inn. She wondered what he'd sensed in her.

"I want what's best for you, Eliza." He raised his hand and pushed back flyaway tendrils of her hair.

She could barely make out his eyes in the gathering darkness. "Thank you," she whispered. "I daresay it's time to eat. I'm famished."

To her surprise, he gripped her shoulders and pulled her closer. She found herself pressed against his hard chest, and his lips touched hers lightly. They were soft and warm, and her whole inner being yearned for more; it was literally standing on tiptoe, begging for a deeper kiss, but it didn't come.

"You are a true friend, Eliza," he said, and gently pushed her away.

She touched her lips, utterly confused. "I know a

route through the hedge and I'll use the back door to get to my room," she managed to say.

"Good night, and sweet dreams," he said, and limped down the lane.

The nerve of the man, she thought, agitated beyond belief. Tears started swimming anew, and she fled back upstairs, grateful that no one had seen her come in.

She thought she'd cried herself dry, but she found that her tears kept falling and that they lasted long into the night. When she finally fell asleep, she was exhausted. The food remained untouched on the table.

FOURTEEN

Eliza only left the room at the inn the next morning as the coach was ready to leave. Under no circumstances did she want to face her *friend* Leo. She had nothing to complain about really; he'd acted like a complete gentleman, but nevertheless he'd trampled her feelings last night. And that only because she'd carried her emotions too close to the surface, she scolded herself. How silly she'd been to allow herself to be vulnerable in front of him, she thought.

"You look peaked," Lavinia said and studied Eliza's face under the speckled veil of her hat. "Are you poorly?"

"The damp has given me a stuffed nose and a sore throat," Eliza said, speaking only half the truth. Her nose was indeed swollen this morning, and she knew her eyes were red and puffy from all the crying and from the lack of sleep.

Lavinia tut-tutted, and Lucy placed a hot brick at Eliza's feet, though it was unnecessary.

"We'll soon be at Claude's, and you shall sleep in a soft feather bed, m'dear." Lavinia patted her knee. "I know you've had a trying time lately."

More than you know, Eliza thought, feeling the acute disappointment of last night. To her relief, Leo had ridden ahead to scout the countryside, and peace reigned inside the coach. The weather was cooler this morning, mist still hanging under the trees. A breeze was building over the hills.

She leaned back against the pillow Lucy placed behind her head and closed her eyes. At least she didn't have to be polite or make any pressing decisions. The swing of the coach on its well-oiled springs soothed her, and she fell asleep, only to be jerked awake a short time later.

Shouts sounded outside, and the coach had halted by the side of the road. She rubbed her eyes and looked out the window. "What's going on?"

"An accident mayhap?" Lavinia said, craning her neck out the opposite window. "Oh, dearest! I don't believe my eyes."

"What is it?" Eliza stiffened with alarm.

"It's Valerie and that miserable Mr. Moffitt. They are more bedraggled than ever, and Valerie is in a fit of fury. She's stomping and gesticulating."

Eliza stuck her head outside the window and watched as Valerie was giving Mr. Moffitt a hideous rake down. Leo watched from atop his horse. He looked as if ready to explode.

Eliza jumped down from the coach. "What happened here?" She looked at Valerie's muddy cloak and boots and knew things had not gone well since their paths had parted. "Mr. Moffitt, what in the world has occurred that you allowed Valerie to fall in such a disheveled state?"

"I'm trying to get the truth out of them, but they've been fighting like cats and dogs ever since I arrived," Leo said.

Eliza took Valerie by the arm and shook her. "Stop this instant! You're sounding like a fishwife, and I can't abide it."

Valerie halted her tirade and stared wide-eyed at Eliza.

She had mud dabs on her face, and her hair had not engaged a brush since yesterday. Her mouth worked as if ready to spew more insults, but Eliza squeezed her arm. "Enough is enough." She turned to Mr. Moffitt. "Tell us what happened."

He looked just as unkempt and muddy. "We've been walking," he said lamely.

"Where's Mr. Findlay?" Leo asked.

"Yesterday afternoon as we rested by the side of the road, he went off in search of a farm to buy some milk and bread. That's the last we saw of him," Mr. Moffitt said in outrage. "The man's a complete bounder."

"How many times do I have to tell you that an accident must have laid him low," Valerie shouted. "I'm sure of it."

"Don't be a ninny. He has abandoned us," Mr. Moffitt said with sudden firmness. "I told you he would."

"You're the silliest, most ineffectual and lackadaisical individual I've ever met!" Valerie cried, spinning off into another rage, and it took Leo's stentorian voice to interrupt her.

"Save your insults, Miss Snodgrass. Sit down!" He pointed at a large rock by the side of the road. She obeyed after sending him a sullen look. "I've had enough of your tantrums," he continued. He turned to Mr. Moffitt. "Nothing but the truth shall fall from your lips, sirrah, or you shall feel my displeasure to the end."

"Ahem," began the young man. He reminded Eliza of a dirty wet cat without a home. A starving wet cat.

"From the beginning," Leo demanded.

"Don't," Valerie shouted, "or I'll let out the *real* truth."

"I don't care any longer," Mr. Moffitt said in a rare show of defiance. "We left Surrey as I explained earlier, but *I* was not the one who wanted to elope. Valerie forced me into this silly charade."

Valerie raged, but Leo cut her off with one stern glance.

"I've known Valerie all my life," Mr. Moffitt said. "We have always . . . well, aided each other, and Valerie has an acrimonious relationship with her father. That much is true. However, he's not as bad as she paints him. In fact, he's rather a levelheaded fellow with a heavy burden to bear."

"Heavy burden?" Leo asked.

"He's *not* married to the bottle as Valerie told you; he's married to a younger woman and has a family with her. Valerie is no longer the center of attention, and she dislikes her stepmother. She asked me to help her run away."

Valerie screeched again, but Mr. Moffitt had gathered strength now that the floodgate had opened. Eliza listened in wonderment.

"She had fallen in love with Mr. Findlay during one of the local gatherings. Evidently he knows Lord Noble who lives in the area, and he spent a fortnight at Noble Manor, where Valerie met him at a dance. Valerie's father took an instant dislike to him—called him a fortune hunter to his face."

"I see," Eliza said, "but how could you help them?"

"By pretending that I was eloping with Valerie, and then she would connect with Mr. Findlay along the road—which happened, as you well know."

"Dear me," Lavinia gasped. She had joined the group without Eliza hearing her approach. "I'll have palpitations if this story deteriorates any further."

Eliza almost felt dizzy herself. "Go on, Mr. Moffitt."

"If we weren't caught, I would take Valerie to that assigned rendezvous, and they would continue on their own to Gretna Green. Her father would never agree to the union, and Valerie would never obey him."

"I thought you had better sense than this, Moffitt," Leo said, his voice icy. "By all that is ramshackle, this is the most decrepit tale I've ever heard."

"True, nevertheless." Moffitt straightened his narrow shoulders and stared Leo squarely in the eye, and Eliza knew he was telling the truth.

"Now, what?" she asked. "Looks as if Mr. Findlay grew tired of the game. Perhaps he found a wealthier prey."

Mr. Moffitt's jaw worked, and he paled visibly. "We could go back home and I'm willing to face Mr. Snodgrass's wrath. As I'm an old friend of the family, he won't call me out—I pray that he doesn't, but I know Valerie's reputation is ruined." His voice petered off. "I could marry her myself . . ."

"But you don't want to," Leo said, and sent Valerie a scathing look. "What does she hold over you, young man?"

Mr. Moffitt squirmed, and Valerie sent him a triumphant look.

"I will *have to* carry on with the mission," Mr. Moffitt said miserably. He stood taller once more. "I'm glad Mr. Findlay ran off. I was ready to shoot him through the heart!"

"Dear me!" Lavinia cried. "Now I will faint." But she didn't, and Eliza had no worry about that threat.

"The arrogant blighter!" Mr. Moffitt continued. "Disrespectful wastrel, arrogant cad, worthless Lothario!" If Leo hadn't held up his hand to stem the flow, Mr. Moffitt would've continued ranting.

"Mr. Moffitt, tell me again, is it true that you don't want to wed Miss Snodgrass?" Leo asked.

The greenhorn nodded convulsively and Valerie shook her head in outrage. "You useless, miserable worm," she cried. "You pushed Mr. Findlay away with your vile manners."

"I did not!"

"Stop right there, children," ordered Leo. He got out of the saddle and went to stand in front of Mr. Moffitt. "If you don't want to marry her, you shan't. We'll find a way to deal with the situation."

"What! What about Valerie's reputation?" Eliza said, outraged. She had to protect the reputation of another woman however much she resented the individual. She didn't want Valerie's life ruined due to silly immaturity.

"We'll have to invent a plausible explanation, and if they join our party once more, she is chaperoned," Leo said. "This problem will not evaporate by itself."

Eliza groaned, knowing he was right.

"I think Mr. Snodgrass will catch up with us," Mr. Moffitt said. "We stayed off the main road the last two days, but I know he's in pursuit, and he'll be angry as a hornet—no, *three* hornets. He's likely to shoot the top of your head off, Captain."

"I doubt it," Leo said with a grim laugh. "Now, get inside the coach and stop moaning, Miss Snodgrass."

Eliza didn't relish the idea of Valerie's theatrical sighs, but they couldn't abandon the two muttonheads on the road.

"What of Mr. Findlay?" Valerie asked as she stumbled into the coach.

"If he shows his face anywhere we stop, I shall deal with him, and I promise you, Miss Snodgrass, I won't be gentle," Leo said gruffly.

"Thank goodness," Lavinia said and made space for the younger woman beside her.

Valerie's eyes swam with tears, and Eliza could sympathize with her for her misplaced tenderness, but Mr. Findlay wasn't worth moping over. "How you developed a *tendre* for that miserable man is a mystery to me, Valerie."

"He's a man of the world, someone interesting, someone who knows how to make conversation, not a country bumpkin like Thomas."

"Mr. Moffitt has a great deal more sense than Mr. Findlay," Lavinia said with a sniff. "He's a nice young fellow, and you've nigh ruined him."

"Balderdash," Valerie cried. "He can't be ruined; he's too thick-headed."

"That's unkind of you, Valerie, and I hope your father takes you to task. A convent would be just the thing for you," Lavinia said, her voice dry with disapproval. "I know a few sticklers for propriety who could teach you some decorum. It sounds to me as if your father doesn't have you in hand, which surprises me, as he is such an ogre."

"At least you understand that he is an ogre, Miss Lytton," Valerie cried.

"She's jesting with you, Valerie," Eliza said, tired from the drama. None of their problems had been solved; they were only starting over.

FIFTEEN

Leo had urged Mr. Moffitt onto the box with Jimmy, who gave the cawker an evil eye. Mr. Moffitt looked no better than a scarecrow, and Leo knew the responsibility of the high-spirited girl was too much for him to carry alone. Leo wished that Miss Snodgrass's father would arrive in time to take the girl home, and he deliberately slowed the progress of the party down, claiming they had to spare the horses as they struggled up the hills. The road finally climbed into Cumbria, giving them a lovely vista of mountains and winding rivers.

They stopped for the evening at Orban, getting closer to their destination every hour. Eliza looked very tired as she climbed out of the coach, and Leo knew the fatigue partly stemmed from Valerie's presence.

Eliza wouldn't meet his gaze, and he vowed to himself he would leave her alone. When they'd begun this trip, he'd felt very comfortable with her, and now he only wanted to avoid her. The tension between them was thick as syrup, and it grew more and more uncomfortable to stay in the same room with her.

He felt like a bottle of fermenting wine, the cork of which was about to explode out of the tight neck. On the previous evening, he'd struggled immensely to stay light and friendly with her, and he'd thought he'd ended their meeting on a warm, affable footing, but he'd been unable to sleep most of the night. Something was wrong within his heart, and he dared not look at the emotion pushing to take over his life. He was afraid of drowning in the feeling, and that he refused to do.

He hadn't bothered to guard the coach last night, and to his relief, nothing more had happened to it in the dark. Jimmy had slept inside, and he'd reported that all was quiet.

"The Violin and Whistle," Lavinia read on the carved red and white sign outside the inn. "I am growing rather tired of this journey and the various inns we've visited." She turned to Leo. "Can we travel with more speed? This trip is taking longer than I ever anticipated."

"We should arrive tomorrow evening, Lavinia."

"Thank God for that!"

"I'm hoping that Mr. Snodgrass will arrive here sometime tonight so that we can deal with that situation."

Lavinia nodded. "It wouldn't be a day too early. Of all the deplorable tales, this is more than I can bear." She brushed the back of her hand across her brow as if to accentuate her opinion.

"At least we're not making the detour to Gretna Green," Leo said. "Mr. Snodgrass will take the young miss off our hands—thank God—and I shall have a word with him about Mr. Moffitt. If the greenhorn was coerced into—"

"Matters not. He still compromised Valerie," Lavinia said in no-nonsense tones, which rubbed him the wrong way.

"Of course, but who needs to know?"

"Captain Hawkins, it sounds as if he's won you over with his tale of woe. I'm surprised to find you that soft-hearted."

Leo laughed. "Soft-hearted I'm not, but I do feel somewhat sorry for the hapless sapskull. He's no match for Miss Snodgrass."

"That's certainly the truth," Lavinia said and tossed her head. "'Tis a pity you're not more soft-hearted, Captain, in an area where it counts."

His chest tightened with an explosive feeling once more. "How is that, Lavinia?"

She did not reply, only stared pointedly in Eliza's direction. Eliza was scolding Valerie and then marching her inside the inn.

"Express yourself, Lavinia. Innuendos are tiresome," he said, his chest tightening even further.

"I have no wish to argue with you, Captain. Anything I say will provoke an argument, I'm sure, but I will state the truth nevertheless: you're an utter fool. It's obvious for anyone to see that you're enamored of Eliza, and she of you. I'll never understand your stubbornness to avoid any tender feelings. At least she's mature enough to accept her burgeoning love, but you hurt her with your contrary behavior. What do you gain from your rejection?"

"I don't intend to discuss any of this with you, Lavinia," he said, his voice hard. "Eliza and I are friends."

"*Friends*? Balderdash!" Lavinia spat. "There's nothing friendly about your situation. Accept the facts as a man, and stop hiding behind your stupid pride." She stomped off toward the inn, and Leo had to admire her for her gumption to speak up.

She was right; he was acting like a coward. Discomfort filled him at the challenge staring him in the face. He'd tried to lie to himself, but it didn't work. Sooner or later that bottle cork that held back his emotions would pop, and he would be lost in love. *Damnation,* he thought.

If only Mr. Snodgrass would arrive to clear up the most pressing problem, he would be a step closer to freedom. Running away might be the only way out of this dilemma, but he filled with shame at the thought. Eliza deserved the truth.

Leo got his wish as Mr. Snodgrass finally caught up with the party. It was almost eleven at night, and his horses were tired, the coach mud-spattered. Leo was smoking a cheroot and drinking brandy in the taproom with Mr. Moffitt when a gentleman of great girth flung open the door and marched inside, filling the room with his commanding presence. He swept off his hat and cloak, and then his beady eyes fastened on Mr. Moffitt. An ugly red stain spread over his face, and his whole body seemed to swell with rage.

"Miscreant, I shall have your hide! You've ruined my gentle daughter, and for that, you deserve to die." He clomped forward, his weight making the plank floor creak. He pulled off his gloves and prepared to slap Mr. Moffitt's face with them, but Leo stepped in front of the pale and cowering young man. Moffitt's brandy glass clattered to the floor and broke.

"Mr. Snodgrass, I presume. If you want to kill Mr. Moffitt, you'll have to wait until I'm done with him."

"What? You're sitting here drinking brandy with him. You're not bamboozling me in the least." He eyed Leo with complete disdain.

"The village is small. There's only one decent inn, and we're all tired. However, at dawn tomorrow"—he heard young Mr. Moffitt gasp behind him, and he wagged a finger of warning behind his back—"I shall shoot him through the heart."

Mr. Snodgrass's eyes widened in disbelief, and Leo noticed he had the same blue eyes as Valerie. "And he would sit here and drink with you without a care in the world? He's not faint with horror?" He pushed Leo aside and stared at Mr. Moffitt, who cringed even more. "Why, you cod's head, you have more gumption than I ever thought. Not afraid to stare death in the eye, eh? If this gentleman, whoever he is, misses, I'll be right behind him, and you know I'm an excellent shot."

Mr. Moffitt emitted a soft moan, but the captain caught Mr. Snodgrass's attention. "Let me introduce myself. I'm Captain Leo Hawkins, formerly of the 14th Dragoons." He shook the soft hand of the other man.

"You know who I am, then?"

"Mr. Snodgrass, I can't miss that fact that you're looking for your daughter, and that you know Mr. Moffitt by name."

"He won't be Mr. Moffitt for much longer. He'll be the late Mr. Moffitt."

"I daresay," Leo said dryly. "Why don't you sit here by this pleasant fire and have something to eat and drink? The sausage is splendid." Leo offered his own seat to the man and waved the cautious landlord forward. "Bring some victuals to this tired traveler," he said. "And a tolerable bottle of claret, not the dredged mud you offered earlier."

The landlord scurried away wringing his hands, and Mr. Snodgrass sank down in the wing chair with a groan. "I'm too old to be traveling like this. I can't hare across England, bouncing over every rock in the road just to save a foolish girl's reputation. When I get my hands on Valerie, she'll experience the full depth of my wrath." He fixed Mr. Moffitt with an evil eye. "You've led her a merry dance, you coxcomb. How did you convince her to go with you? I thought she loathed you."

Mr. Moffitt looked offended. "A merry dance, sir? *She*

led me in a merry dance. You more than anyone would know that."

"You can't talk yourself out of this." Mr. Snodgrass laughed coldly, his large frame shaking. "Slithery snake, ain't you? I should expect you to push the blame on her, lowly creature that you are."

Mr. Moffitt's eyes lit up with angry fire. "You know me better than that, sir! Have you ever known me to step out of bounds before?"

Mr. Snodgrass rubbed his chin in thought. "Come to think of it, no. You always were a cowardly sort."

"Sir!" Mr. Moffitt stood, his body bristling with affront. "I prefer peace to war, that's all, and Valerie's whole life is a great war."

"Hmm, you might be right on that score, whelp, but the chit is innocent. You've ruined any chances for her to make a decent match."

Mr. Moffitt chewed on his bottom lip as if desperately searching for words. For guidance, he glanced at Leo, who had sat down on a chair nearby. Leo only shrugged his shoulders, and Mr. Moffitt shifted from one foot to the other. "To protect her reputation, I . . . *ahem,* plan to marry her myself," he muttered. He looked extremely beleaguered for one long moment, and then he deflated.

"Well, ain't that the whole reason why you eloped, you idiot?"

Mr. Moffitt stood mutely, his shoulders slumping. If he divulged the truth, he was still responsible for aiding Miss Snodgrass. Leo felt for the young man.

He spoke. "Miss Snodgrass should consider herself fortunate to gain this young man's affection. She isn't exactly the easiest to please."

"What? Not half an hour ago you swore you're going to meet the whippersnapper at dawn, and now you're defending him? Dashed rum business if you ask me." He leaned forward, pinning the young man with an awful glance.

"You shall never wed my Valerie, Moffitt, and as she sips coffee tomorrow morning, your blood will seep into the earth of some meadow close by."

Mr. Moffitt caught his breath and looked frightened. Leo winked at him, but he didn't appear to notice. When the landlord brought in the food, Leo went to the door with the pretext of stepping outside. He waved at Mr. Moffitt who joined him with utmost alacrity.

"He means to kill me," the young man whispered as they hovered on the porch, braced against a chilly breeze rolling down the mountain.

"You're right on that score. If I were you, I would disappear just as soon as Snodgrass goes to seek his rest tonight. You can't help Valerie any more, and the game is over. She'll have to return back home with her father."

Moffitt heaved a deep sigh, but it was clear to see he wasn't happy. "I daresay you're right, Captain."

"Once you're gone, I can convince Snodgrass that it's all for the best, and point out that Valerie has returned to his care, hearty and whole. If I assure him that he won't clap eyes on you again, all will be well."

"But that means I can't return home to Surrey, and if I do, and he gets wind of it, he'll seek me out. You don't know it, but the man holds a grudge for a long time."

"Once Valerie is safely married, he'll forget the whole matter."

"You're very optimistic, Captain. She may never get married due to her vile temper. She's just like her father. He *never* forgets anything, and he has always disliked me, as I have no standing to offer. It was a dreary day Valerie convinced me to fall in with her wild schemes."

"Yes, it's easy to see that, but what is her hold over you?"

Moffitt squirmed. His gaze darted to every corner of the yard before focusing anew on Leo. "I . . . er, well, borrowed money to pay for my gambling debts."

"Cent per centers?"

Moffitt nodded miserably. "I owe them a monkey plus almost as much interest. Valerie swore she would tell my father, and I know he'd have an apoplexy."

"Hmm, it's odd that she's willing to marry someone who is as deeply in debt as you are, Moffitt. It's as if she just wants to get married to go through it."

Moffitt sighed. "She doesn't want to marry *me,* Captain. As I explained before, she'd planned to wed Mr. Findlay over the anvil. I'm just a cover for the truth, but I'm sick and tired of the manipulation. All my life, she's been my tormentor."

"Well, it's about time you stand up for yourself, then. I assure you that you're free of this burden from this moment on, and Miss Snodgrass won't marry Mr. Findlay. I doubt that scoundrel will show his face here again, but if he does, he shall deal with Mr. Snodgrass. I won't stand up and protect Mr. Findlay as I protected you."

Moffitt looked relieved. "This whole plan was wrong from the very beginning, but a lesser evil than my father finding out about my gambling debts."

"Dashed difficult, but perhaps you've learned your lesson by now. You still have to find a way to pay back your debt."

Moffitt groaned, and his shoulders slumped once more.

Leo slapped him on the back. "Greenhorn, you have to stand up as a man and take control of your life."

"I have always wanted to buy a commission in the army, but Father is against it due to my weak chest."

"Mollycoddling won't aid you. I might be able to drop a good word for you in the right ear at headquarters. A discipline and a purpose would serve you well."

Moffitt's eyes began to shine. "You would, Captain? You would do that for me after all that has happened?"

Leo nodded. "Yes. I think you're basically a good man, Moffitt. You need stability and guidance, and a prospect for the future. Meanwhile, you'd better come clean with your father about your debt, so that you can move on. If he doesn't help you, the cent per centers will keep on hounding you. They are a ruthless lot, and not people you can ignore."

Moffitt nodded. "You're right. I'll have to begin a new life."

Leo gave him a small push. "I told you to wait until Snodgrass goes to bed, but there's no time to lose. Even if it's late, I'd see about a horse if I were you."

Moffitt held out his hand to Leo. "Thank you, Captain! I'm fortunate that you came across my path."

Leo reached into his waistcoat pocket and pulled out one of his cards. "Contact me in London in two weeks, and I'll make sure you'll meet the right people." He glanced over his shoulder to the window. "I'll find your things and bring them outside when Snodgrass isn't looking."

"I never went to my room. The bundle is in a corner below the stairs."

Leo nodded and slapped the young man's shoulder. "God speed."

"I pray Valerie can write a different chapter in her life," Moffitt said.

"I understand your concern, but you're not responsible for her wild ways any longer."

Moffitt nodded and loped off toward the stables.

When Leo returned inside, he found Mr. Snodgrass concentrating on his food and groaning with pleasure as he downed a tankard of ale. He'd already finished the bottle of claret.

Leo went to retrieve Moffitt's bundle and thought he heard a sound upstairs, a floorboard creaking, and a sigh, but he saw nothing move in the gloom. He waited, straining to notice something out of the ordinary, but no more sounds followed. Shrugging his shoulders, he walked back the way he'd come. Mr. Snodgrass's eye followed him, and the captain smiled. "I'll join you in a moment. I have to give some orders for tomorrow about the horses."

"I see." The words hung heavy with foreboding, but Leo ignored them. He found Moffitt at the stables saddling a horse with the help of one of the grooms.

"I'll take care of the cost," Leo said. "Just get as far away as you can, Moffitt."

The groom was all ears, but Leo said no more. He placed the bundle in Moffitt's arms, and returned to the inn.

"Nothing like a good meal to mellow your ire," Mr. Snodgrass said and wiped his mouth with the back of his hand. He burped and took another slurp of ale. "Good brew, this."

The landlord overheard the compliment and hurried over with more ale. He beamed, but looked very tired. "Will there be anything else, Yer Highnesses?"

Leo shook his head. "Not for me. Looks as if you need forty winks, my good man."

"Bring me two more tankards," Mr. Snodgrass said.

"Directly, Your Highness," the landlord said in awe.

Snodgrass thought for a moment. "And a dish of strawberries and milk. You have made up my bed, haven't you? And there's fresh water in a glass on the bed stand? I get thirsty at night. And you have to wake me up before dawn!"

The captain chuckled. "I doubt you're going to have to leave the comforts of your bed, Snodgrass. By the time I'm through with Moffitt, there won't be anything left for you."

Mr. Snodgrass gave him a calculating stare. "Hmm, I suppose I'll have to take your word for it. Fact is, I don't rise early if I can help it. A good night's sleep does wonders for a tired complexion. I like to look my best in the morning."

"I daresay," Leo said dryly. "I'd better find my rest, then, or my complexion will be in a dismal state tomorrow."

"I would polish my Mantons if I were you. You *did* bring your dueling pistols, didn't you?"

"Wouldn't leave home without them," Leo lied. He rose and wished the other man a peaceful night. As he walked up the dark stairs, candle in hand, he listened for unusual sounds, but heard nothing. He stopped for a moment outside Eliza's room, wondering if she was enjoying a good night's sleep. No sounds came from her room, so he suspected her rest was peaceful.

Tomorrow they would all need their strength as Mr. Snodgrass's wrath would know no bounds. At least Miss Snodgrass would be restored into his care, and that was a victory in itself—another burden lifted from his own shoulders, Leo thought. He was tired of the constant drama, and wanted only to get on with the trip.

As he undressed in the light of the one candle, he recalled how frustrating the entire trip had turned out to be.

He unfolded his neck cloth and put it over the back of a chair with his waistcoat. The problems with the young people had overshadowed the situation between him and Eliza, but he could not push away the images of Eliza's smiling eyes and rosy mouth, or her soft words when she'd asked him if he wanted to marry her. If he were to be honest, he knew he loved her and indeed wanted to marry her, but it would never work. His pride would never allow for the act to happen.

SIXTEEN

Lavinia shook Eliza's shoulder urgently, jolting her out of a dream that involved a snowstorm. She sat up, wiping the snowflakes out of her face, and found that she was snug in a bed in an unfamiliar room. "What—?"

"Eliza! Valerie has disappeared," Lavinia cried. "I woke up and Valerie was gone. Lucy never heard a thing even though she rose before dawn."

"Good riddance," Eliza muttered and fell back against the pillows. "Dear God, what have we done to deserve this? It was a day of ill fortune when we decided to take them along."

"Don't be melodramatic, Eliza. You could not have chosen differently than you did, and you know it."

"We should've known last night there was some skullduggery afoot." She sighed and rubbed her eyes. "'Tis too early in the morning for this, Aunt Lavinia."

Lavinia pulled the curtain aside and looked out the window. "No one is about except the stable grooms, and Jimmy. He looks as if he didn't sleep much; he's yawning repeatedly and looks as if he has a bellyache."

Eliza laughed at that. "How could you tell?"

"He has a bilious expression on his face and he's rubbing his stomach." She turned back to Eliza, and there was a knock on the door. Lucy stepped inside with a pot of tea and cups on a tray. She looked as serious as ever, and the journey had left her in less than perfect condition because she had no place or time to iron her own garments. Her simple blue round gown had creases and her mobcap wilted over her ears.

"Good morning, Lucy," Eliza greeted her. "Did you see Miss Snodgrass this morning?"

Lucy shook her head. "I saw her last night as she went into her bedchamber, Miss Lytton." She set down the tray on a table and stirred milk and sugar into a steaming cup, which she handed to Eliza.

Lavinia shook her head. "What a senseless girl Miss Snodgrass is! She must've run off with Mr. Moffitt again, but I don't know how. Unless they stole some horses, or convinced someone to take them along."

"I doubt it. Miss Snodgrass was not dressed for riding, and rarely do people travel at night."

"I think she'd throw herself into anything, even if she wore a ball gown," Lavinia said. "She's that willful."

Eliza nodded. "I shall step downstairs and discover the truth shortly." She threw her legs over the side of the bed and stuck her feet into her slippers. Her white nightgown fell around her as she stretched, yawning. "I've had enough of this strange business, haven't you?"

Lavinia agreed heartily and drank some tea. When they'd finished and Eliza had dressed in a burgundy muslin dress with a dark brown spencer and a matching bonnet, they went downstairs.

To her surprise, Eliza came face to face with a stout gentleman who'd dressed with extravagant flair in very tight yellow pantaloons, a garish green brocade waistcoat that clashed with his red complexion, and such high and stiff shirt points that they stuck him in the cheeks every time he turned.

"Damn, more womenfolk," he muttered and bowed as far as his bulk would allow. His blue gaze held no pleasure at seeing them, but he adhered to polite behavior. "I'm Mr. Snodgrass at your service, ma'am," he addressed to Lavinia, who fluttered her fan in agitation.

An imposing personage, indeed, Eliza thought, as she studied Valerie's father.

"Where's that whelp? Dead, is he?" Mr. Snodgrass went on. "I overslept, alas. Had too much ale in my belly. Is the captain back yet, and did he make short shrift of that greenhorn?"

"Whelp? I take it you must be referring to Mr. Moffitt, but why he would be dead is beyond me," Eliza replied. "Last I saw of him he was hale and hearty."

"The captain shot him through the heart at dawn," the gentleman said with satisfaction.

"He did?" Eliza thought the man had windmills in his head. "I doubt the captain is that bloodthirsty at the first rays of dawn."

"They had an appointment in the meadow, ma'am. Moffitt's blood is staining the earth even as we speak."

Lavinia gasped. "Have you gone mad, sir? As I passed the captain's room this morning, I heard him snore."

Mr. Snodgrass looked thunderous at this piece of news. "What?"

"He's still asleep."

"Abed? How odd. He must've gotten down to business much sooner than he planned." He stomped to the bottom of the stairs and bellowed, "Captain Hawkins, are you up there?"

Eliza and Lavinia exchanged incredulous glances.

"Come down this instant and make an account of yourself. I want to know what happened this morning."

He took a deep breath and continued in that stentorian voice, "Valerie! I expect you downstairs in ten minutes."

"The man is about in his head," Lavinia whispered. "What will happen when he discovers that Valerie is gone?"

"He most certainly will break something."

"Oh, dear. Perhaps he'll call out Captain Hawkins. He has an awful temper. At least Valerie didn't lie about that."

"I hared across the country at breakneck speed to save my daughter, and no one has an inkling of the despair I feel," he shouted, "and people are still abed as if nothing has happened. Such ignorance should not go unpunished!"

"I daresay," Eliza muttered. She cleared her throat. "Can you explain yourself further, Mr. Snodgrass?"

"That whelp who ran off with my daughter should by all rights be drawing his last breath, if he didn't already. If Captain Hawkins missed his mark, I should have the chance to finish Moffitt off—per our agreement last night."

"We were not witnesses to any such agreement."

Mr. Snodgrass grew redder in the face. "Because today is the first day I clapped eyes on you! So, unless you lurked behind a curtain last night, you could not have overheard the conversation."

"Sounds very serious to me," Lavinia said. "Very serious, indeed."

"It is, blast it all!" His eyes shot fire, and he was slowly turning purple. He bellowed once more up the stairs, and Leo appeared, straightening his cuffs. Due to the dark rings around his eyes it was clear to see that he hadn't slept much. He wore fawn breeches and top boots, and a simple black Belcher neckerchief around his neck.

"What's the matter?" he asked as his gaze locked with Eliza's. "Is there a fire somewhere?"

Yes, in my heart, she thought, and averted her eyes.

"Did you put an end to that miserable wretch, Captain?" Mr. Snodgrass demanded to know.

"Alas, I found him gone. He fled the coop last night, Mr. Snodgrass."

"*What?* You didn't lock him in his room?" Mr. Snodgrass's eyes bulged.

"I would never dream of doing that, Mr. Snodgrass. I trust a man's word, but I miscalculated this time. I thought he was man enough to meet me in the field, but—"

"Faradiddle! You let him run away. I saw you putting your heads together last night, which I found suspicious. As things stood, you ought not to be on speaking terms with him."

The captain's voice held an edge of ice. "Mr. Snodgrass, calm yourself. I reminded him of our encounter. When you see him next in Surrey, you'll have your chance to set things straight. I'm sure you know where he lives."

Mr. Snodgrass balled his hands into fists. "Have no doubts about that, sirrah. That black-hearted defiler of young women shall get his comeuppance. I have a special bullet saved for him!"

Eliza could barely suppress her giggles. This was more than absurd, she thought. She swallowed her mirth and pinned Mr. Snodgrass with a firm eye. "Mr. Moffitt is not a criminal," she said. "I found him rather gormless. Annoying to be sure, but surely not evil."

Mr. Snodgrass had a retort ready, but he halted himself and stared at her for a long moment. He said at last, "Miss Lytton, your opinion matters not."

She glanced at Leo. A smile lurked at the corners of

his mouth and she realized he was laughing. Something had happened in the night. She went to the door. "I'll take a look at the coach while everyone is getting ready," she said as an excuse to leave the room.

The captain followed her, and as he walked across the yard, she asked, "Tell me the truth about Mr. Moffitt. Were you really going to meet him at dawn?"

Leo shook his head. "No, absolutely not. I gave Mr. Snodgrass that impression so he wouldn't kill Moffitt on the spot. He would have to wait until I was done with Moffitt. I advised that impudent young puppy to disappear in the night. He's probably halfway to Manchester by now."

"I can understand that you wished to keep his life intact, but—"

"Miss Snodgrass bullied him into running away with her, and I sensed that a long time ago, but the cawker was not willing to speak about it."

"What a bumble broth! At least our problems are almost over, and I can't tell you how happy I am about it."

They arrived at the coach and discovered that Jimmy had everything ready. Lucy had seen to the transfer of the boxes, and they had been piled into the coach. "Just as soon as the matter with Valerie has been cleared up with Mr. Snodgrass, we're leaving," Eliza said. "I'm eager for the journey to be over, and so is Lavinia. Too much friction, don't you agree?"

"Yes," he said. "I wish I could've protected you from these events, but when you go on the road you make yourself vulnerable to unforeseen difficulties."

"That's what makes travel interesting. An unforeseen event can be positive, indeed."

He smiled. "That's true, and perhaps I'm looking at this with a jaundiced eye, but we did have the misfortune of meeting Mr. Moffitt and Miss Snodgrass."

"I daresay it's not over. If we are fortunate, Mr. Snodgrass will whisk Valerie into his coach and go south, but—"

A furious bellow penetrated the walls of the inn, and Eliza looked at Leo. "That sounds like Mr. Snodgrass in a full-blown rage. He must have discovered that Valerie is missing."

"I'd say you're right. He has not calmed down, quite the contrary."

They hurried back to the inn and found Mr. Snodgrass throwing things around the taproom. Crockery shattered, chairs flew into the fireplace, and a tankard of ale splattered its contents all over the floor.

"Stop this nonsense!" Leo barked over the din, and everyone fell silent under his sharp command.

Mr. Snodgrass stood in the middle of the chaos, his neck cloth askew and his hair in wild disarray. He breathed heavily, and his eyes shot fire. "She's gone! The blasted greenhorn stole my daughter!"

"Don't be ridiculous, Mr. Snodgrass," Leo said.

"They're both gone. Explain *that*, Captain!" He stomped across the floor and stood in front of Leo, his hands clenching and unclenching. "*You're* behind this."

"Nonsense. Why would I support their elopement? There's absolutely no reason for such an act on my part."

He looked from Leo to Eliza. "Then it's *you!*" He stuck an accusing finger into her face, and she took a step back.

"I didn't bundle them off in the small hours of the night," she said. "Valerie is very stubborn, and she would never allow anyone to sweep her off anywhere unless it were part of her own plans. She's willful and spoiled."

"*What?* Are you accusing me of spoiling my daughter?"

"Or failure of keeping her under your control. I surmise she's managed to get her own way most of the time," Eliza said without concern for his reaction to such a bald truth. "I also presume she's been left to her own devices a lot as she developed a high degree of manipulation. Her bold disappearance is just another act proving my point."

Mr. Snodgrass tore at his hair. "She was a handful from the moment she was born, and she quite wore me down, but that she should escape from right under our noses is beyond the pale."

Eliza had no explanation.

Lavinia said, "Since they're both gone, we have to suspect that they are together and heading for Gretna Green."

Mr. Snodgrass moaned. "I'm in utter despair. She would do this only to spite me." He gave Leo a narrow stare. "You were supposed to take care of any further involvement of Mr. Moffitt."

"He must have left before dawn, Mr. Snodgrass," Leo replied.

Leo pulled Eliza out of earshot of the older man and began to pick up parts of the broken chairs. "As you know, Moffitt didn't leave with Miss Snodgrass. He left last night, and we witnessed that she went upstairs with Lavinia."

"There's no telling. Perhaps he climbed through Valerie's window and awakened her. 'Tis suspicious that they're both gone. Lavinia is a sound sleeper and usually falls asleep the moment her head hits the pillow. Valerie would've sneaked downstairs without anyone being the wiser."

"I was there with Moffitt for at least an hour, and no one came downstairs. Mr. Snodgrass stayed up even later. Moffitt left shortly after midnight. I watched him head to the stables, but not actually ride off, but there's no doubt in my mind that he took the opportunity to flee from this distasteful situation."

"You're right on that score. It was clear he abhorred this whole situation. Then what do you think happened to Valerie?"

"Perhaps Mr. Findlay returned," he said grimly.

She caught her breath, and worry swam through her. "You may be right."

Leo made a pile on the floor of broken wood. The landlord was wringing his hands and she could see that he was close to tears. "Don't worry, Mr. Long, we'll see to it that Mr. Snodgrass compensates you for the damage."

"A wild 'un, and I don't need that kind of clientele. Me grandfather made those chairs."

Eliza got angry and addressed Mr. Snodgrass. "I believe you have something to settle with Mr. Long here." She pointed an accusing finger at the damaged goods. "It's the outside of enough."

He shrugged. "Very well, what does it matter anymore? I have plenty, but what does it matter when I've lost my daughter?" With a theatrical sigh, he extracted a roll of bills from his pocket and peeled a few off and handed them to the proprietor.

"Don't think the worst of Valerie," Eliza said.

"I'd rather be dead than see her shackled to that nincompoop!" he roared and stomped outside.

"I suppose he'll head for Gretna Green," Leo said. "I suggest we take our time to keep away from him and his wrath. He'll be even more apoplectic when he discovers that she's not with Moffitt. It's clear for anyone to see that Mr. Findlay is a fortune hunter—if what Valerie told us about her ample inheritance was true."

Eliza looked out the window, watching Lucy crossing the yard with a bandbox. "I have a feeling we haven't seen the last of Mr. Snodgrass."

SEVENTEEN

A lot of time had been wasted before they left the inn at Orban. Threatening clouds were gathering on the horizon, and Eliza feared the day would be cut short by inclement weather.

The captain opened the door to the coach, and she looked inside. To her surprise, she found her boxes and her lacquered dressing case in wild disarray on the seats and on the floor.

"Oh, no!" She clapped her hand to her mouth to suppress the sharper expletives hovering on her tongue.

Leo pushed her aside in his urgency to find the reason for her distress. "Blast and damn," he swore. "What is going on here?"

"Lucy brought the articles downstairs, and there was nothing amiss when we looked earlier." Her heart pounding, Eliza stepped gingerly over her toilet articles strewn on the floor and looked in the box that held the most important thing—her father's beloved papers.

Someone had sifted through the contents, but nothing appeared to be missing. The manuscript was still there with the string tied neatly around it as always. Eliza stepped back outside. "Everything seems to be intact, but it's hard to say. No one wanted my silver brushes. A common thief would've stolen those."

Leo looked around. "Where is Lucy?"

"I don't know." Eliza looked up at the bedroom window behind which she'd slept on the previous night. No one stared back, and she wondered if Lucy had gone back to the room to fetch some last articles.

Lucy appeared two minutes later from behind the inn. "Where have you been?" Eliza asked.

Lucy turned red and looked uncertainly at the captain before she replied. "To the . . . well, you know, Miss Lytton."

"For how long were you gone?"

"A few minutes, Miss Lytton." Lucy looked affronted. "I didn't know you were looking for me, miss."

Eliza pointed at the disarray in the coach. "Do you know anything about this?" She studied her maid closely as Lucy looked inside.

The maid gasped and cried out in distress. "I've only been gone—who could've done such a dastardly thing?"

"You tell me, Lucy," said the captain sharply. "You must've have seen something before you decided to leave these articles unattended. Why would you make a slip now? You've guarded Miss Lytton's personal things admirably so far."

Lucy shook her head, her mobcap flopping farther down over her ears. "I have no idea," she said, her eyes cold. She never took criticism well, even if it was warranted. A lesser servant would've succumbed to a fit of crying.

"Are you sure you didn't see some stranger lurking about?" the captain pried.

"No. Jimmy and the grooms, that's all." Without waiting for the order, she stepped into the coach and began tidying the mess.

Leo went to speak with Jimmy and the stable grooms.

Eliza joined Lucy inside the coach and helped her straighten the things. "Why would anyone want to create such havoc?" she asked herself. "What is he or she looking for?"

"Your guess is as good as mine," Lavinia said as she stuck her head inside the coach. She looked grim. "I witnessed the commotion at the inn as I finished my tea. I suppose Miss Snodgrass did this out of spite."

"I doubt it," Eliza said. "So far as we know, she wasn't anywhere near here this morning."

"The whole thing is odd, to be sure," Lavinia said. "No one ever saw the villain defiling your coach, and now this." She brushed off a hair comb and handed it to Lucy, who fitted it into the dressing case.

"I'm tired of this, Lavinia. It's as if the whole trip has been cursed, and it's about time we shake off these mishaps and arrive at Uncle Claude's, even if it means traveling until midnight."

"I agree," Lavinia said. She stared at the door that had been damaged. "Sometimes I think these marks look like foreign letters, but it might just be my imagination."

Lucy stepped down and stared at the scratches on the door. "You might be right. In the right light, they faintly resemble hieroglyphs."

"Hmm, yes." Lavinia looked at Eliza. "I'd say your jilted suitor might lie behind these furtive attacks."

"Mr. Homer?"

"Yes. He has knowledge of the Egyptian culture and he might be looking for something to steal, sore loser that he is."

"He's a coward, Lavinia. He would never dare to go through my things in broad daylight and look for something to steal."

Lavinia sighed and straightened her hat and fumbled

in her reticule for smelling salts. "You're right; all the upheaval must've gone to my head. I'm exhausted."

Eliza placed a soothing hand on her arm. "I know, and I'm sorry that you had to be part of this, but as I said, we'll drive straight through. I don't care how long it takes."

Leo questioned the grooms, and everyone had been busy with the horses, including Jimmy. They had not seen any stranger on the premises in the last hour. "If 'e'd been 'ere, I would've seen 'im, Captain. 'Tis broad daylight, an' it would take a crafty 'un to creep up unnoticed."

Leo could not have said it better himself. "It's odd."

"We're ready to go, Captain." Jimmy led one of the horses outside and backed it in between the shafts of the coach. Leo followed and watched as Lucy and Eliza finished the task of cleaning up.

Eliza faced Leo as she brushed the dust off her hands. She looked angry. "I've had enough, Leo," she said, her voice trembling "I know you can't be everywhere at once, but I expected some results from you—that you would discover something that would put us on the right track to discovering the villain's identity."

Leo stiffened, feeling her anger like a whip on his every nerve ending. "You're right, and I should've spent the night guarding the coach. I got distracted with the arrival of Mr. Snodgrass, but that's no excuse."

She was about to speak again, but changed her mind. She pinched her lips together, and he saw tears twinkling in the corners of her eyes. He longed to pull her into his arms, but it was impossible. "We're ready to leave. I assure you it will be the last time someone goes through your things, Eliza."

She gave him a curt nod, her lips trembling. She

stepped back into the vehicle. As she sat down and he was about to close the door, she said, "I want to travel straight to Uncle Claude's tonight—come hail or high water."

Just as she said those words, a faint spattering of rain could be heard on the roof, and she made a small grimace. Leo swore she wouldn't have to suffer any more hardships. He'd failed to protect her, but if anything untoward happened along the rest of the way, he would be in charge.

And he would have to speak with her about that other matter—the one waiting in his heart.

The rain intensified as they traveled north, and the afternoon stretched dreary as the fog thickened and the quality of the road deteriorated. Cumbria was a land of rocks and water, and spectacular vistas, even though none could be seen through the fog in the darkening day. Leo's clothes felt damp despite the heavy cloak covering his shoulders. His mood worsened as the day turned grayer, and Eliza had not spoken to him at any of the infrequent stops they'd made.

It rained harder, and the ground was soggy, the road flooded in places, and Jimmy confided he thought it was a poor idea to travel in the dark.

"There's no moon, and I can't see the lane a'ead of me, Cap'ain. I think it best we stop for the night even if we're not far away from Broadmoor. I can continue for another hour, but that's the limit."

"I agree," Leo said. "We'll find somewhere to stop. There's a village up ahead, according to the map, and I'll convince Miss Lytton that we have to take shelter for the night."

Lights appeared twenty minutes later out of the darkness, and as they drove closer, Leo saw the cluster of buildings huddled together on the meager soil of a hill.

Cold air hung over the mountains. The stone cottages looked as if they had grown out of the earth on which they stood. Leo saw no sign of an inn, only a tavern at the edge of the village. Jimmy pulled the horses to a halt, and as he waited, Leo went inside to inquire about accommodations.

The taproom was dark and dank, smelling of stale beer and rancid food. A fireplace filled with damp logs smoked in the corner, making his eyes burn. The landlord, a brusque Scotsman, dressed in a dirty white shirt rolled up to his elbows and a green apron, claimed he had two modest rooms upstairs, and Leo realized the chambers would have to do for one night.

He opened the coach door and looked inside. Lavinia was snoring, and Eliza sat with her head back. Lucy was the only one still alert.

Leo touched Eliza's arm, and she started, her eyes flying open. "Why have we stopped?" she asked, her voice thick with sleep.

"The horses can't go on. The road is too treacherous and the fog is growing thicker every minute. Without the moon, Jimmy can't see the road. I don't want an accident to happen. I know you wanted to go all the way." He braced himself for an argument, but she only gave him a look of resignation.

"Very well. If that's the way it is, we'd better break the journey."

He helped her down from the coach, and Lucy followed, carrying two of the boxes. Eliza awakened Lavinia, and they trundled toward the tavern to take occupation of the chambers. Leo had decided to sleep in the coach with Jimmy, and there was a shelter for the horses at the back of the tavern, and fresh mounds of hay. He followed the women inside and made sure they were as comfortable as they could be.

He was surprised they accepted the simple accommodations, but they must be too tired to complain. Eliza gave him a veiled glance as she closed the door, and he longed to take her into his arms and hold her, assure her that everything would be perfect from now on.

He helped Jimmy to wipe down the horses and feed them, and then went to make a bed for himself in the coach. Lucy had left three of the larger boxes in the coach, and he had to rearrange them to stretch out his long legs on the seat.

Jimmy arrived just as Leo was drifting off to sleep, and staggered inside, emitting many groans and sighs. He settled on the opposite seat, muttering to himself. Before long, he started snoring, and Leo fought an urge to strangle the man. Now wide awake, he lay on his back, his head propped on his hands, and stared into the darkness. Sleep finally overcame him, but it was almost dawn.

A light sleeper, he awakened to a slight squeak that penetrated Jimmy's rhythmical snores. At first he thought a mouse had entered the vehicle, but then it came again, a very faint creak. He stared toward the door and saw the grayness outside grow wider. Someone was in the process of opening the door. As he strained to see, a shadow loomed.

The outlines sharpened as the person moved closer, and Leo tensed, ready to pounce as the figure tried to enter the coach. He held his breath, and it was as if the intruder also held his breath, waiting. Jimmy kept snoring, and then the figure moved forward.

Leo leaped up and threw himself over the person, knocking him back onto the ground and gripping the throat with the aim to squeeze the very life out of the villain if need be.

The neck was rather slender for a man, he thought

through the haze of his anger. He heard a moan and realized he was on top of a woman. He let go of his grip and pulled her upright by a quick twist of his arm. He grabbed the back of her neck and held her steady.

"Captain," she moaned, and Leo recognized Lucy's voice.

"Lucy! What in the world are you doing here?"

"I couldn't sleep," she said. "And I was worried about the boxes. Now my cloak is ruined by mud."

He peered at her closely, but couldn't really see any details of her face, whether she was telling the truth or not.

"You should not walk around in the middle of the night. The customers at the tavern looked rather unsavory, and I don't want you to come to harm."

"No one saw me," she said and looked over her shoulder. He sensed her nervousness, and wondered if she was alone. He strained to see if someone moved in the shadows by the wall, near which Jimmy had parked the coach, but everything seemed quiet.

"Do you need one of the boxes?" He indicated the inside of the coach. "I don't know why you would need it in the middle of the night."

"I told you I was worried about it," she said with a tremble in her voice.

His instinct that something was wrong sharpened. "How important is it? You must've known Jimmy at least slept in the coach. He would protect his mistress's things with his life."

"As he is now?" she commented contemptuously.

She was right, he thought. Jimmy would sleep through an earthquake. "I understand your point, Lucy, but I'm here tonight, and nothing passes by me—as you've found out. I think you're acting very nervously, and perhaps you're afraid of the dark, but I don't believe it. You want something that is in one of the boxes."

"No!" she cried. "I told you I couldn't sleep."

Leo hurried across the few yards that separated the tavern from the carriage with the aim to startle anyone lurking in the shadows. It didn't surprise him when a larger, deeper shadow detached and someone rushed headlong toward the back of the building.

Leo ran after him and almost caught him, but the stranger leaped toward a moving shadow, clearly a horse, and after some fumbling, hurled himself into the saddle. He galloped down the road, and Leo shouted in frustration.

"You coward, come back here!" he yelled in frustration as the rider disappeared around a bend.

Blast and damn, he thought, and hurried back to the coach. There was no sign of Lucy now, and he stormed into the tavern and found the proprietor slumped in front of the fire, snoring deeply. Leo bounded upstairs and knocked on both doors. Eliza appeared wearing a white nightgown, and Lavinia stuck her head outside the door of the other room.

"Is Lucy with either of you?"

Eliza looked back over her shoulder. "No . . . she's not here. She was sleeping on the floor earlier, on a pile of horse blankets."

"She's gone, then, with her cohort," Leo said, and swore under his breath. He marched back and forth on the landing to vent his anger. "Lucy is the person whom we were looking for," he said. "She was right under our noses as she defiled the coach."

"How? What happened?" Eliza asked.

"Put on your dressing gowns. One of the boxes will be missing from the coach, you mark my words."

Eliza and Lavinia obeyed. Their expressions worried, they followed him downstairs. He lit a torch with the flames from the fire and went outside. He led the way to the coach, and Jimmy's snores reverberated in the night.

Leo lit up the interior and showed Eliza. "Look, there are only two boxes. There were three when I went to sleep in here tonight. I personally stacked them."

"How do you know? These are all alike," Eliza asked.

"I counted them, and I knew Lucy carried two in her arms when you went upstairs earlier."

"I carried my dressing case, and Lavinia carried a bandbox," she explained. "The box with my father's papers is upstairs. I saw to it that Lucy brought that up as it is the most valuable of our cargo."

"I see, but someone might have put something in another box," Leo said.

"We thought someone was following us, but it was Lucy all the time. But why would someone wait until Cumbria to retrieve the box?"

"The person might live up here. We won't know the reason until we see Lucy again."

"She's probably gone for good, the saucy wench," Lavinia said.

"I don't have any valuable jewelry with me, or other desirables," Eliza said. She pulled the first box out of the coach and Leo shone a light at it as she began untying the string holding the top down, and the contents looked intact, neatly folded and untouched. The other was untouched as well.

"It's puzzling. The one missing contained some Egyptian tablecloths and an embroidered shirt and fez for my uncle I purchased in Cairo. Nothing remarkable, just gifts you give to friends after a trip."

"Yes," Leo said. "I daresay Lucy had a burning desire to give someone Egyptian male attire."

Eliza gave him a sharp glance. "Flippancy is not needed."

He cleared his throat. "What I mean is that something else had been packed among the layers of fabric."

"It could be anything."

"Did you bring something valuable from Egypt besides your father's writings?" He shone the torch on the box as she laced the string back up.

She shook her head. "No. Nothing that I can think of right now. I brought some minor artifacts to England, and one gold ceremonial cup that government officials gave my father for his dedicated work. It was a simple article, but very old, of course."

"Just that fact tells me it's extremely valuable."

"But I left that in London, locked up in a strongbox," Eliza said, clearly puzzled. "No one but me knows where that strongbox is located."

"Lucy may have ferreted out the location. She had access to every corner of the house, didn't she?"

Eliza nodded. "Yes. I trusted my servants. There would be no reason to mistrust Lucy, but Mrs. Brown, who recommended her, was wrong this time."

"Yes, she was, alas." He looked at the others watching the proceedings. "Did you trust Lucy, Lavinia?"

"I had no reason to distrust her, but her constant lack of animation was annoying. I avoided her as much as possible."

"Do you know what happened to her before you hired her, Eliza?"

"No, but Mrs. Brown researched Lucy's recommendations and found them all to be legitimate. She's always very thorough."

Leo heaved a deep sigh, his head still groggy with

sleep. He wondered if he would ever get a full night's sleep again, but that was not important in the face of this latest problem. "I suspect Lucy's referrals might have been falsified. It's possible she's a thief or works with someone."

"What about the marks on the coach?" Eliza said. "Are there more?"

"No, I would have heard something. I doubt that she would've left any marks; she was only interested in the box."

"This has been a cursed journey," Lavinia said. "I, for one, am tired of it. I'm going back to bed." She returned to the tavern, and Jimmy shifted uneasily from one foot to the other as if awaiting orders.

There was no reason for the coachman to stay up, and there was nothing they could do until daybreak.

"Go to bed, Jimmy. On the morrow I'll report Lucy to the local constables, and after I've delivered you to your uncle, Eliza, I will personally set out in pursuit of her. It galls me no end that she would steal a box right under my nose."

Eliza stared at him mutely, and a feeling of guilt washed through him. "Mark my words, I shall get to the bottom of this."

"When you catch her, I want to know what the box contained even if I have to question her myself."

"Don't worry about that. The authorities will wring the truth out of her."

EIGHTEEN

They ended up sleeping late the next morning, and the sun was high in the sky when Leo awakened. The coach was hot inside, and he climbed outside and stretched his tight muscles. The seat wasn't the most comfortable sleeping arrangement, he thought, and remembered last night's events with disgust.

He washed his face under the pump in the yard and raked his hands through his hair. The stubble on his chin would have to stay until he could rent accommodations with a washbasin and a pitcher of hot water.

Jimmy was feeding the horses and Leo went in search of a cup of coffee. He found Eliza outside on a bench finishing a slice of toast and drinking the last of her coffee. Filled with self-loathing, he realized he might be the last one to rise. He straightened his wrinkled neck cloth and smoothed down the front of his waistcoat. She didn't seem to notice his unkempt appearance as she stared straight through him.

"Did you find some rest last night, Eliza?" he asked.

She focused her attention on him at last. "What? Oh, good morning, Leo. Please join me when you've found something to eat. The fare is meager at best."

He accepted and went in search of breakfast. She would surely berate him for his failure to protect her possessions, but he wasn't in any mood for arguments. He knew his plans had gone wrong, but he could bring everything back to order. He'd always fulfilled his assignments successfully while in Wellington's army.

The coffee was strong, and the owner of the tavern offered him some fried ham on thick bread, which Leo accepted. His stomach growled with hunger, and he returned outside. The wind had increased, blowing away the fog. The view of the mountains and a lake in the distance was breathtaking. The air had a crystalline clarity, and he breathed deeply.

He sat down beside Eliza on the rickety wooden bench and began chewing the food. He waited tensely for her to start berating him, but her voice was soft when she spoke.

"I realize you must be extremely aggravated by the goings-on, Leo, and I want you to know I don't hold you responsible."

"You don't?" His shoulders slumped with relief. He gave her a searching glance. "Are my ears playing a cruel trick on me, or did I just hear you—?"

"You did," she said with a smile. Her eyes glowed warm as she gazed at him. "You've kept Lavinia and me safe, and that's the only thing that counts. We ought to have discovered the identity of the person—Lucy—who marred my coach earlier, but we can't be everywhere at all times. Besides, I trusted her. I never thought she would do such an underhanded thing. We might never discover why she did, but clearly her mind is in shambles."

For a short moment, his throat clogged with emotion. "Thank you. I expected you to be very angry this morning. This took me wholly by surprise."

"We're all guilty of not keeping a closer eye on the baggage after that first occurrence when someone vandalized the coach, but nothing besides my father's papers was that important. It appears I was wrong."

"Yes, but as I said last night, I'll find Lucy if it's the last thing I ever do. She was calculating and deceitful."

"How dramatic," she said with a laugh. "I surely hope it's not the *last* thing you do. I have grown rather used to having you in my employ."

"Truthfully, despite our difficulties, I've enjoyed my post very much." He drank some coffee, scalding his tongue. He swore silently. A fragile feeling hovered between them. He felt the urge to speak, yet found it almost impossible.

"I—" she began.

"I need to speak to you honestly." He plunged in after clearing his throat. "In fact, Lavinia scolded me severely for not allowing the truth to be revealed."

Eliza stiffened beside him, and he could read the fearful questions in her eyes.

He smiled. "Not to worry. Lavinia did not whip me into doing this, my heart did." He sighed. "I'm very nervous about it, but there's no going back."

"Tell me before I explode with curiosity, Leo." She wrapped her hands around her coffee cup as if she needed to hold on to something.

"I've been a total cloth-head, Eliza. Truth is, my heart is overflowing with feelings for you." He waited for a long breathless moment for her comment, but nothing happened. She seemed to have turned to stone, barely breathing.

"Do you hear me, Eliza? I think that ever since I laid eyes on you, my heart has slowly cracked open, but I've been stubborn and suppressed my feelings."

She took a long, shuddering breath. "Well . . . then

you're willing—?" She couldn't finish the sentence, and he knew she was thinking about the proposal she'd given him in the past.

"I . . . well, I daresay it's a bit early to speak of anything more," he said lamely. "This took an enormous effort on my part. Besides, I'm horrified at the idea that you might consider me a fortune hunter."

"There's a world of difference between you and, say, Mr. Findlay. He's naught but a calculating adventurer. You're not selfish and manipulating, Leo, but I understand your pride. I find it endearing, yet wholly useless."

"I always adhered to the right code of behavior. As a gentleman, I'm expected to act in an honorable way."

"I don't think you know any other way, Leo, but I shan't pressure you." She turned her face toward him and he noted her warm smile and the glitter of joy in her eyes. He so longed to kiss her, and he took a deep breath and leaned forward. His lips touched hers, and the connection was sweeter than anything he'd ever experienced. She was soft and sweet, and she smelled of coffee and roses. The morning light around them seemed to brighten even further. He reluctantly lifted his face from hers.

"This, for example, is breaking the code of which I just spoke," he said huskily.

"Drat the code," she said, her eyes slightly unfocused as she tried to get her bearings.

"I'd like to do something farther outside that code of politeness," he continued. "I long to hold you in my arms and squeeze you so tightly you beg for mercy."

She laughed. "That doesn't sound very comfortable, but my heart responds to that yearning." Her eyes were frank as she looked at him. "Truthfully, I long for more. I'd love to know you better, Leo."

He failed to respond, because an urge to kiss her silly

and ravish her right then and there overcame him, and he blushed. He gulped down more coffee to distract himself. The cup wobbled as he set it down. He reached out and touched her cheek, reveling in the round smoothness. As he pushed a wayward curl behind her ear, and readjusted her hat that had tilted over one ear, he heard applause behind him. The moment felt fragile as his eyes spoke to Eliza's of the love in his heart, and she responded.

"Bravo!" Lavinia cried. "I daresay you took my advice, Captain."

He groaned and closed his eyes. "You forced me to speak the truth, Lavinia."

Lavinia's face was radiant as she sat down at the other end of the bench. When she began to talk, Eliza put a finger across her lips.

"Leave it be, Lavinia. Another time."

"Very well. I suppose we have more pressing business at hand." She clapped her hands together. "We're almost at Claude's and I look forward to seeing him again despite the fact that we always argue. It's been a year."

"As long as there are no more mishaps, we should be there shortly," Leo said, still feeling the sting of failure as he thought about the trip, even though Eliza had assured him that she didn't judge him. Where would he ever find a woman of a kinder heart? he wondered. He wouldn't, and he didn't intend to look if he couldn't claim Eliza for himself.

By midday they entered Carlisle, a city close to the Scottish border. A brisk business in special coaches that brought elopers the last miles to Gretna Green for a fee flourished, and Eliza looked out the coach window for any sign of Valerie and Mr. Findlay. She did not see them.

Mr. Snodgrass's coach happened to be traveling right behind them, but she lost view of the equipage as Mr. Snodgrass stopped at the establishment that offered the wedding coach to Scotland. If Valerie and her escort had availed themselves, he would find out. He must be beyond furious by now.

Eliza watched as Leo spoke with some other peddlers along the street, but she was eager to reach Uncle Claude's house so that she could rest and write in her journal. She had so much to report, most of all her very tender feelings for the dashing captain. Her heart was singing, and for the moment, it bothered her not one whit that someone had marred her carriage and stolen some of her property.

She could never quite understand when she'd become so smitten with Leo. It must have been that first kiss that triggered her feelings, she thought, or perhaps it had happened when she first laid eyes on him. She'd liked him from the start.

"Look at the flower seller," Lavinia said, pointing out the window. "The captain has stopped there." She craned her neck to see better. "He's buying some tulips."

Eliza's heart expanded as she thought of flowers, and when he rode up to the window, she pulled it down. He reached inside with the sweet-smelling bouquet.

"To celebrate that we have almost reached our goal," he said, his smile wide. He rode off again, and Eliza buried her blushing face in the pink flowers.

"How lovely," Lavinia said. "And I always claimed the man was smitten. At least he's admitting it now, which is a great improvement."

"Don't blame him totally for his lack of expression or remote behavior. I did something extremely mortifying."

She explained how she'd proposed to him earlier in the week.

"You did not!" Lavinia looked aghast.

"I did, and he rejected me. I've never felt more foolish."

"And so you should. It's not your place—"

"Don't berate me, Auntie. I'm shocked at myself, and I will never overcome the shame of it."

"Don't be silly. He has rallied, and the next thing will be a proposal. You've only known him for a short time."

"It feels like years, but it's only been a few days. Strange, how much you learn about people during a time of travel."

Lavinia nodded. "We've learned a lot. For one, never take up stranded elopers, and never trust new servants."

Eliza laughed ruefully. "You have a point there, Lavinia."

She glanced out the window, and to her surprise, she saw Valerie outside a modiste shop buying lemonade from a young boy. The woman still looked bedraggled, and it was clear no one had offered to pay for any articles in the shop that might help to improve her appearance. "Look, Lavinia, there's Valerie."

"Bold as brass," Lavinia said with anger in her voice. "I have a few choice words to say to that vixen."

Before Eliza could stop her aunt, Lavinia had jumped out of the carriage and stormed up to the young woman. "You hussy! I've never been more angry in my life," she shouted at Valerie. "You have the nerve to accept our assistance, only to throw it right back into our faces. Not only do I have to worry about our own welfare, I have to feel responsible for yours as well."

Valerie took on an expression of disdain. "I have no use for you any longer, Miss Lytton."

Hearing those words, Eliza filled with rage and jumped out of the carriage. "Of all the ungrateful things to say!"

The girl fled into the modiste shop.

"She'll get her comeuppance," Eliza cried and followed Valerie.

Inside, she searched among hat stands and shelves of gloves and fans. To her surprise, there was no sign of Valerie. The dratted girl could not have disappeared without a trace. The old shopkeeper stared wide-eyed at Eliza and pointed wordlessly at the back door.

Eliza sprinted around a stand of parasols and found the back door ajar. She pushed it open and came upon Mr. Findlay's carriage. Two men were fighting outside, and Eliza immediately recognized young Mr. Moffitt and Mr. Findlay. Their clothes had been torn, and dust covered their faces and their blood-spattered hands.

They were shouting insults at each other and had gathered quite a crowd that cheered them on. Brisk betting among the onlookers was underway. Eliza took two steps toward the combatants, but hesitated to engage in any sort of action. Valerie was standing beside the carriage chewing on her nails. Her lovely face was filled with wrath, and Eliza knew that the younger woman's plans had been squashed.

"I hate them both," Valerie cried over the melee as she laid eyes on Eliza.

"You ungrateful minx," Eliza cried back. She saw Leo rounding the corner of the square brick building, and behind him came Mr. Snodgrass's coach. The alley was soon packed so tightly that no one could move forward or back. The crowd shouted crude encouragements and clapped their hands. Some of the men threw hats into the air to celebrate this unexpected spectacle in the middle of town.

Just as Mr. Moffitt punched Mr. Findlay's nose and drew more blood, Leo jumped out of the saddle. He plowed through the crowd and gripped Mr. Moffitt by the back of his collar. "Damned impudence," he shouted and pushed the young man behind him.

Mr. Findlay charged, but he was already exhausted, and when Leo punched his jaw, he fell over. Dust covered every inch of his elegant attire, and a string of obscenities erupted from his bloodied mouth. The crowd cried for more action, but Leo demanded that they disperse, and before long, two constables arrived to enforce his order. Protesting, the men left the alley, and Leo helped Mr. Findlay to stand up.

The constables had taken hold of the livid Mr. Moffitt and were pinning his arms back. He spat on the ground and kicked to get free, but they kept him imprisoned.

"Miserable worm!" Mr. Moffitt directed at Mr. Findlay.

"How come you're here and not on your way south?" Leo asked the cursing man.

Mr. Moffitt took a deep breath and said, "I came upon this vermin as I was leaving the inn at Orban, and he was helping Valerie to climb out the window. I guess she got wind of her father's arrival. Before I could raise hue and cry, Findlay punched me unconscious."

"I didn't ask you to meddle," Valerie cried.

"I could not rest easy knowing you were in this scoundrel's clutches, so I followed you."

Mr. Snodgrass ambled forward, his face purple with rage. He pointed at his daughter. "Valerie, go to the coach this instant."

"I will do no such thing," Valerie spat, her hands braced on her hips.

Eliza gripped her arm none too gently and steered her away from the men. Valerie protested, but Eliza pushed her forward. "You're not of age, and as such, you're under your father's command. I feel sorry for him."

Valerie gave her a sideways glance. "You have no right—!"

"We have a right to put an end to this farce," Eliza shouted. "I'm grateful that your father caught up with you. You've made a spectacle of yourself long enough. We're all tired of it."

Valerie muttered something under her breath, and Eliza was glad she couldn't hear the words. She pushed the younger woman into the coach, slammed the door shut, and stood guard.

Meanwhile, the men talked, and she overheard the conversation. Both Mr. Moffitt and Mr. Findlay had their cheeks slapped, and Mr. Snodgrass was ready to slap Leo as well, but he laughed and stepped aside.

"Wait a minute here, Mr. Snodgrass. I'm not your enemy. You ought to thank me for taking care of your daughter all this way. Frankly, it was an ordeal, and you should thank this young man"—he pointed at Mr. Moffitt—"for saving the day. Without his help, Miss Snodgrass would now be Mrs. Findlay, and I daresay you would dislike that immensely."

Mr. Snodgrass stared narrowly at Mr. Moffitt. "He was part of the action that brought her to this . . . scandalous place."

"But he has Valerie's best interests at heart, don't you see?" Leo pointed at Mr. Findlay. "Your villain is there. I suggest you focus your anger in that direction if you have to do so, but I also suggest you take back your challenge to Mr. Moffitt."

Mr. Snodgrass stomped in a circle, his hands behind his back. He was deep in thought, but Eliza noted that his anger was boiling dangerously close to the surface. He faced Leo at last. "Due to these whippersnappers,

I've had to hare across England to put an end to this folly, and you ask me to be grateful?"

"Your trip has been a great inconvenience, no doubt," Leo said. "Gather your wits for one moment. Miss Snodgrass is still unwed, and we've prevented this fortune hunter"—he pointed at Mr. Findlay once more—"from getting his claws into her."

"She's going to a strict young ladies' academy until she's of age, you mark my words," Mr. Snodgrass snarled and sent an angry glance toward his carriage.

Eliza cheered his decision silently, but Valerie moaned inside the coach.

Mr. Snodgrass looked at Mr. Moffitt, whom the constables had set free. He was brushing off his clothes, which had been in a sorry state even before the fight. The constables listened silently, shaking their heads.

"Very well. I forgive you, Moffitt. I know that Valerie most likely forced you into this charade, but you should've come to me."

Mr. Moffitt slanted a dour glance in Mr. Snodgrass's direction. "No matter what I did, I would incur your wrath."

Mr. Snodgrass flung out his arms in frustration. "You're a young whelp; what use could I ever have of you? But you've proved yourself loyal to Valerie—and to me—and that I appreciate."

"Very well," Leo said. "I suppose the challenge is null and void." He turned to Mr. Moffitt. "I believe that this time, you'd better turn south."

"With great pleasure," Mr. Moffitt said heatedly and smashed his hat onto his head. I could've been halfway home by now."

Mr. Findlay was wiping the blood off his face with a handkerchief. "You'll meet me one day, Moffitt, properly," he said to himself.

"I heard that," Leo said. "No, he won't. Someone will make short shrift of you long before that." He indicated Mr. Snodgrass. "He will."

Mr. Snodgrass puffed himself up. "I suggest we ride out of town and settle this right now."

"In broad daylight for anyone to see?" Leo asked. "That's not a good idea as there might be any manner of witnesses to report you to the authorities."

"No, there won't! This is in strictest honor and I doubt anyone would try to foil that. We're not in London. I don't want to tarry here, and Valerie needs to go home. I have a mind to marry her off to the local vicar in Surrey. He's seventy if he's a day. That would teach her."

"No need to be cruel, surely. A stringent academy for young ladies will be just the thing, or even a convent." He pulled Mr. Snodgrass aside. "Did you bring your dueling pistols?"

Mr. Snodgrass looked affronted. "Of course I did! Do you take me for a flat?"

"I'll force Findlay to go with us now in your coach. Let's get it over with. The Misses Lytton will look after Miss Snodgrass."

Mr. Snodgrass nodded grimly. "I'm loath to spend any more time here in Carlisle, but I have to deal with that villain."

"I know just the place outside of town. We drove past it."

"My only worry is that the ton will hear about this escapade, and then Valerie's reputation will suffer." He sighed. "I have to get her off my hands before she becomes the end of me."

Leo smiled. "It's quite understandable, Mr. Snodgrass. Let me remind you that you have Mr. Moffitt to thank for the fact that the elopers never made it to Gretna Green, even though it was close."

"I'll have to put a guard in Valerie's room tonight to make sure she doesn't escape again."

"She has no reason to now." When Leo turned around, he was taken by surprise as Mr. Findlay threw himself upon Mr. Snodgrass's massive back and started pounding his head. He shouted with rage as Snodgrass shook him off. In one quick motion, he pulled a knife from his boot. Leo witnessed the move and grappled with Mr. Findlay, going down in the dust as the younger man swung at him. He held on, dragging the younger man to his knees. The knife went flying onto the ground.

In one fluid movement, he got up and planted a right hook to the man's chin and then chopped a fist to his neck. Mr. Findlay screamed and fell face first into the dirt.

Leo pulled him up by the back of his coat, ripping all the buttons in the process. They fought, but Leo's military training came to his aid as he punched the younger man several times with blinding speed. Mr. Findlay fell at last, his face buried in the dust.

Suddenly a shot rang out, and the young man convulsed and his leg jerked as a bullet slashed his thigh. He screamed as a red gash appeared in the ruined pantaloon leg. Leo stared in surprise at Mr. Snodgrass, who held a smoking pistol in his hand.

"What?" Leo shouted.

"No time like the present," Mr. Snodgrass said with satisfaction in his voice as the constables rushed to aid the fallen man.

"I have a feeling he won't bother us again," Leo said, brushing off his clothes.

The constables bound the wounded leg with a neck cloth and pulled Mr. Findlay upright. He leaned on their shoulders, his head hanging down, his legs dragging.

One of the lawmen spoke to Mr. Snodgrass. "We were witnesses to this debacle, and rightly ye should be taken to task for the shootin', sir. However, this man provoked ye underhandedly with a knife, and in my opinion, ye had a right to protect yer daughter's honor."

"Thank you." The older man staggered to the coach and opened the door.

Eliza stepped aside, her legs weak after what she'd witnessed. "Valerie is still in there, but not very happy."

"Hmph! She never is, and I'm sure this setback will keep her in high dudgeon all the way to Surrey." He heaved a sigh of defeat. "That's the burden I bear as her father, I suppose." He leaned inside and placed his pistol on the seat. He pointed at Valerie. "Stay in your corner, you ungrateful chit."

Leo stepped up to the group, hat in hand. "I wish you a safe and speedy return trip to Surrey, Mr. Snodgrass."

Mr. Snodgrass smiled and shook Leo's hand. "Thank you for your help, Captain. I appreciate it more than I can ever say."

Leo turned to Eliza. "Good work. You spotted Miss Snodgrass before it was too late to save her reputation."

Eliza smiled. "Sometimes Lady Fortune turns her eye my way."

Mr. Snodgrass bowed to her, his expression rather humbled. "Thank you again, Miss Lytton. I'm in your debt for everything you did to protect my ungrateful daughter."

"Don't mention it, Mr. Snodgrass. I could not have done differently."

Leo joined her as she walked around the building to join Lavinia waiting in the carriage. The older woman was full of questions, and Leo helped Eliza into the coach.

"We'll soon be at Broadmoor, and your trials and tribulations will be over."

Eliza laughed. "I like the sound of that, but I'm not utterly convinced as we haven't found Lucy. Until that mystery is cleared up, I won't sleep easy."

"Another impudent hussy," Lavinia said, eager to hear about the events behind the modiste's shop.

Leo held Eliza's hand a little too long, and she felt her heart beat faster.

"I'll be right behind you. Another hour and you'll behold Broadmoor."

Lavinia rubbed her hands together with pleasure. "We've wasted too much time already, and I, for one, can't wait to feel the rocky mountain under my feet. Claude will complain about the upheaval of our visit, but pay him no heed, Eliza. He'll be eager to go through your father's papers."

"Perhaps he can shed some light on the mystery of what Lucy found worth stealing from us," Eliza said.

"I can't fathom why she would go off with some stranger in the dark. She must have planned the assignment, or the man was following us on the road."

"Perhaps he caught up with her and demanded the goods," Eliza said with a sigh. "We won't know until we find Lucy and the missing box."

NINETEEN

Broadmoor sat in a wide valley between two crags that loomed gray against the ever more cloudy sky. Grass and heather covered the meager soil, and a silver ribbon of water wound around the mossy outcroppings of rocks in the valley. Sheep grazed on the slopes of the hills, whitish dots against the darker background. The air was crisp and cool, and a light breeze ruffled the clumps of coarse grass.

With every breath, Leo felt the air lift his spirits. Broadmoor, so much reminding him of a medieval stronghold, was welcoming him in the diminishing light. Lights glowed here and there in the windows. Dogs roamed the land and barked at the advancing coach, but did not approach.

The coach lumbered across an arching stone bridge over the river and through a gate. The winding drive took them to the huge oak front door, and the carriage halted before it. As Leo helped the ladies out, he heard commotion at the door and saw a tall, rather robust man come out onto the front steps. He wore an old-fashioned coat with wide cuffs adorned with braiding, black knee breeches, and an antiquated gray wig on his head. His idea of high fashion had been lost in the past.

"Claude!" Lavinia cried as large Irish wolfhounds circled the group of people, tails wagging.

"Lavinia! Not a day older." Claude's round, heavy-lidded face beamed. "And my niece, Eliza. How excessively pleased I am!" He took Eliza's hand and kissed it tenderly. "You are beautiful, just as your father described."

She laughed. "You're exaggerating, surely."

"Not at all." He turned his kind blue gaze on Leo. "And who is this splendid gentleman?"

Eliza made the introductions, and Leo immediately liked the older man. As they went into the house, and as the servants brought bandboxes and trunks inside, Leo spoke to Mr. Lytton. "Did anyone arrive here earlier inquiring after us, or ask you any questions about our whereabouts?"

He shook his head, clearly puzzled. "No. Should I expect someone?"

"No, but I'll tell you later what happened on the way here." Leo looked around the hallway with its curving oak stairway and many family portraits hanging on the walls. A marble bust of a forefather stood in the center of the entry, his severe expression daunting as Leo walked past toward other regions of the house.

The ladies disappeared upstairs to their chambers, and Mr. Lytton invited Leo to the library for a brandy. Leo accepted, happy to have a chance to speak with the man in private. Just as soon as they'd sat down with their snifters by the fireplace, he told Mr. Lytton everything about the tedious trip, not leaving anything out.

"Deuced nuisance," the older man said as Leo finished. "You say that Eliza's maid stole one of the boxes?"

"Yes. Do you know if Sir Walter had sent you anything of great value other than the papers?"

Mr. Lytton shook his head. "No, he never indicated he'd held something for me for later use. Besides, I have all that I need. Artifacts are all that is good, but I need no more." He pointed toward the mantelpiece and Leo noted two tall, slim statuettes made of gold. "The purpose of our research was not to take artifacts out of Egypt, but to study them. Walter shared my opinion in this. I have some scrolls that I'm studying, but they will be returned to Egypt in due time."

"I've promised Eliza to discover the truth about the theft, but it may be hard to find Lucy and the missing box now."

Mr. Lytton rubbed his chin in thought. "She must have had an accomplice, someone who knew about Eliza's purpose for traveling here."

"I suspect Mr. Homer. Eliza jilted him and he took that rather badly." Leo went back over the events with Mr. Homer and his mother.

"I never took to that character," Mr. Lytton said, his forehead pleated with worry. "I could see why he would become an enemy, but stealing things from the carriage is the outside of enough."

"And something that baffled us was the time. Why wait to perpetrate the theft until we reached Cumbria?"

"If an artifact was involved, there are several collectors that I know in Scotland. It wouldn't surprise me if one of them made an offer on an object."

"You think Homer waited to steal it so that he didn't have to carry the box all the way through England?"

"Perhaps. The box would be safer in your care since you traveled in a group. It's anyone's guess at this point." Mr. Lytton finished his brandy and went to top off Leo's glass and refill his own. "So far as I know, Homer has pockets to let. Always did."

Leo nodded. "Eliza indicated as much. Speaking of pockets . . ." He fished in his waistcoat for the gold fob. "I found this at the site of the crime when someone vandalized the coach the first time." He handed the fob to the older man, who turned it over in his hand.

"I recognize this, Captain. If I remember correctly, Walter gave Mr. Homer this fob on his fortieth birthday. The leaf design is rare, made by a local goldsmith, in fact. I ordered it myself. Walter asked me to send the gift to Egypt since he couldn't find one there."

Mr. Lytton sat back down with a groan, and Leo let out the breath that he'd been holding as the older man spoke about the fob. "Mr. Lytton, if Homer is involved, it's pure vindictiveness, don't you agree?"

"Melvin Homer always struck me as a strange man. Emotions run deep with him, and I believe he might turn vindictive when thwarted. Then there's his sickly mother, always at his side. I think she would be a threat to any bride Homer might pick out for himself. That lady would not be pleased by a change in the family structure."

"Now we'll have to see if there's a connection with Lucy and Mr. Homer. I shall ride out shortly and start my investigation. Really no time to linger here, and I feel responsible for clearing up the mystery."

They pondered in silence for a moment. Mr. Lytton gave Leo a long stare, and cleared his throat. "Now, then, tell me when Eliza became Eliza and not Miss Lytton any longer."

Leo gave a hollow laugh. "You don't miss anything, do you, Mr. Lytton?"

"Rarely. If you want to be a decent scholar, you have to notice the details." He gave Leo a frank stare, and Leo fidgeted in his seat.

"I've grown very fond of . . . Eliza, and I believe she's fond of me, Mr. Lytton. I'd like to make an offer for her hand, but sadly to say, I don't have a lot to offer her. I'll eventually gain a useful government position, but it'll take some time. I have solid connections, and I expect a crony will recommend me, but the truth is, I could never support Eliza in great style." He gave his host an earnest stare. "I told her I don't want to be viewed as a fortune hunter, though many will say that I am. I don't have any kind of defense other than that I love her."

"Hmm." Again Mr. Lytton rubbed his chin. "I see."

"I understand if the proposal is offensive to you, sir."

"Eliza is of age, and I doubt that she cares much for social position. She lived a rather simple life in Egypt, and she's a levelheaded woman, I believe. Fact is, she would not be taken in by the wiles of an adventurer."

"I take that as a backhanded compliment, Mr. Lytton," Leo said with a laugh.

The older man chuckled. "I suppose it is."

Leo shifted in his seat. "Does this mean I have your blessing to pursue my acquaintance with Eliza?"

"Truth is, I knew your father, Captain. We went to university together; he's a good man. We were friends, but I'm sad to say, I've lost touch with him as he lives so far away." Mr. Lytton sipped his brandy and looked out at the sky. The clouds had begun to break up, and the sun peeked through, gilding everything. Leo took that as a good omen. "I sense you're a good man, and that is more important than social standing. I wouldn't mind your future presence in the family."

Leo felt as if a great burden had been lifted off his shoulders. "Thank you. I think I needed your approval, Mr. Lytton, since your brother is no longer with us."

"I don't know Eliza very well yet, but I've gathered through our correspondence that she is a sharp woman."

"That she is. The only fly in the ointment is the disappearance of Lucy, and I feel I can't approach Eliza with my offer until that matter is cleared up. I failed in my duty in that respect."

"You couldn't very well know that the maid was involved. Who would suspect one's closest servants to be villainous?"

"You have a point, yet . . . I can't help but feel responsible."

"You'll propose to Eliza properly, won't you, young man? And may I offer you to have the wedding at Broadmoor? A family gathering of sorts. I have two cousins in Scotland, and more distant relatives in Yorkshire."

"I'm sure Eliza would be pleased with that arrangement, but let's not put the cart before the horse."

Mr. Lytton chuckled and sipped more brandy. "You speak with great wisdom, old fellow."

Later that evening, the ladies came downstairs after resting in their rooms. Leo couldn't wait to tell Eliza about his conversation with Mr. Lytton, but he would have to wait until he could offer for her hand properly.

He kissed her fingertips and held them longer than was necessary. To his delight, she blushed and lowered her eyelashes. The current running between them was unbearably sweet, and he longed to take her into his arms and rain kisses all over her face. He found the delay hard to bear, but soon he would declare himself.

Only two weeks ago he didn't know Miss Lytton existed, and now he carried his heart on his sleeve for her. How quickly things could change, and to his surprise, he felt as if he'd known her for a very long time.

"You look rested, Eliza."

"It's a pleasure to be off the road and feel solid ground under my feet. My room is all that is comfortable."

"Mine, too," Lavinia piped in. "When I've had my tea, I'm going back upstairs. I'm going to sleep without interruption for twelve hours, and tomorrow I'm going walking!" With a smile, she left them alone.

"What are your plans, Eliza? Are you going walking, too?"

"I might," she said with a smile. "Do you like to walk? If you do, I might join you."

He pointed to his foot. "I don't walk much, but for you, I'll do anything."

She laughed at that. "I had forgotten, but I'm glad you reminded me."

"About my foot?"

She blushed. "No . . . that you would do, er, anything for me."

"It's true." He touched her soft cheek. "Once the issue of Lucy and the missing box has been cleared up, I shall be at your beck and call." He explained about his plan to go in pursuit of Lucy, and then showed her the gold fob.

"Your father gave this to Mr. Homer as a birthday present."

"Mr. Homer? So he was present on the night someone broke the shaft of the coach?"

"I'd say so. I'm certain he's smarting from your rejection and had revenge on his mind. I can't wait to get my hands on that bounder."

"Be careful. I think he's capable of great anger, and subsequent action."

"I can handle myself, Eliza, but your concern warms my heart."

Her eyes glittered with pleasure, but soon clouded over. "I never suspected he would go to that length to avenge what he perceives as a personal insult." She went to stand by the window and looked outside. He joined her, waiting for her to speak. The sun shone and swallows wheeled overhead. The distant bleating of sheep could be heard across the valley.

"At least we're closer to solving the riddle that has plagued us ever since we started this trip," he said to her thoughtful profile. "I should have paid more attention to Mr. Homer's anger, and then his unexpected appearances along the road."

She nodded. "Yes, it bothered me that he would go to such length to follow me. Perhaps he knows something about Father's work that I don't."

"It's possible, but keep in mind that more than anything he planned to gain financial security through you."

"Yes . . . he was rather forceful about it." She turned to Leo, her eyes troubled. "I hope he doesn't come here to bother me."

"No, he's not welcome at Broadmoor, I'm sure. Your uncle does not seem overly keen on the fellow."

"You're right." She threw another glance outside. "It's so lovely here, isn't it?"

"You're right on that score, Eliza. Majestic splendor."

They pondered the view in silence, and Leo took Eliza's hand in his, caressing the smooth skin on her palm.

"I'm going in search of Lucy now. There's no time to waste, and I won't be back until I have succeeded with my mission."

She nodded. "Thank you."

He bent down and touched her rosy lips with his and felt that dizzying feeling in his stomach. She leaned into his chest, and he pulled her close. He didn't want to allow an inch of air between them, and she sighed against his neck. Warm and soft, he thought as he pulled her even closer. They stood in silence, bathed in the afternoon sun. He didn't want to let go, but finally had to. With a groan, he pushed her away gently. Her eyes were half closed, and he thought she would lose her balance.

"Dearest," he whispered. "You are the most important person in my life." Not trusting himself to say anything further, and slightly afraid of her reply, he headed toward the door. "I'll return when I find Lucy," he said before he left. "Keep close to your uncle."

His legs trembled with the aftermath of kissing her, but he pushed aside his longings. Nothing could stand between them, and they had no future until he could get his hands on Lucy and restore Eliza's property.

TWENTY

Eliza went from room to room looking out the windows for any sign of Leo. He'd been gone for five hours and she could not expect him to return quickly, but she worried. She'd rather keep him at her side. Her heart had not slowed down since their last embrace, and she longed for him so much her stomach ached.

Darkness had fallen, and she could not see the winding drive in the dark. She decided to take a walk to see if she would meet him. Surely he would come back even if he didn't find Lucy tonight, she thought. She went in search of a cloak and gloves, and put on a sturdy pair of walking boots. Before long, she'd let herself out and felt the brisk breeze against her face. It invigorated her as she set out at a quick pace along the drive. She should've brought a servant to accompany her, but she didn't fear the dark, and in this remote idyll she doubted that villains abounded.

The gravel crunched under her feet, and she enjoyed the exercise. The moon hovered just below the horizon and would soon spill its silvery light across the earth.

Where was he? She needed to speak with him, to find out the truth in his heart and what he intended to do about it. She wasn't going to propose again, but she prayed that he would. When had she fallen so deeply in love with him? She had realized how much she loved him when she'd written about it in her journal, and he'd called her a "friend." That had been most awful, but she'd forgiven him for not allowing himself to see the truth. She'd known he had deeper feelings for her, but how could she make him accept them? But he had, without her prompting, in fact. The thought made her spirits soar.

She heard a crunching sound farther down the drive. Stopping, she listened intently. It was unmistakably a horse. Filled with joy, she ran forward. "Leo?" she cried.

He didn't reply, but perhaps he hadn't heard her. "Leo, is that you?"

The horse advanced, slower now.

"Can you hear me?"

"Yes," came the reply in the darkness. "Eliza?"

"Yes, it's me. Did you find her?"

Silence. Her heart began to thud, and unease rose like ice through her veins. She sensed someone else listening to her, and she knew it wasn't Leo.

Turning around, she began to run blindly. The lights inside the house beckoned, and she whimpered as she stumbled and almost fell. The horse was coming up behind her, and before she could scream, someone had gripped her arm. The horse pressed against her, and the man stepped down, still twisting her arm. She fought back, punching and kicking, but she was no match for the larger man. He pushed her hands together and tightened a rope noose around them. He threw her up in front of the saddle and climbed up behind her. Pulling her back against him, he held her in a steely grip.

She squirmed and tried to get a foothold against the slippery horsehide but failed. Crying out, she discovered that he'd turned the horse around and they were trotting down the road. Something about him seemed familiar—perhaps the smell. She gathered herself to scream, but he hissed in her ear to be quiet.

"Mr. Homer!" she sputtered, her anger flaring. "What in the world—?"

"Shut up, you ingrate," he ordered against her ear. "Sit still, or we'll both fall off and be trampled to death. The stallion is vicious."

"Nonsense," she cried. "What are you doing?"

"Taking you to Gretna Green, where you were supposed to go."

"Of all the foolish— Have you gone completely out of your mind?"

"*Au contraire*, my sweet. I'm doing what I should've been doing right from the beginning—putting you in your place and taking what's mine."

"You have no right to treat me like this, Mr. Homer. Take me back to Broadmoor right now!"

He only laughed. "You were allowed too much freedom, but I shall soon take care of that. I cannot abide your high and mighty ways. A woman should know her place, not giving orders, but taking them."

Fueled by fury, Eliza threw her head back hard and hit him in the face. He swore under his breath and clutched her so tightly her chest ached. She sent a shoulder into his chest, but it barely connected. He laughed derisively and she thought of ways to batter him further, but couldn't find any leverage as the horse bounced her with every move. She'd never felt so uncomfortable, but she fought as best she could.

She was afraid he would hurt her, but if he loosened his grip, she would fall off the horse. But at this point, anything was better than staying in his power. She fought to no avail; he was a lot stronger. Broadmoor lay behind them, and they'd reached the open road.

To Eliza's surprise, he ordered the horse to stop a mile closer to town, and she saw the outlines of a coach. The coachman was waiting for them, and he opened the door as soon as Mr. Homer let her slide down. Her legs barely carrying her, she made a dash for a copse of trees, but the driver caught her and pushed her brusquely into the carriage. She fell face first into the squabs and bruised her shoulder against the back of the seat. Scrambling to a sitting position with difficulty as her hands were still tied, she found that Mr. Homer had pushed in after her and closed the door.

The coachman got the equipage rolling, and it bounced over the uneven ground and onto the road. She could hear the horse tied to the back whinnying.

"Where are we going, again?" she demanded to know, so angry she could barely speak. She knew, but had to ask as if the force of her voice could change the destination.

"I told you. Gretna Green. No need to get into a pelter over it," Mr. Homer said, his voice triumphant. "What luck! I never expected to find you walking in the dark all alone. You saved me a heap of difficulty."

"Whatever you think you'll gain from this won't work, Mr. Homer. I have no desire to fall in with your schemes."

"You have no choice, Eliza. When I'm done with you, you'll beg me to make an honest woman out of you."

"You are mad." She rubbed her ears, disbelieving his words. Dismay filled her, and she worried about her safety. The man had truly lost his mind. She had underestimated him as she'd brushed him off as unimportant. She should've known he wouldn't give up.

"Mad for not taking care of this problem sooner," he replied.

"Problem? Do you imply that I'm a problem?"

The coach went through a pothole and she was jarred sideways. She readjusted herself as she gained her balance.

"Not for very long. Once we're wed, all my problems will be over. I just had to make you see sense, and since you didn't, I took matters into my own hands."

"*Married?* Never! I'm never going to marry you."

"No one will care about your protestations. I've paid the blacksmith a large sum to get this handled, and he's waiting."

She froze. He was serious about Gretna Green. He planned to take her across the border into Scotland. She'd heard of women being forced to marry against their will, or being drugged and pulled half unconscious into the ceremony. Any protest on her part would go unheeded as she might appear inebriated to the blacksmith. She knew that Gretna Green nuptials were as binding as a standard marriage.

She would have to escape before they got to the border. The carriage bumped along at high speed, and the moon spread a ghostly silver light over the landscape. She could not see Mr. Homer's features in the darkness, but she sensed his determination. The man was ruthless, to say the least.

"You're making a great mistake."

He laughed. "No, I'm not. Once we're leg-shackled, you'll be packed off to the country and you'll have nothing to say about it. If you behave—which I highly doubt—I might allow you to spend some time in London once in a while."

"I would rather throw myself in front of the horses than marry you."

"You shan't have the opportunity, so don't even think of it."

"Your mother can't support this cruel scheme."

"She does as she's told, but she likes the fact that her life will be easier just as soon as we have more funds to support us. I'll set her up in style in London with me, and she will enjoy the twilight days of her life."

"She birthed a monster in you," Eliza spat. "It's beyond me that she would condone your evil plans."

"She's my mother; she sees no fault with my plans, and so it'll always be. She recognizes that I put her comforts before my own, and that pleases her no end."

"But you would pack your wife off to some drafty old house in the country?"

He shrugged his shoulders. "A wife such as *you*, I would. If you hadn't been so stubborn and accepted my offer in the first place, I would've considered a more lenient treatment of your future, but as it is"—he spread his arms wide—"I have no hopes that you will change, Eliza."

"Don't call me Eliza," she said between gritted teeth. She was so angry she could barely talk, but fear also curled through her body. He had the upper hand. Where was Leo when she most needed him?

"Leo will save me," she said defiantly, "and he'll kill you."

Mr. Homer laughed. He made a mock show of looking out the window. "Well, where is he?"

Eliza sent out a silent thought to the man she loved, wishing he could feel her distress. No one knew she had disappeared, and she'd never suspected she would be attacked in the wilds of Broadmoor. "My uncle will call you out."

He snorted. "Yes, definitely," he said with utter derision. "I daresay he'll shoot me with a book."

"How cruel you are. My contempt for you increases with every word you say."

"Then don't provoke me. After tomorrow I shan't have to set eyes on you, or listen to your unruly tongue any longer. That defiance will be beaten out of you. You might as well prepare for it. From now on, your life will be very different."

Eliza swore that she would fight him to the end.

The coach rolled past the turn to Carlisle and headed north. Within the hour they arrived near the border, and Eliza was pushed out of the coach at a small inn by the road. To her utter surprise, she came face to face with Lucy outside the building.

"What are you doing here, Lucy?"

The former maid looked somewhat uncomfortable. "None of your business," she said, her voice cold.

"You have a lot of explaining to do. I want to know what happened to the box that you stole."

Lucy stepped forward and pushed a rag soaked with something that smelled very strong over Eliza's face. Eliza struggled, her throat constricting with fear, and her eyes watering. Mr. Homer tightened the noose around her hands behind her back, and she fought to get free. Her head started to swim, and tears clogged her throat as the acrid substance overcame her. She lost touch with her knees, and the world seemed to tilt upside down. She kicked out, but did not connect with Mr. Homer's leg. Lucy removed the rag, but Eliza's head kept swimming. She thought she would throw up.

A stranger walked up to her, a man wearing a simple gray coat. "Do you need to hire horses for the last mile over the bridge to Gretna?" he asked, staring curiously at Eliza. Her mouth moved, but she couldn't utter a word. *Help!* she cried within.

With one hand at the back of her head, Lucy forced her to nod. "She's overcome with emotion," Lucy explained.

"I take it the nod is a yes?"

Again Lucy forced her to nod. Eliza moved her feet and found herself losing grip. Her legs gave way and the ground came up to meet her.

"Look at her, fainting for all the excitement," Lucy said and sat with Eliza's head in her lap. "And riding in the coach makes her sick to her stomach."

No! Eliza cried, but no words came out.

"It happens," the stranger said. "A long, tiresome journey and the emotions will get the better of you. How about parson's money and the witnesses? Is she going to pay for that, too?"

Lucy nodded. "Yes, she spoke of it, didn't she, Mr. Homer?"

"She certainly did. Bring us over the bridge, old fellow. She gave me a guinea to give to you."

Eliza saw everything moving slowly, and Mr. Homer's arm undulated snake-like as he handed the man something. Eliza kept her eyes open, because if she closed them, the whole world went mad.

The man left to make arrangements, and Mr. Homer pulled Eliza to her feet. She couldn't stand, so he lifted her up into his arms, and she started butting her head against his chest, but without strength. "We'd better keep her quiet before she draws attention to herself," he said.

He set her down on a hard bench outside the inn, and she slumped forward. If she put her head between her legs, perhaps her head would clear. She struggled with that simple maneuver and finally succeeded. Her skirt smelled of horsehide and mud.

Lucy sat beside her. "You'll be waiting on me shortly, Miss Lytton," the maid said. "Quite a change, don't you agree?" She laughed uproariously, and Eliza was surprised to hear the sound. She had never thought Lucy was capable of laughing.

Eliza never bothered to answer that. She kept praying that someone would help her, and she looked up at passersby on their way into the taproom, but they only laughed, thinking she was three sheets to the wind as she called out in a feeble voice.

"You were so stupid, helping those young people," Lucy chided. "Thinking you could dictate their lives."

Eliza felt relief as she sat with her head down, and she decided to gather all of her strength and run away before they could cart her to Scotland. She had to listen to Lucy going on about their journey north and how much she'd hated waiting on people such as Eliza.

"No more. Melvin will set me up in style, and I'll be his wife even if I won't carry his name. He loves me, not you, Miss Lytton. He loathes you." She laughed again. "We decided we could get so much more from you than the artifact. You *owe* Melvin for all that thankless work he did for your father."

The artifact, Eliza thought. Lucy must have stolen one and wrapped it in the box for later disposal. "Where . . . is it?" Eliza dared to ask, her voice weak and unsteady.

"The old cup? Sold to Mr. Grogan in Scotland who collects these ugly things. Not the first time I dealt with him, but no need to continue that trade. I don't know what he sees in those trinkets, but he paid well—one hundred guineas."

The artifact is priceless, Eliza thought, but she couldn't find the strength to speak further. Anger coursed through her blood, and she felt even sicker.

A few minutes later, Mr. Homer returned with another man, and they shook hands outside the inn. The door stood open, and sounds of laughter and people talking could be heard. A rectangle of yellow light spilled out onto the yard, and Lucy dragged Eliza through that to join Mr. Homer at the other side of the building.

Eliza tried to tear away, but Lucy was stronger. Whatever they'd used to befuddle her mind had made her lose the strength in her extremities. She wobbled, and Lucy cursed at her side. The noose loosened and fell off. The former maid almost pulled Eliza's arm from her shoulder to make her stand back up.

Eliza moaned. "Help!" she cried feebly. "Help."

"Damn you to hell," Mr. Homer hissed and pulled her other arm. "Shut up."

She staggered forward. "Help, please, someone!" Eliza's voice grew stronger, and she heard voices behind her.

"Unhand her!" a man cried, and Eliza's heart jumped with joy as she recognized Leo's voice. He had been here all along, or he'd just arrived.

Mr. Homer lost his grip, and Leo knocked him to the ground. Leo fell upon him, raining blows to the prostrate form. Another gentleman separated Lucy's grip from Eliza, and Eliza rubbed her sore arm. She could barely stand, and leaned up against the coach, watching the scene before her.

Lucy was screaming like a fishwife. "Let me go, you lout!"

"Shut yer gob, ye thief," the man shouted. "This is 'er," he told Leo, who got up and brushed his hands off.

Mr. Homer lay unmoving on the ground. "And this is the other villain," Leo said and pointed at the fallen man.

Eliza took one step toward Leo and he gathered her into his arms. *Safe,* she thought, tears streaming down her face.

"Darling," he said, caressing her face and hair. "I

could not believe my eyes when I saw you with Mr. Homer. I heard your call for help as I came outside."

"You—f-found Lucy here," she said between sobs. His strength seeped into her and she felt better with every breath.

"Yes. Evidently, she'd stolen a bowl in a shop in Carlisle, and this constable has been in hot pursuit of her since yesterday. When I asked around in Carlisle, they directed me to this fellow, and we rode north. Someone saw Lucy and Mr. Homer going north, and we asked at every tavern along the way."

"She admitted to stealing the ancient Egyptian cup. They sold it in Scotland to a Mr. Grogan. I suppose she didn't think anyone would catch her. Careless wench." Eliza stared at her erstwhile servant, who was shouting insults as the constable shackled her hands behind her.

Mr. Homer came to and slowly rose to his feet. He was clutching his head as if in awful pain.

"This is her accomplice," Leo explained.

"Accomplice? Not at all. I don't know that woman." Mr. Homer pointed at Lucy.

"Mr. Homer is from London," Leo continued. "We can prove he knows Lucy, but we can't prove he stole anything. He tried, however, to abduct Miss Lytton here across the border for a hasty ceremony over the anvil."

"Is she an heiress?" the constable asked.

Leo nodded. "That she is, and I know for a fact that she doesn't want to wed Mr. Homer."

"He's right," Eliza affirmed. "Under no circumstances do I want to marry Mr. Homer. He forced me onto his horse in the dark, threw me into his carriage, and treated me completely without respect. When we arrived here, Lucy pressed something to my face that made me groggy. We were about to embark to Gretna Green when you came to save me." She began to cry again, and Leo held her tightly. She felt safe in his arms, yet embarrassed.

Mr. Homer's face turned ugly. He moved toward her, but Leo stepped between them and forced the older man to turn around. The constable had a rope, which he handed over, and Leo tied Mr. Homer's hands. "You'll explain this to the magistrate in the morning, Constable, and I'll stop by and make a statement."

The constable yelled toward a group of men coming out of the taproom, "Bob and Johnny, 'elp me with this wicked lot. They're goin' back to Carlisle."

Two large farmhands joined them and gripped Mr. Homer by the arm without ado. "Come along," one of the said gruffly.

"Damned yokels," Mr. Homer spat. "Let me go." He tried to break free from their sturdy grips, but they held him tightly.

The constable brought up the rear with Lucy. "To the gaol they go," he said to Leo over his shoulder.

"As I said, I'll join you tomorrow and I'll bring witnesses, Constable Jenkins," Leo said, still holding Eliza.

She hugged him fiercely, so happy that she'd escaped from the nightmare. "Thank you," she whispered, feeling better. "I'll have to thank my Maker who sent you to me. If you hadn't come along, I would've been Mrs. Melvin Homer by now."

"You sound strange, darling."

"It's from the substance they made me inhale. I'm feeling stronger now—with every breath." She breathed the cool, fresh air deeply and smiled up at him.

By the light spilling out of the inn, she saw the tender expression in his eyes.

"I almost had an apoplexy when I saw you, Eliza," he whispered and kept stroking her hair. "I would've been beside myself if I'd lost you, and I'm furious with Mr. Homer for trying to abduct you. I could never have looked myself in the mirror if he'd succeeded."

"I would've done everything in my power to annul the marriage."

"You don't know how difficult that is, Eliza."

She sighed. "It's over now." She clung to him. "I'm safe here with you."

His grip tightened. "Eliza, I don't have anything to offer you," he said, his voice tight with anguish.

"You have yourself, and that's enough for me," she said. "As long as you honor me."

"Honor you? I could not live any other way." He took a deep breath. "I love you. I love you more than I can ever express, but I find it very difficult to ask you to become my wife."

"Do you want to ask me?" she whispered.

"More than anything," he whispered back. "But how can I do it?"

"Just ask," she said.

He stared at her hard as if to see if she was serious. "Eliza Lytton, can you find it in your heart to become my wife?"

A warm smile played over her lips. "I never thought you would ask. Yes, with all my heart, I desire nothing more."

This time she thought she would swoon with happiness. Her knees were still soft, but now it didn't matter. When he kissed her with every fiber of his being, she knew they would be happy together.

She played with the hair at the back of his neck. "You know, Mr. Homer paid the man who would take us across the border. Perhaps we ought to take advantage of that service?"

"What? Marry now? Over the anvil?"

"Yes, what's there to stop us? I don't want someone such as Mr. Homer to abduct me again."

"I doubt that it would happen, but if you're serious, I'm game. I think, however, that it's unfair to your relatives to marry in haste."

"We'll arrange for a proper wedding afterward." She pulled his hand and approached the man who'd retreated to the taproom door. "We're ready to go to Gretna if you are."

He gave them a long uncertain look. "Very rum business, this," he muttered, but led the way to the waiting carriage. "There's another witness inside waiting."

Ten minutes later they trundled over the bridge and found themselves in Scotland. The hamlet of Gretna Green did not live up to its reputation; it was insignificant. The blacksmith, Mr. Julius Weston, met them at the inn, and before two witnesses they told him their names and affirmed that they both were unwed and present by their own free will.

He filled out the certificate and asked that the groom place a ring on the bride's finger. Leo looked appalled. "I don't have one."

Unruffled by such carelessness, one of the witnesses produced a length of string, which Leo tied around Eliza's finger. "This will have to do until later. I shall give you my mother's wedding ring."

She smiled into his eyes. "I'll always cherish this piece of string."

Mr. Weston cleared his throat and continued, "What God joins together let no man put asunder." He then pronounced them man and wife.

Leo kissed her, and she responded with all her heart. "I love you, Captain Hawkins."

He held both of her hands in his. "And I love you, Mrs. Hawkins."

This time Eliza didn't care when her legs gave out. She knew she was safe in his arms forever.